THE MATCH

A Baby Daddy Donor Romance

WINTER RENSHAW

Copyright

COPYRIGHT 2021 WINTER RENSHAW
ALL RIGHTS RESERVED

COVER DESIGN: Louisa Maggio, LM Book Creations
EDITING: Wendy Chan, The Passionate Proofreader
LINE EDITS: Kelley Harvey
BETA READER: Ashley Cestra
PHOTOGRAPHER: Wong Sim
MODEL: Igor Augusto

All rights reserved. No part of this book may be reproduced or transmitted in any form, including electronic or mechanical, without written permission from the publisher, except in the case of brief quotations embodied in critical articles or reviews.

This is a work of fiction. Names, characters, places, and incidents either are the product of the author's imagination or, if an actual place, are used fictitiously and any resemblance to actual persons, living or dead, business establishments, events, or locales is entirely coincidental. The publisher does not have any control and does not assume any responsibility for author or third-party websites or their content.

E-Books are not transferrable. They cannot be sold, given away, or shared. The unauthorized reproduction or distribution of this copyrighted work is a crime punishable by law. No part of this book may be scanned, uploaded to or downloaded from file sharing sites, or distributed in any other way via the Internet or any other means, electronic or print, without the publisher's permission. Criminal copyright infringement, including infringement without monetary gain, is investigated by the FBI and is punishable by up to 5 years in federal prison and a fine of $250,000.

This ebook is licensed for your personal enjoyment only. Thank you for respecting the author's work.

Important!

If you did not obtain this book via Amazon or Kindle Unlimited, it has been stolen. Downloading this book without paying for it is *against the law*, and often times those files have been *corrupted with viruses and malware* that can damage your eReader or computer or steal your passwords and banking information. Always obtain my books via Amazon and Amazon only. Thank you for your support and for helping to combat piracy.

Also By Winter Renshaw

THE NEVER SERIES

Never Kiss a Stranger

Never is a Promise

Never Say Never

Bitter Rivals

THE ARROGANT SERIES

Arrogant Bastard

Arrogant Master

Arrogant Playboy

THE RIXTON FALLS SERIES

Royal

Bachelor

Filthy

Priceless (an Amato Brothers crossover)

THE AMATO BROTHERS SERIES

Heartless

Reckless

Priceless

THE P.S. SERIES

P.S. I Hate You

P.S. I Miss You

P.S. I Dare You

THE MONTGOMERY BROTHERS DUET
Dark Paradise

Dark Promises

STANDALONES
Single Dad Next Door

Cold Hearted

The Perfect Illusion

Country Nights

Absinthe

The Rebound

Love and Other Lies

The Executive

Pricked

For Lila, Forever

The Marriage Pact

Hate the Game

The Cruelest Stranger

The Best Man

Trillion

Enemy Dearest

All Books Available here!

Free Content Available here!

Description

All I wanted was a baby. No daddy? No problem.

That's what anonymous donors are for ...

But when the fertility clinic accidentally sends me a letter addressed to a man whose ID matches my paperwork, I discover my child's father is none other than world-renowned tennis champion Fabian Catalano—famous for his gorgeous face, chiseled abs, and broody, wildcard reputation.

Only everything changes when the clinic calls us in for damage control—and Fabian drops the bombshell of the century. Turns out the intense Adonis wants to get to know his daughter.

So I invite him to stay with us—*temporarily*.

Ground rules and all.

And our arrangement is simple ... until it isn't.

Between 2 AM confessionals and stolen kisses, my sweet little simple life has taken a very complicated left turn.

But oh, baby ... what happens next—is a game changer.

To all the baby mamas—past, present, and future. ;-)

Prologue

Two Years Ago

Rossi

"HEY, WHAT ABOUT THIS ONE?" My sister, Carina, slides a piece of paper across my dining room table. "Donor A77462J. *Trilingual Sailor*."

I cringe. "When I think of a sailor, I think of a hot guy screwing beautiful women all over the world, and then *that* makes me think of STDs."

"The agency isn't going to give you a sperm donor with STDs." She rolls her eyes.

"I know. I'm just telling you those are my connotations."

"Ooh." She plucks another from the pile. "*Eager Engineer*."

I wince. "Makes me think of a socially awkward genius."

"Smart is good though. You want smart. The father of your child should be a freaking prodigy."

"Yeah, but what if he's one of those guys who are so freakishly intelligent they lack common sense and street smarts? Like your last boyfriend?" I wink. Reminding her about the time the poor guy got mugged in New York City and thought he could use intelligent conversation to convince his attacker to drop his knife and run away isn't necessary.

My sister crumples the page before hurling it across the room. "Moving on. Okay, what about this guy … Donor K87338L … This donor *puts God above all else and is always willing to help those in need. In his free time, he volunteers at local nursing homes and youth clubs, as well as fosters homeless elderly cats—*"

"—stop." I lift a palm. "He clearly has a saint complex. And he sounds too good to be true. Pass."

My sister chuckles, retrieving the next page from the stack. "Pile's getting thin here …"

"Who's next?"

"Donor W44321G … *Ambitious Athlete* … Tall with chiseled cheekbones, dimples, and a sun-kissed bronze complexion, this donor is not afraid to stand out in the crowd. Naturally athletic, physically fit, intellectually gifted, and driven, there's nothing he can't do once his mind is set. He would describe himself as adventurous and well-traveled, with a focus on collecting experiences, not things. Heritage: Italian and French."

"Let me see that." I feast my eyes on Donor W44321G's profile. "Athleticism is good because we definitely don't have that on our side of the family … and ambition is never a bad thing. Dimples are a bonus." I purse my lips, studying the rest of the limited details. "He's six two. Black hair. Brown eyes. It says his closest celebrity lookalikes are Eddie Cibrian, Eric Bana, and Benjamin Bratt."

"So basically he's hot as sin."

A strange flutter tickles my chest, but I remind myself that I'll never see his face, that he'll be nothing more than the other half of my future child's DNA. And then I quiet the palpitations and get back to business.

"You know, Dad was full-blooded Italian and Mom's mom emigrated from Normandy," she says, sharing things I already know. "Maybe it's a sign?"

I lift a brow. She isn't wrong. But she's also been combing through these with me for the past six weekends. I'm sure a part of her is ready to be done with this exhaustive search. I know I am. But this isn't the kind of thing I can take lightly. This is the biological father of my future child we're talking about. I can't pick someone who's good enough.

He has to be *perfect*.

"There's no such thing as the perfect match." My sister waves Ambitious Athlete's profile like a white flag in front of my face. "But this is pretty damn close."

I examine his paper, reading through the sparse information as if I could possibly glean something extra, something subtle, something hiding in plain sight. Closing my eyes, I picture his face, a mish-mash of handsome actors with the kind of fist-biting, knee-weakening physique you only see on giant billboards in New York, Paris, and Milan.

"You said Dr. Wickham matched you genetically to these donors?" Carina asks.

"He has some kind of state-of-the-art algorithm that pairs us genetically," I say. I read all about it in the brochure months ago when I first embarked on this single motherhood journey. A week after I met with the doctor's team and signed the contract, they mailed me a mountain of questionnaires focused on genetic history, psychological tendencies, and personality traits, and once I'd finished, they brought me in for bloodwork. After months of analysis, they sent me a semi-thick manila envelope of prospects.

And now here we are.

"Well, my vote is for *Ambitious Athlete*." She leans back in her chair, finished. "Don't think it gets better than that."

I read his description once more.

"You're smiling." My sister points at my face. "Did you make your decision?"

Laughing, I clutch the page against my chest. "Yeah. I think so. He's the one."

Chapter 1

Present Day

ROSSI

I READ the letter three times.

DEAR FABIAN CATALANO—

PER YOUR REQUEST, we have destroyed the remainder of your frozen donation. Please know that your specimen has been utilized successfully in the past. For your records, your donor number is W44321G. Please also know that your donor number is registered on the National Donor Sibling Registry in accordance with the Hemlock-Patterson Act of 1997. Should you choose to connect with any offspring in the future, you may do so via the aforementioned organization.

If you have further questions, please contact our clinic manager, Rhonda Bixby, and she would be happy to assist.

RESPECTFULLY,
Dr. Wickham and Team
Wickham Fertility Clinic
Chicago, IL

"CARINA," I call to my sister in the next room. A second later, she appears in the doorway of my home office, my nine-month-old daughter, Lucia, on her shoulder. "Read this."

I hand her the letter. Her nose wrinkles and she squints. "What's this mean?"

"Why would they send that to *me*?"

"Clerical error."

"Clearly." I take the letter back and scan it once more. "Why does that name sound familiar? Fabian Catalano. I swear I've heard that before."

"Wait." Hoisting the baby on her other hip, she slides her phone out from her back jeans pocket and impressively uses her thumb to tap his name into Google. "Oh my god."

"What? What?"

Flipping the screen toward me, she all but shoves it in my face. "Fabian Catalano—the *tennis* player. He beat Rafael Nadal last year in the Spanish Open, remember? And then they got into some kind of fist fight after their match in Paris?"

"I literally don't watch tennis. You know that," I remind her before feasting my eyes on the muscled Adonis in the images before me. He's a beautiful man, I will admit.

His thick black hair is shoved back carelessly with a Nike sweatband, his shirtless torso glints with sweat, and his generous hands are wrapped tight around the base of a neon-yellow tennis racket. Sports—or anything involving competition—has never been my thing, but I'm sure I've heard his name in passing before. Maybe in a news clip or on a billboard somewhere.

"What if *he's* your donor?" she asks, covering my daughter's ears despite the fact that she's still very much a baby and wouldn't be able to comprehend any of this. "Remember his donor name? Ambitious Athlete? And he was half Italian. Isn't Catalano an Italian surname?"

"There's no way." This kind of thing doesn't happen. For starters, it'd be a careless and expensive move on the clinic's part. And one as advanced as Wickham surely has a system in place to prevent this kind of privacy breach.

I steal her phone and scroll through the images again.

Lucia came out with a head of thick black hair when she was born—a far cry from my God-given chocolate-dirt locks. My dad called her Priscilla Presley the first week and thought it was the funniest thing in the world.

But lots of people have black hair. It's not like it's rare or anything.

"Did you save the sheet?" she asks.

"What sheet?"

"The Ambitious Athlete one? With his donor number and description?" Carina points to my filing cabinet. She knows damn well I save everything. I'm an informational pack rat.

Rising from my desk, I head over to the cabinet where I keep all of Lucia's medical records—and every piece of paper the fertility clinic ever sent me home with. Blood-work. Test results. Appointment confirmations. Follow up schedules. Sliding the drawer out, I pluck out Lucia's file and flip to the pack, where I kept the original sheet describing Ambitious Athlete.

"Let me see." Carina reaches for it, but I swipe it away.

"If it *is* him," I say, "and it *isn't*. It's not going to change anything."

She bounces Lucia on her hip, eyes wide and impatient. "Come on. Let's see."

"I don't know if I want to know though." I chew my bottom lip. "The whole point of this was for it to be anonymous. And then what, when Lucia gets older, I'll have to make the decision of either telling her who he is and explaining that even though we know who he is, he'll never be a part of her life—or lying to her and acting like I don't know. I don't want to be put in that position."

"Don't you think the cat's already out of the bag?" she asks. "Either it's Fabian Catalano or it's not. From here on out, you're going to hear his name and think of this moment. This question. It's going to haunt you and you know it. Don't you want to put your mind at rest? It's not like it'll change anything. He's not going to suddenly have parental rights or be a part of her life. Your day-to-day isn't going to change. You're still going to be a single mama doing your thing with the most beautiful baby girl this world has ever seen. Whether or not you know the name of her father won't change that."

I place the sheet of paper next to my laptop and fold into my chair, tugging fistfuls of hair and exhaling.

"I'm happy to compare the numbers for you ... I could keep that information safe until you decide you want it someday," she says. It's not unlike the gender reveal we did last year. Carina accompanied me to my twenty-week scan and the technician wrote the baby's gender in an envelope, sealing it and giving it to my sister for safekeeping until we could reveal at a small friends and family gathering at my parents' house.

When I first decided to have a baby, gender wasn't important.

And I'd have been thrilled either way.

But I'll never forget the way I felt when that pink confetti flew through the air after I popped the balloon. I was plucking it out of my hair for days after, smiling every time as I daydreamed about a little mini me. About mommy-daughter mani/pedis. Barbies and babies. Lazing by the pool together in matching swimsuits in the summer. The enormous collection of dresses and hair ribbons I was about to start for her. I'd have been just as excited to have a baby boy, but being able to visualize this next chapter of my life without effort quashed any tiny voices in my head telling me I was crazy for doing this.

"You realize the irony in all of this, don't you?" Carina asks. "You're a genealogist. You study family histories and make family trees for a living. Legacies are your jam. Now you've got the opportunity to fill in the other half of your daughter's family tree and you're content just to leave it … leafless?"

She has a point, but I'd accepted that half of her tree would be bare the second I agreed to go the sperm donor route. It was a trade-off I was willing to make in the grand scheme of things. Plus with DNA technology advancing every year, it's not like she wouldn't be able to figure out her heritage when the time came.

Lucia coos, clapping and reaching for me.

Typically we have a no-baby-in-the-office-during-work-hours policy, but I can't not hold her when she gives me that look.

Carina slides her into my arms, and I kiss her warm, pink cheek before studying her deep brown eyes.

My sweet, perfect, beautiful, brown-eyed girl.

My whole world, really.

It's funny, despite being thirty-five, I hardly remember life before her. All those memories feel like they belong to someone else. The rebellious college years. My brief marriage to Brett. Launching my genealogical services business. Starting over single, fabulous, but still aware that something was missing …

"Nonna always says everything happens for a reason," Carina quotes our vivacious Italian grandmother. Though the cliché words don't belong to her, it's something she says all the time, about everything. If it rains, it means the grass needs watering. If a guy ghosts Carina, it's because his presence in her life would've thrown off her entire path. After my husband left me for another woman, she swore it was because my soul mate is still out there.

I don't know about all of that—but she's never been wrong.

The things that don't work out for us are because something better is waiting in the wings.

Lucia is worth every painful moment of my failed marriage, every tear, every headache, every embarrassed explanation I had to give friends and family.

"She kind of looks like him," Carina studies my baby's face.

"You did not just say my nine-month-old baby girl looks like a thirty-seven-year-old Greek god." I snort.

"The hair and eye color," she says. "It's his."

"A lot of people have that combination …"

Pulling out her phone, she taps something into the screen and flips it to show me. "Look at his eyebrows. The shape of them. Those are Lucia's brows."

"I don't know why you're trying to hard to sell me on this when it doesn't matter."

Carina blows a puff of hair between her lips and slides her phone away. "Fine. You're right. It's none of my business. I just think ..."

"What? Everything happens for a reason?" I finish her thought.

"Exactly." She gathers Lucia in her arms and kisses her temple before brushing her jet-black hair from her forehead. "But it's your life. And Lucia's. And it's not my decision. I just would hate for you to spend the rest of your life wondering ..."

"Yeah, yeah, yeah." I swat her away. "I really need to get back to work."

"You called me in here." She points, winking. "Just remember that."

She's not wrong—when I first opened the letter a few minutes ago, my heart fluttered at the thought of this secret information landing in my lap on an ordinary Wednesday afternoon. But the more I think about it ... it's not for me to know.

Then again, the more I think about it, what sense would it make that someone as famous and successful at Fabian Catalano would ever need to be a sperm donor?

There's no way it's him.

Rising, I refill my coffee in the kitchen before returning to pace my office—or at least the single window that looks out onto our little front porch. Sliding the sash, I inhale a burst of fresh spring air. A year ago, I was six months pregnant, happily and comfortably so.

I loved being pregnant. Relished every minute of it. I studied a million baby books, listened to her little heartbeat on the at-home doppler at least ten times a day, and snapped hundreds of belly photos.

She was my first pregnancy—but also my last.

I know my limits.

Motherhood is hard. Single motherhood is even harder. Not that I'm complaining. I'm simply rationalizing my decision to be one-and-done.

I've caught myself daydreaming of having just one more, a sibling Lucia can grow up with, someone to play with and fight with like Carina and I had, someone to make fun of me when I do something embarrassing during their teen years, or someone to call and vent to when I'm getting on their nerves. Someone to hold and hug them long after I'm gone.

A decade ago, I thought I wanted that boring, typical, traditional family—and Brett and I tried for years to get pregnant before going in to see Dr. Wickham and discovering that Brett was the issue. He refused to so much as consider using donor sperm, which left my hopes and dreams of having a family with him on the cutting room floor. He was also adamantly against adoption, calling it a parental form of Russian roulette. At the time, I thought he was simply being bitter because of his infertile diagnosis. I didn't think he meant those harsh words, and I was one hundred percent convinced he'd come around with a little time.

Everything changed the night his best friend came over, drunk as I'd ever seen him. Brett was out of town for work and Ethan knocked at the door, asking if he could crash at our place. We lived in a trendy neighborhood with popular bars, and Ethan had done it a million times before so I didn't think twice. But it wasn't ten minutes into getting him settled when he said he had to tell me something.

I'll never forget the tears in his eyes. I'd chalked them up to far too many beers and the toll his recent breakup was having on him.

"Brett doesn't love you," he'd blurted next. Followed by,

"Two years ago, he got a vasectomy. That's why you can't have kids."

I stood in the doorway of our guestroom in stunned silence as he proceeded to tell me my husband wasn't alone on his latest business trip, that he'd brought along another woman for company. And he rattled off half a dozen names of other women who'd kept him company over the short course of our very new marriage.

At the time, it felt like a bad dream and seemed like a ploy—because when Ethan was finished ratting out my husband, he tacked on a confession of his own … he'd been in love with me for years.

I quickly ended the conversation, tucked him in with a bottle of Gatorade and two Advil, and hid in my room the rest of the night.

He was gone by the time I woke up in the morning, but I spent the entirety of that day verifying and confirming all of Brett's "activities."

"Think I'm going to go for a walk," I call to my sister as I slip into my tennis shoes, grab my ear buds, and jet out the front door. All these thoughts and memories swirling in my head is making me stir crazy, and I can't possibly finish the Valdez project like this.

Striding around our picturesque little neighborhood, I gather as much fresh air as I can while an eighties pop station plays in my ear. The synthesized sounds and funky beats always break me out of my strangest moods. They've never failed me once.

Thirty minutes later, I'm back to our street when a silver Lexus pulls up and rolls the window down. I pause Blue Monday—which is a shame because it's one of my favorites.

"Hey, stranger." My next door neighbor, Dan, flashes a megawatt smile and flips his shiny sunglasses over his head.

"Oh, jeez. Didn't recognize you. New car?" I approach his window and the scent of new leather floats on a breeze.

"Fresh off the showroom floor. Whatcha think?"

I give it a careful inspection, making a show of it as I nod. It's spectacular compared to my trusty Subaru, but I've never been one to care about this sort of thing.

"Going to miss seeing you come down the street in that bright red BMW though," I say.

"Psh." He waves a hand. "That thing was a lemon. Always in the shop. And my ex picked the color. Always thought it was obnoxious. Lease ended today—couldn't have happened sooner."

When Dan first moved to the block a few months back, I did the neighborly thing and brought him a tray of made-from-scratch caramel brownies and introduced Lucia and myself. Within seconds, he'd invited us in and gave us a tour of the place. A corporate accountant, he'd just gone through an ugly divorce and was excited about starting over. It didn't take long for us to bond over failed marriages and our love of this little boutique neighborhood where all the houses look like they're out of some movie set and all the neighbors won't hesitate to bake you a casserole *and* stick their nose in your business. I called it a miniature Wisteria Lane, and then we spent the next few hours talking about our favorite TV shows.

We'd been hanging out—in a casual neighbor sort of way—for a few months when he asked me on a date.

A real date.

I had to let him down gently, informing him that Lucia was my priority, and I wasn't in a place to start thinking about that sort of thing. I'll never forget the way his lips curled into a gracious smile, but his eyes were a deep shade of glassy blue. Either way, it changed nothing between us. He still shovels the snow from my sidewalk in the winter and hand delivers my mail when he accidentally receives it. He also texts me movie recs and has gifted Lucia miscellaneous toys—always soft ones, never the noisy ones. We've also made a couple of jaunts to the farmers' market together—all three of us, that is.

"Nice day for a walk," he says, buying time. "You should've waited another half hour and I'd have joined you."

That's another thing—he loves our walk-and-talks, always offering to push the stroller when Lucia's along and never complaining when we stop at the park to let her enjoy a few minutes in the baby swing. I can't count how many times passersby have stopped to fawn at my daughter and then tell us what a beautiful family we are.

I shrug. "Just needed a little fresh air. About to head in and get back to work."

Splaying a palm across his pristine dress shirt, he feigns an injury. "Ugh. Should be illegal to work on a gorgeous day like today."

"Just tell that to my boss," I tease, referring to my ball-busting alter ego. While I love being self-employed, some days it's a struggle to find motivation to stay on task. A schedule—a strict schedule—is the only way around that. "Hoping she gives me a day off soon."

"I meant what I said the other week. Name the date and we'll go." Two weeks ago we were drinking wine, chowing on pizza, and bingeing some trendy Netflix series when Dan suggested we take a road trip—the three of us. His grandparents had a farm in Wisconsin and he insisted it'd be fun for Lucia to see the animals. Plus, he said his mom loved babies more than anything in the world, and she'd be happy to babysit if we wanted to go into the city for a night.

His offer was tempting …

I haven't taken a proper vacation since before the pregnancy, but I didn't want to give Dan the wrong impression —not to mention the thought of leaving my only child with a complete stranger made me want to vomit on the spot.

I'm not there yet.

"I'll let you know." I point to my house ahead. "Going to head in and get back to work. Congrats on the new wheels ..."

I trot along the sidewalk, skirting around the back of his shiny new car, heading back before he can stall me another minute. Dan's a pro at that. He can turn any kind of casual small talk situation into a forty-five minute full-on conversation. Deep down, I imagine he's lonely. The man was married for ten years—to his high school sweetheart no less. They'd been together since they were fifteen and then poof. And the house he bought is better suited for a family. Two stories with a finished basement and five bedrooms. Plus a fenced back yard and a playset leftover from the previous owners. Waking up to all that emptiness, all that wasted potential must get to him somedays. I can only imagine he chose this home hoping he could one day fill it.

And I have no doubt there's someone special out there for him—it's just not me.

Kicking off my tennis shoes in the foyer, I drop my ear buds on the entry console and duck into my office before Lucia hears me. Taking a seat, I find myself face-to-face with that damn letter again.

The odds of Lucia's donor being a famous, crazy-hot tennis player are slim.

And if for some insane reason it is him—nothing about my life is going to change.

Also, my sister's right ... the answer to this question is

going to haunt me the rest of my life if I don't put it to bed now.

I tug a handful of hair, gather a deep breath, and place today's letter next to the donor form from the file cabinet.

And then I compare the donor numbers.

W44321G ...

and ...

... W44321G.

It's a match. Holy shit. *It's a match.*

"Carina!" I yell for my sister. "Carina, hurry—get in here!"

Three seconds later, the office door swings wide, slamming against the wall.

"What?" she asks. "What is it, what's wrong?"

Clamping a hand over my mouth, I hand her both papers. "It's him. Fabian is the donor."

Examining the numbers for herself, she sucks in a sharp breath. "I ... I didn't think ... I mean, I thought it was a long shot ... I didn't ..."

She's as speechless as I am.

"I know," I say, letting the information sink into my marrow, where it'll live the rest of my life.

"What are you going to do now?"

Steadying my breath, I force myself to get a grip. I need to come back down to earth. I had my mini freak-out but now it's back to reality.

Folding both papers together, I tuck them into the file cabinet folder where they belong. I wanted my answer. I got it. And someday, when the time is right, I'll share it with my daughter—for whatever it'll be worth at that time.

"Nothing," I say. "There's nothing *to* do. My life—*our* life—is staying exactly the same. Only difference is, now I can fill in the donor side of her family tree if she wants me to do that someday."

Carina lingers in the doorway, hand on the knob as she studies me.

"I'm fine," I insist, despite the fact that she hasn't asked. I can read her thoughts—they're practically broadcasting off her forehead. Glancing at the clock on my desk, I add, "Should be about time for Lucia's afternoon nap, yeah?"

Carina closes the door on her way out, and I wake my laptop, diving back into the research I've been conducting on the Valdez family—a project initiated by a woman named Mimi who was adopted in the fifties as an infant. She never wanted to trace her biological roots, fearing it would offend her adoptive parents who were nothing but wonderful to her. But now that they're gone and she's nearing the twilight of her own life, she wants to answer the unanswered questions that have silently plagued her for the last seventy years.

In fifth grade, Mrs. Wesley assigned us each a family tree project for a social studies unit we were working on. At first, it seemed tedious and monotonous. I knew the names of my aunts and uncles and cousins and grandparents and great-grandparents. By the time Mrs. Wesley made her way around the classroom and back, I'd already filled my tree in completely. Birth dates and all. So then she challenged me to take it further. To interview my family and see how far back I could go—to get as many names as I could, until the trail dried up.

So that's what I did, tracing my father's side all the way back to Colonial New England times and my mother's side to the mid-1700s. My great-grandma Bianco, who was still living at the time, fished out a hat box full of old photographs from her time as a small child in northern Italy, and she spent hours telling me all about her cousins and aunts and uncles. There were scandals.

And there were stories—some heartbreaking and some that made me snort chocolate milk through my nose. I took meticulous notes, typed them up and placed them in a binder later that night. Later on, I emailed copies to everyone on that side of our family. It wasn't long before I was the designated family historian. And I did the same for my mother's side—the French half of me. For my senior trip, my parents took us to Europe for two weeks, and we stopped at every landmark, gravesite, and still-standing home we could find that was in any way connected to our ancestors.

I was a year into college when my university came out with a new degree program, one that combined genealogy and DNA studies.

The rest is history.

As Nonna always says, everything happens for a reason.

Double-clicking on my family tree software, I create a new file for Lucia and type the name of her father next to mine. And then I lean back, taking it in for a surreal moment.

Rossi Alessandra Bianco (mother) and Fabian Catalano (father).

Lucia Evangeline Bianco (daughter).

Our own little, tiny family tree—one with enormous roots waiting to be explored.

All in due time.

I hit 'save' and return to Mimi Valdez's project. I'm so close to uncovering the name of her biological mother, who gave birth to her at fifteen. There's a chance she's still living. Slim, of course, since she'd be in her mid-eighties. But I have hope. Logging into my Ancestry account, I send a message to a woman connected to Mimi's DNA—a possible second cousin, it says. When I'm finished, I log out and shove my chair away from my desk … only to have second thoughts.

Biting my lip, I scoot back in, pull up Google, and hesitantly type in Fabian's name, one reluctant keyboard peck at a time.

Despite the fact that this feels every variety of wrong, suddenly my curiosity is in the driver's seat and she's throwing caution to the wind in the name of personal interest.

The first result is his official website. One click of the mouse and I'm met with a shiny black page highlighted with neon accents and peppered with modern, sexy fonts. Various menu options offer up videos, articles, and ways to get in touch with his team. I click on the image gallery, soaking in the highly-edited action shots as well as a few menswear pictures that have probably graced the glossy pages of GQ and Esquire at some point.

I study the sharp angles of his jaw, his straight nose, and the perfect angles of his eyebrows which are neither bushy or unmanageable and identical in shape to Lucia's.

I'll never forget lying on that cold table, my feet in stirrups, a fluorescent light stinging my eyes overhead.

"All right. Time to make a baby," Dr. Wickham said as he perched on the rolling stool at the foot of the exam table and his associate handed him a long tube full of donor sperm. It wasn't exactly magical. Definitely not romantic. And of course it wasn't how I imagined starting the journey to motherhood. The doctor told me to lie back and relax—impossible, but I tried. Thirty seconds later, it was over. *Ambitious Athlete's* unfrozen seed was officially inside of me. The rest was up to my body.

We did a natural round, no hormones necessary since I've always had an impeccable twenty-eight day cycle. The doctor told me I had a fifteen to twenty percent chance of it working in any given round, and not to be disappointed if it took two, three, four, even eight rounds.

But she took the first time.

Nine months later, I held Lucia in my arms, my mother and sister beside me, each of us weeping tears of joy—save for Lucia who was simply hungry.

I've occasionally daydreamed about meeting her donor someday, but in these scenarios it's always when Lucia is older. Maybe she does a DNA test and discovers a half sibling or two. They meet up. Her biological father is there. That sort of thing. And in these daydreams, I'm there, too—but only because I want to thank him for the beautiful gift he gave me.

Running another search on Fabian, I glean that he has no children of his own. Only a string of relationships with young, beautiful, international models. A deeper search shows he wasn't making headlines until closer to his mid-twenties. His life before that is a mystery, save for a one-paragraph personal life summary on his Wikipedia page.

Fabian Catalano was born in Chicago, Illinois. After attending Wakecrest University on a tennis scholarship, he moved to California to train under famed tennis coach Reed Cartwright. His parents are the late Grace (DuBois) and Gianni Catalano. He has never been married, is currently single, and keeps a primary residence in Los Angeles.

That's it.

Mere scraps.

I spend the rest of the afternoon combing through various interviews he's done on talk shows—and I stop when I get to the one where the invasive, chatty blonde host asks if he and his then-fiancée (who happened to be his long-time coach's daughter) had thought about how many kids they wanted to have after they tied the knot. And before he had a chance to answer, she rattled off some witticism about how beautiful their babies would be.

Fabian scoffed, going off on the woman for assuming that every couple who marries automatically wants children. After that he yanked the microphone off and stormed off stage while the host gathered her composure.

This particular interview took place a mere two months ago.

It's impossible to know when he donated his sperm. I can only assume it was during his college days. Maybe he needed some extra cash? Men that young aren't necessarily thinking about the long-term repercussions of their actions.

I re-read the letter one last time, letting the realization sink in that he had recently requested the remainder of his sample be destroyed.

Tightness floods my chest when I think of my daughter someday knowing who he is and having her heart broken when she sees this interview. The man clearly has no desire for children. Which is fine. That's his prerogative. But if a nosy little interview question about babies sets him into a hot-headed rage on a television set, how would he act if his own daughter were to someday reach out to him?

I glance at the file cabinet, and I decide to tuck this entire day into the recesses of my mind.

We never needed him anyway.

And we never will.

Chapter 2

Fabian

"HEY, you have time for a phone call?" My new assistant, Taylor, sashays across my private tennis court.

While everyone in my camp assumes I hired her because she's got perky tits and a tight ass, I simply chose her because she's young and malleable. There's nothing worse than hiring someone's used assistant and having to break them of all their old habits. This one's fresh out of college, and this gig is officially her first job.

I have hope.

Wiping the sweat from my brow, I nod toward my coach on the opposite end of the court. "I don't know, Taylor. Does it look like I have time?"

I almost feel bad biting her head off like that, but this is how she's going to learn.

That and I've only reminded her six separate times since she started last week that my court time is sacred.

Coach Cartwright tosses his hands in the air, his annoyance taking the shape of a grimace on his face.

Biting her overinflated lips, Taylor skips closer, phone in hand. "They've called several times in a row. I let it go to voicemail at first, but then they kept calling. They said it's urgent."

"Take a message ... that's what I pay you to do."

"I tried, but they insisted." She pouts like a damned toddler. Hesitating. Then she steps closer, tucking her chin. "It's a doctor's office." Her attention spans to Coach and back. "Dr. Wickham. In Chicago. It's a fertility—"

Before she can finish her sentence, I shove my racket at her and trade it for the phone, heading inside to deal with this nonsense. Last month I had my attorney draft up a destruction mandate for some sperm I donated back when I was a broke college kid. At the time I was barely twenty-one, a senior in college, and in desperate need of cash to replace the catalytic converter in my piece of shit Oldsmobile. A clinic in the next town over was offering five hundred bucks per donation—all I had to do was fill out an application, submit some bloodwork, and if accepted, it was easy (if not awkward) money.

I must have donated half a dozen times that year—and that summer Cartwright hand-selected me as his next "project." He'd seen me play in some college invitationals and was convinced I was going to be the next big thing in the tennis world.

He wasn't wrong.

"This is Fabian," I answer once inside and out of earshot of staff.

For the past sixteen years, my life has been a whirlwind of beautiful women, trips around the world, endorsement deals, and fat checks.

It wasn't until the catastrophic end of a recent engagement that I remembered the donations I'd made to that clinic outside Chicago. While the contract I signed at the time was ironclad, I hired one of the most powerful law firms in that area to draft up a proposal to destroy any remaining donation. My attorneys said it shouldn't be a problem given my "celebrity status," but legally, they owed me nothing.

"Hi, Fabian, this is Rhonda Bixby. I'm the clinic manager at Dr. Wickham's office." Her voice is saccharin-sweet, dripping with honey. Sometimes people get like this when they're starstruck, but in this case I've said a mere three words. "We received your request last month to destroy the rest of your donation." She pauses, clearing her throat. "And I'd like you to know that we have done so."

"Okay ... so why are you calling?"

She clears her throat a second time. "We've had a little ... clerical mishap."

"And what the hell does that mean?"

"The letter that was intended to you," she says, "was actually sent to a recipient of your donation."

I take a seat in a leather armchair, massaging my temple. "And what did this letter say? Exactly?"

"Well, it had your name on it." She chuckles even though nothing about this is funny. "As well as your donor ID number. It was just a confirmation that we had fulfilled your request."

"So you're saying that because of a careless mistake your clinic made, there's a woman out there who now knows that I'm the biological father of her child?"

"That's precisely what I'm saying, Mr. Catalano." The sweetness in her tone is gone. Now it's all business. "I want you to know that Dr. Wickham and I, we understand the gravity of this breach of information, and we're prepared to offer you a settlement."

"Money's the last thing I need." I sniff, insulted. "And it sure as hell isn't going to fix this."

"Yes, we realize that, but the law states—"

"—the law is nothing more than a liquid guideline," I interrupt. Pinching the bridge of my nose, I examine my options. I could sue the hell out of that place until they're forced to shutter their doors, but that would mean putting innocent people out of work. Not to mention, taking this to court would make it public record. Neither of those options are going to undo any of this. It'd be a lose-lose-lose situation.

Rising, I pace the space in front of the floor-to-ceiling windows. Outside, my coach stands in the middle of my tennis court on a phone call, waiting patiently while I sort out this shit show.

If the recipient of my "donation" realizes who I am—and if she's got half a brain cell, she will—she could try to extort me in exchange for her silence. And if that doesn't work (and it won't), she'll go to the news. She'll garner enough publicity to make *me* look like the villain, not the clinic. I'll be painted in every light imaginable. "Cancelled" on social media. The kind of jerkoff other guys laugh about in locker rooms.

"I want to meet her," I say.

"You want to meet … the recipient?" Rhonda asks, over-enunciating.

"Yes." I check my watch. It's not quite noon here. I could hop on a flight and be to Chicago in hours—assuming that's where she lives.

"Oh, I don't know if that's possible, Mr. Catalano. You see, if I give you her name, that is a breach of privacy for her and the child as well."

"A little late for that, don't you think?"

"I see what you're saying, but unfortunately it doesn't

work that way," she says. "Like I was about to say before, Dr. Wickham is prepared to offer you a generous settlement for this … inconvenience. I can give you our attorney's information if you want to pass it along to yours."

My skin heats.

Nothing infuriates me more than being brushed off.

"You're not hearing me," I raise my voice, though I'm far from shouting. "I don't want your money. I want to meet my child's mother."

"I heard you perfectly, Mr. Catalano, but like I said, legally we aren't allowed to give you her information."

"Then call her." I switch my phone to the opposite ear, head to the kitchen, and grab a bottled water. "Ask if she wants to meet me."

I don't know what her situation is, obviously. She could be a single mother or she could be a married mother raising six of my genetically perfect offspring. Either way, all I need is a private meeting where I can speak to this woman, adult to adult. I can explain to her that I've no intentions of pursuing custody or being in any kind of fatherhood role, but I'm happy to ensure that the clinic establishes a healthy college fund for any and all children that came from this arrangement. I'll even insist the clinic throw in a new car and a little something special for her. A family vacation or something. After that, I'll have her sign an NDA and we'll both be on our way.

It'll almost be like it never happened.

"I can try," Rhonda says. "But I can't make any promises. And you have to respect her decision."

"Just make the call." I hang up, chug my water, and head back to the court, ready to hit some balls.

"Everything okay?" Coach asks.

No—but it will be.

I grab a ball, toss it high, and deliver one of my signature, impossible-to-hit serves.

"*Jaysus*," he says, ducking. "Take my head off, why don't you?"

Smirking, I lob another one at him—this time it's gentler. "There. Better?"

He returns it with a hard smack—and I fucking miss it.

"See what just happened?" he asks. "You just let someone get inside your head. And you allowed me to manipulate you. Don't do it again."

Chapter 3

Rossi

"COME ON, I know you like this ..." I lift a spoonful of pureed butternut squash to Lucia's mouth, but she puckers up, refusing it. And then to make it worse, she grabs the spoon with her chubby little hand and sends the goopy orange substance flying everywhere. In her hair. On the wall. All over me. "Baby girl. You literally ate this last week. Three jars, I might add."

Rising, I grab a rag by the sink and attempt to clean what I can before it dries and I have to break out the Magic Eraser.

"Fine." I sigh. "Hawaiian Delight it is. Again. But tomorrow you're getting peas, sister."

Heading to the pantry, I pull out a glass jar of her favorite baby food and grab a clean spoon from the drawer on my way back to the high chair. No sooner do I sit down when my phone rings. Ignoring it, I feed my daughter—

and she doesn't miss a drop. When we're done, I sneak her a couple bites of my Greek yogurt because girlfriend needs some protein in this fruity equation. Lord knows I do too. I'm still holding onto a little bit of pregnancy weight—not that it's a major concern of mine. This little cherub was worth all the late-night Snickers ice cream runs.

My phone rings again.

"Ugh." I steal a glance at the Caller ID—only to be met with WICKHAM FERTILITY CLINIC. "Oh."

Clearing my throat, I press the green button. "Hello?"

"Ms. Bianco?" A woman's voice asks.

"Speaking."

"Hi, this is Rhonda Bixby at Dr. Wickham's office. Do you have a moment?"

Lucia kicks in her high chair. She's over the confinement, ready to crawl all over the living room and try to stick her fingers in places they don't belong.

"Um, I have a couple of minutes." Thinking quick, I grab a baggie of yogurt melts from the cabinet and place a small handful on her tray to keep her occupied. "Is this about the letter I received in the mail earlier?"

She's quiet for a beat. "Yes. Yes, it is."

"Okay?" I don't know what she could possibly say in this situation other than they're sorry for the privacy breach, but I'm not the one they should be apologizing to—unless they sent my name to Fabian? Though I can't imagine why they'd do that. I haven't communicated with them since they discharged me to my OB after the first trimester almost a year and a half ago.

"Have you had a chance to look over the letter in any detail?"

"That's an odd question." I imagine she's trying to get me to say whether I realize Fabian is my donor because if she admits it first, that could come back to her. "If you're asking if I matched up the donor number on the letter with the donor number on my original papers, the answer is yes."

Rhonda exhales into the receiver. "All right. That's what I was wondering. And that's also why I'm calling. I just spoke to your donor, and he would very much like to meet you."

No.

No, no, no.

This wasn't supposed to happen.

"Absolutely not," I counter before I have a chance to think it through. A man with all the money in the world can hire the best lawyers that money can buy. "So now that he's aware he has a child, he wants to be in her life? What —does he want some kind of split custody arrangement? Does he want to suddenly be her father? Why would he want to meet us?"

For a flicker of a moment, I'm taken back to my painful divorce a decade ago. My ex got the house, our dog (a black Labrador retriever puppy he claimed was his exclusive hunting dog), and over half of the furniture we bought together (because it was placed on a credit card in his name). As soon as everything was finalized, I vowed to never let a man take anything away from me again.

"He … he actually hasn't mentioned the child yet. He simply said he wanted to meet you."

"Obviously I'm the gatekeeper to said child." I lean over my kitchen island, watching my daughter pick a half-melted yogurt dot off the back of her hand. Our eyes catch and she flashes a smile that half-melts my heart. "My baby isn't a pawn. We didn't ask to know who her donor was. And even after getting that letter yesterday, I have no expectations of having Fabian Catalano in my life in any capacity."

"I completely understand," she says, though her tone is less than convincing. "This situation is less than ideal for each of us. And the clinic is extremely sorry for the complications this is causing you. In fact, I just spoke to Dr. Wickham a few moments ago, and he's prepared to offer you a generous settlement."

Money for nothing?

I'm not exactly hard-up. My car is paid off. My mortgage is very much affordable thanks to a recent refinance. My retirement account is healthy for my age. And my business has grown leaps and bounds in the last few years, to the point where I'm going to have to hire an assistant.

But turning away money that I can sock away for my daughter's future would be a prideful move.

"If you could come in tomorrow, our legal team will be there to answer any questions," she says, "and to go over the terms of the offer. We would just ask that you sign an NDA in exchange for your settlement."

Of course …

They're a business and they have to protect themselves. As a fellow business owner, I understand. I'm a liability to them, and they're essentially paying for my silence. In the end, my daughter will benefit from this. I'm willing to sell my silence for her. Besides, it's not like I'm going to go on social media and blast their clinic for this careless mistake. That won't change what's been done and it would only broadcast my personal business to the world.

"What time tomorrow?" I ask.

"Would two PM work?"

"That's fine." Carina will be here with Lucia, and it'll give me enough time to run to the clinic and be back before dinner. "But just to reiterate, I do *not* want to meet my donor."

"Are there any circumstances in which you might reconsider?"

"Can't think of a single one," I say. "I'll see you tomorrow, Ms. Bixby. Two o'clock."

Chapter 4

Fabian

"MR. CATALANO, MR. STEEN, MS. FARBER," Rhonda says the following afternoon as I take a seat at the head of the twenty-foot table, sandwiched between my attorneys. "Thank you so much for flying out. I know your time is valuable, but I'm positive we can walk out of here with a satisfactory agreement that benefits us all."

The conference room door swings open a second later, and in walk two men with matching silver beards and black suits.

"I'd like to introduce you to our legal counsel from Hawthorne and Gideon LLC," Rhonda says. "Dr. Wickham will be in here shortly and then we can begin."

Yawning, I peer out the window, toward a half-filled parking lot. We took a redeye last night from LAX to O'Hare. Tomorrow we fly back first thing in the morning.

"Where's the recipient?" I ask, scanning the room.

The Match

Rhonda folds her hands, eyes averted. "I'm afraid she wasn't open to meeting you."

I see red for a moment, and my skin flashes hot.

For the bulk of my adult life, anything I've ever wanted has been a snap of the fingers away. "No" isn't a word I'm accustomed to hearing. What mother wouldn't want to meet her child's donor father if given the rare opportunity?

"I don't understand." I sit straight, jaw tensing as my gaze bores into her. "That's half the reason I agreed to this in-person meeting."

Not to mention, the meeting is costing an arm and a leg in legal fees. The flights alone were several grand on such short notice, though I intend to have the firm bill Wickham's office. Had I known the recipient wasn't going to show, we could've fucking Zoomed this shit show.

Rhonda's gaunt, papery cheeks flush. "When we spoke on the phone yesterday, Mr. Catalano, I informed you there was no guarantee. I spoke with your recipient yesterday and there was no changing her mind. She was adamant that she not meet you. I'm sorry."

I shoot Steen and Farber a look, but they remain impressively stone-faced. As soon as we're alone, we'll have to discuss our next move and hopefully get ahead of any impending storms. More than likely this woman is looking to cash in on this ... unfortunate mishap.

The door opens again, this time ushering in a tall, reedy man with salt-and-pepper lining his temples and thick rimmed glasses. The white lab coat covering his suit identifies him as Dr. Martin Wickham.

"Sorry I'm late, folks," he says in a humble Midwestern tone. "Was just finishing up an embryo transfer. Can't rush those."

He chuckles as he takes a seat at the far end of the table, opposite of me, and he meets my stare without an ounce of reservation. His casual buoyancy is impressive given the circumstances.

"Mr. Catalano, as the founder and owner of this clinic, I want to first offer my sincere apologies. This entire thing has been a blemish on our pristine history, and quite frankly, we're disappointed and embarrassed. We'll do everything we can to ensure it never happens again," he speaks as if he memorized a script his lawyers gave him. "In the meantime, we're happy to offer you a settlement. I know it won't change what's already taken place, but it's a show of good faith."

The older-looking of his lawyer team slides a folder to Steen, who flips it open and scans the top document.

"Is this a joke?" Steen asks, sliding the folder to his partner. "A *million* dollars?"

A million? I make that in my fucking sleep.

"You do realize Mr. Catalano is worth *hundreds of millions*—and your actions have adversely affected the rest of his life," Steen adds.

"All due respect, Mr. Catalano knew exactly what he was getting into when he first made his donation sixteen years ago. While the breach is unfortunate, it doesn't change the fact that he was okay with the prospect of having a child or children out there who he'll never know about."

Farber clears her throat, tapping her glossy power-red nails on the folder. "This isn't about that. Obviously our client knew what he was getting into when he signed on for this. This is about the recipient knowing the name of her donor and that donor being one of the richest athletes in the world. There's a lot at stake for Mr. Catalano. She could make things extremely complicated for him if she wanted to. With cancel culture in the media lately, a single unflattering interview could affect his reputation—which would trickle down to endorsement deals and sponsorships and—"

Wickham's first lawyer lifts a palm. "Yes, okay. We understand that. The issue is Dr. Wickham's insurance company places limits on what they'll pay out. In this case, they were only willing to pay a hundred grand. But because of who you are, Dr. Wickham is willing to front the other nine hundred from his personal funds. In our opinion, it's an extremely generous gesture—one he isn't legally obligated to do. And while we all know you're not in need of the money, this is our best and final offer."

"Everything's negotiable." Steen chuffs, shooting Farber a knowing glance.

"If you want to draw this out despite the fact that your client has no need for any of it, then by all means," his second lawyer chimes in. "But I'd highly recommend putting this to bed so we can all move on."

"How'd this happen anyway?" I interject. "Who's responsible for sending that letter?"

Rhonda steeples her fingers. "It was a new hire. She'd only been on the job a few days. Somehow she cross-referenced your address with the recipient's address. Even *she* was shocked at the error. Carelessness, I assume. We have no reason to believe it was intentional. In fact, she's the one who realized the mistake after the mail had gone out. She came to me immediately."

"This employee is no longer with the clinic," Dr. Wickham adds, messing with the pen in his jacket pocket.

I never met him back in the day. I dealt only with his office staff and the nurses who took my blood and processed my donation. I'd seen his face on a business card by the front desk once. Nice smile. Lots of letters after his name. That's about all I recall.

"I don't want the settlement," I say.

Farber taps my hand and mutters something I can't hear.

"No," I say. "I want part of that money to go into a college account for the child. And I want the rest to go into a trust for her. On top of that, I'd like a little extra for the mother."

"We're currently in the process of negotiating a separate settlement with her," Wickham's first lawyer says. He raps his meaty knuckles against the table top.

"Similar terms to what you're offering me?" I ask.

His team exchanges looks before the second one answers, "We're not at liberty to discuss another patient's settlement with you. I'm sorry, Mr. Catalano."

I should be back in LA right now, practicing for next week's Rosemont Open, not sitting here banging my head against the wall with a bunch of apes. Dragging in a ragged breath, I grab a fistful of hair before rising and shoving the chair out from under me.

"Where are you going?" Steen asks.

"Getting some air." Abandoning the conference room, I storm toward the first exit I see—and wind up in the rear parking lot, stopping short in front of a sapphire blue Subaru with an empty gray car seat in the back.

"*Shoot.*" A soft voice steals my attention, and when I follow the sound, I find a curvy brunette in skin-tight black leggings that stop just below her calves, a white tank top that scoops low enough in the front to showcase her generous tits, and a faded jean jacket cuffed at her elbows. In a haphazard rush, she gathers the strewn contents of her spilled purse from the sidewalk—lip gloss, car keys, hand sanitizer, Kleenex, wet wipes, a packet of pureed applesauce ...

Crouching, her silky chocolate waves spill down her shoulders, hiding her face, and the sunglasses that were perched on the top of her head tumble off, skidding across the concrete.

I seize a bullet of lipstick from the grass—and her scratched sunglasses.

And then I wait.

By the time she's finished, she reaches for the top of her head, feeling around before scrunching her nose when she realizes her glasses are gone.

"Looking for these?" I wave, her belongings in my grip.

Sucking in a stunned breath, the woman gazes up at me with the bluest eyes I've ever seen, so blue they can't possibly be of this world, so icy and vibrant I lose my train of thought. Framed with a fringe of thick dark lashes, she peers up at me and quickly looks away—the way most people do when they recognize me.

"Thanks." Biting a full, rose-colored lower lip, she rises and takes the lipstick and glasses from my hand. "There's an uneven crack in the sidewalk back there, so be careful …"

"Will do."

Tucking a strand of hair behind her ear, she steals another glimpse at me before fishing her keys from her bag and striding toward the sapphire Subaru with the baby seat in back.

"You're Fabian Catalano, aren't you?" she asks before she climbs inside.

Most people typically don't ask that—they just know. Regardless, I nod and pray she doesn't ask what the hell I'm doing at a fertility clinic outside Chicago. This is how blind items and TMZ articles get started. Last thing I need is some nosy internet sleuth digging into my business because they saw some gossipy post on Instagram.

Without another word—and before she has a chance to ask for a selfie with me—I shove my hands in my pockets and strut down the sidewalk, ensuring I avoid the place that caused her to take a spill.

"Wait," she calls.

I turn around and spot her leaning against her car, arms folded casually across her chest as she examines me.

"I don't do pictures. Sorry." I turn away when she calls out again.

"I don't want a picture." She steps toward me, her white Adidas scuffing against the pavement. "I just ... this is going to sound weird, but I just wanted to thank you."

Facing her again, my gaze narrows. "For what?"

We're separated now by a handful of feet, and I find myself momentarily distracted by her pointy chin, her delicate nose, that rosy pout, and those hooded, hypnotic blues. She isn't like the women back in LA. I swear there's a legion of clones, all of them with the same overfilled lips, the same wavy blonde extensions, the same fluffy lashes, and expressionless, Botoxed faces.

Her tank top is tugged down in one spot, revealing a hint of a lacy white bra barely containing her spilling cleavage, but I do my best to keep my eyes trained on hers.

"I didn't want to meet you," she says. "But running into you now—it'd be weird not saying something, right?"

"What are you talking about?"

"Rhonda said you wanted to meet me. I told her no, but ..."

My heart hammers in my ears as I stitch this together. "So *you're* the recipient."

Her pink lips press into a hard line as she scans the parking lot. I follow suit. We're alone. Thank God. But for how much longer is anyone's guess.

"I *love* my life." Her left hand splays over her heart, and I can't help but notice there's no ring. Not that it matters. It's merely an observation. "*Exactly* the way it is. I don't want any part of it to change, so that's why I said no to meeting you. But since you're here, standing in front of me, I just wanted to take the time to say thank you for the beautiful gift you've given me."

Before I have a chance to process her words, she unlocks her car, climbs in, and starts the engine.

Strutting up to her door, I rake my hand across my jaw, smirking. So ... she doesn't want to meet me because she thinks *I'll* upend *her* life?

I rap on her window. She slides her scratched sunglasses over her perfect nose before rolling it down.

"So ... if you didn't want to meet me, why were you here?" I ask.

"They wanted me to sign an NDA." She exhales. "I was meeting with their legal team."

"And did you sign it?"

She winces. "No."

Pinching the bridge of my nose, I sigh. I've a feeling this is going to go exactly how I originally imagined, but I'm willing to hear her out.

"So let me get this straight, they tried to buy your silence, you refused, and on top of that, you refused to meet with me?"

The woman nods. "The offer was laughable. Insulting, really."

Yeah, tell me about it ...

"I can't possibly imagine what reason you'd have to meet me." She runs her hand along the steering wheel, staring forward.

"How do you know I wasn't going to offer you some kind of financial support," I shouldn't plant the seed, but I doubt the thought hasn't already crossed her mind.

"Why would you do that? You have no legal obligation to support this child," she says. "I don't want your money. And honestly, the clinic can take their sorry offer and …"

She bites her lip, silencing herself.

"*You* didn't do this," she continues. "You didn't sign up for fatherhood, so I don't expect you to suddenly be a part of the baby's life."

Baby.

I hadn't thought about the age of the child.

"Honestly," she continues. "I wish I could unlearn this information. It was a lot easier when you were just some nameless, faceless guy that I didn't have to think about."

"So you don't want anything from me?"

"You've literally asked me that how many times now and my answer hasn't changed." She half-laughs, though I suspect there's an undercurrent of annoyance there. "Almost feels like you're interrogating me."

Sassy.

I can respect that.

"Anyway … I need to get home." She checks her watch before shifting into reverse, but I'm not ready for this to be over. I don't even know her name—or the sex of the child we share. Granted, the kid is hers, and legally I don't have a right to know anything about it. But now that it's all within arm's reach, I know I'll spend the rest of my life wondering. One of these days, I might kick myself for not asking when I had the chance.

"Boy or girl?" I ask.

Head tilted, she flattens her pretty mouth. "Does it matter?"

"Of course not," I say. "Just curious."

She hesitates, knuckles turning white as she grips the steering wheel. "Girl."

"Does she look like me?"

She exhales, pausing again as she stares straight ahead. "Spitting image. Eyebrows and all."

"Healthy?"

"Extremely," she answers.

"What's she like?"

Her lips begin to move, but then she stops. Flicking her sunglasses over her head, she angles her attention my way. "I saw an interview you did once. The lady asked you something about when you were going to start a family and you stormed off the set. I guess I'm just confused as to why you're suddenly interested in a kid you never knew existed … and you don't even want kids in the first place."

Ah, yes. The Katherine Kingman Show a few months back. In the pre-interview, my team had informed her on numerous occasions not to mention my engagement (which was already on thin ice), only the defiant gossip queen proceeded to not only bring up the impending nuptials, but she then took it a step further and brought up children—a hot button topic between my then-fiancée and me at the time.

Saying on camera that we weren't going to have kids would've started WWIII at home.

Saying we were considering it would've given her false hope.

No matter what answer I gave, I'd have been fucking myself over.

So rather than respond, I tore off my mic pack and exited stage left. I wasn't going to sit there like a doormat and be disrespected by a spray-tanned, fake-toothed woman gaming for ratings at the expense of my personal life.

Although I have zero desire for a family of my own, storming off her set had absolutely nothing to do with my feelings toward children and everything to do with respect.

Respect for myself, for my relationship at the time, and for the boundaries that woman crossed without a second thought.

"I'm navigating this minute by minute—just like you," I tell her. "Half the time, I don't know what to think."

"I just think maybe it's not a good idea to talk about her anymore." She bites her lower lip and offers an apologetic expression. Cupping a hand over her heart, she says, "Thank you again, Fabian."

Her car begins to roll backwards and she glances in the rearview.

"Wait." I hook my hands on the frame of her open window. "I don't even know your name."

Looking away, she drags in a breath so hard it lifts her shoulders. "And we should keep it that way."

I release my hold on the door and watch the nameless mother of my child drive away, her license plate so dusty I can only make out three letters—SRY.

Sorry.

Yeah, me too.

An empty, dented soda can rolls past me, coming to a stop in the grass. I scoop it up and drop it in a trash can on my way back. Never in my life have I related to a piece of garbage before, but I can't help but notice the hollowness in the center of my chest that wasn't there an hour ago.

Heading back to the conference room, I walk back into a war zone, both sides quarrelling over ethics and legalities, spewing threats and ultimatums.

I tune them out, focusing on the window that showcases the parking lot, replaying the last few minutes' events in my head on a loop. That hypnotic blue gaze. Those bitten-pink lips. The soft curves. And the sass. All of that and she's the mother of my child—a part of me grew inside of her.

Whether I know her name or not, we'll always be connected.

I think about the healthy baby girl who looks like me—the one I'll never meet.

Rising, I interrupt their quarrel. "If you'll all excuse me, I'm going to head back to the hotel. Steen, Farber, make sure you negotiate a killer deal for my recipient. It's the only way I'll sign a damn thing."

With that, I head out. And within minutes, I'm driving back in radio silence. By the time I pull into the hotel valet lane, I have no recollection of the drive. My mind was too focused on her.

The beautiful, mystery baby mama who wants absolutely nothing to do with my money, my time, or me.

Chapter 5

Rossi

"HOW'D IT GO?" Carina asks the instant I walk in the door.

I drop my purse and keys on the kitchen island and head to the living room, where my daughter drops blocks into a bucket. Her eyes light when she sees me, and when I take a seat beside her, she hands me a blue wooden cylinder.

"You seem ... frazzled." Carina takes a seat across from me and pages through a soft ballerina book. "What'd they offer?"

I blow a puff of hair between my lips. "Twenty-five grand. Can you believe that?"

"That's it?"

I nod, rolling my eyes. "Their lawyers claimed they didn't legally owe me anything because the breach didn't involve my name—only his. But they were sorry and they wanted to offer this."

"If they don't legally owe you anything, why have you sign an NDA?"

Shrugging, I say, "Who knows. Maybe it's a precaution."

"The whole thing sounds shady. Did you sign though?"

"Nope." I reach for a purple triangle and hand it to Lucia.

"So … what are you going to do?"

"Going to find a lawyer of my own, have them go over the contract and just make sure everything's kosher," I say. "And then I'm going to act like none of this ever happened."

"Is that even possible?"

"Probably not—but I'm going to try." Lucia crawls to the far corner of her blanket to grab a stuffed elephant. Once there she promptly shoves the snout in her mouth. I envy her blissful unawareness, and I intend to keep it going for as long as I can. Her life is so easy, so uncomplicated. And that's exactly what she deserves.

That said, if there's one thing I've seen in my career that has completely decimated families, it's secrets and lies. My baby's not even a year old yet, and already I'm burdened with hiding her father's identity from her until she's grown enough to comprehend this.

"So … I met him," I blurt. The entire way home, I debated bringing it up to Carina. It all happened so fast, our little exchange in the parking lot. And for half the drive home, I wondered if I imagined it."

"Wait, what? You met whom?" She scoots closer. "Fabian?"

I nod. "By accident. We were both outside at the same time. I tripped and spilled my purse. He handed me my lipstick and sunglasses, and my god, Carina. We locked eyes and it was like someone had used a stun gun on me or something. My entire body went numb. My thoughts were racing in every direction. My mouth went dry. I kept telling myself to keep walking, to get in the car and drive away—but then half of me thought I should thank him because I'm never going to see him again, and I truly am so grateful for the gift he gave me."

"Rossi." Her tone is low and her hand clamps over her open mouth.

"He wanted to know why I didn't want to meet with him. He said something like how did you know I wasn't going to offer you money or something like that," I say, "and then the next thing I know, he's asking if it's a boy or a girl, if she's healthy, what she looks like …"

"Seriously?"

"It's clear he wants to be a part of her life—which was exactly what I was afraid of."

"Did he say that? Did he explicitly state that?"

I shake my head. "He didn't have to. Why else would he be shoving money in my face and asking questions about her?"

Carina's brows furrow and she tugs her hair tie out of her dark hair before twisting it into a messy bun.

"He wanted to know my name," I say. "But I left."

She winces. "This is tough because … you have his name. Isn't it only fair he has yours now? And before you protest, hear me out. What if ten years from now he finds out he has an inheritable heart condition and wants you to know for Lucia's sake?"

"They did extensive hereditary testing on him during the donor process—he's clean."

"What if … years from now … he has no other children and he wants to leave his estate to his one and only biological offspring? What if Lucia could inherit hundreds of millions of dollars?"

I laugh. "No one needs hundreds of millions of dollars. I want Lucia to work for what she has, not have everything she's ever wanted handed to her simply because she won the genetic lottery."

Carina rests her elbows on her knees, picking at threads of carpet. "Okay, then what if someday, eighteen years from now, when you tell Lucia who her father is, she finds out that he wanted to be a part of her life and you denied her of that?"

I hate that she has a point.

I bury my face in my hands and breathe through steepled fingers. "I'm just scared, Carina."

"Of what? Of not being a single parent anymore? Of allowing your daughter to know her roots?" She laughs. "You realize how ridiculous this sounds coming from you of all people? You're the queen of family trees."

"My whole thing is—what if he wants joint custody? Can you imagine having to ship my baby off on some private jet every other week so she can spend time with her father?"

"You're forgetting that the man signed away all of his legal rights to this baby the day he made the deposit at the sperm bank …"

"And you're forgetting he has an insane amount of money and access to the best lawyers in the country," I say. "There's not exactly a precedent for this kind of thing. Believe me, I spent a couple hours googling it this morning. In all the custody cases I found, the judge almost always instated parental rights of some kind to the parent requesting it. Courts tend to favor uniting families."

"You're catastrophizing," Carina says. "Let's flip this. What are all the ways this could be the best thing to ever happen to the two of you? Maybe he wants to be a part of her life, but not legally. They could have a relationship of some kind, whatever that looks like. And maybe nothing would change except you have to let them FaceTime a couple times a week. Maybe he sends her Christmas gifts or visits on her birthday. You'd be okay with that, right?" Her lips inch up at the corners. "Or what if the two of you spend time together and somehow … maybe … accidentally … fall in love?"

Chuckling, I grab a throw pillow off the sofa behind me and pretend like I'm going to toss it at her. "You had me until the love part."

She straightens her shoulders. "All I'm saying is this can go a million different ways. Right now you're a ship drifting at sea, waiting for a wave to carry you somewhere. But if you get behind the wheel of that ship and steer it yourself, you can get exactly where you want to be."

"Thanks for the analogy, captain."

"This is what I'd do," she continues. "Call the clinic, have them put you in touch with him, and if he's still in town, invite him over tonight to meet Lucia. Make it clear it's a once-in-a-lifetime meeting. Maybe take some pictures for Lucia to have when she's older so she doesn't end up hating you for keeping him away. And then the two of you can talk about this. At the end of the day, you're a family. Maybe not a traditional family. But you're in this together and you can figure this out together. That's what families do."

Scooping my baby into my arms, I trace my thumb across her perfect dark eyebrows and sweep a lock of her wispy hair from her forehead.

"You're thinking with your heart, sis," she says. "And I know the idea of everything changing is terrifying. But you need to think with your head on this one. Step back and make a rational decision with Lucia's best interests in mind. I know you can do it."

The Match

My sister says a lot of crazy things. She drives a bright yellow Mini Cooper she lovingly calls Rupert, occasionally highlights her hair various shades of unnatural colors, and dreams of opening a solar-powered greenhouse someday called Plant Parenthood. She's always marched to the beat of her own drum, and I love her for it. She's never been one to dole out nuggets of wisdom, but she has a point.

"If you sit back and think about it, there are way more pros than cons here," she adds.

Dragging in a breath, I slide my phone from my back pocket, close my eyes, and gather my composure.

With sweaty palms and trembling fingers, I dial the clinic and ask for Rhonda Bixby.

Chapter 6

Fabian

I'M RECLINED in a leather arm chair, bouncing a tennis ball off the hotel suite wall, when my phone rings.

"Rhonda, hi." I answer after checking the caller ID.

"Mr. Catalano," she says. "So glad you answered. I'm calling with good news."

"If this is about the settlement, I would advise you to call Steen and Farber. They can relay any information to me."

"No, no." There's a rush of excitement in her tone. "I just got off the phone with your recipient—she's decided she's open to a meeting after all."

Never mind that we already met …

Wonder what changed?

Sitting forward, I release the yellow ball, which rolls out of sight. Then I make my way to the expansive windows overlooking a gray Chicago skyline. Just when I was thinking this entire trip was a waste of valuable time, it seems I may be proven wrong.

"She'd like you to call her," Rhonda says. "Let me know when you have a pen and paper handy."

Trotting to the writing desk in the corner, I grab a pad of hotel stationery and a monogrammed ballpoint pen. "Ready."

"Okay, her name is Rossi Bianco and her number is 555-786-8851."

"Got it." I end the call and dial her number. There isn't much in this world that makes me nervous, but pacing the window as the phone rings, a subtle burst of nausea floods my middle.

"Hello?" A soft-sweet voice answers.

"Rossi," I say, her name foreign on my tongue. "It's Fabian."

"That was fast … I hung up with Rhonda not five minutes ago." She chuckles into the receiver.

"I'm only in town for tonight," I say, a feeble attempt to cover my enthusiasm. I wouldn't normally jump at an opportunity to call someone back, but *this* someone isn't just *any* someone. "Rhonda said you were open to meeting?"

"Yeah. I thought about it a little more," she says. "But before I agree to anything, I wanted to get some clarifications on expectations."

"Naturally. Go on," I say.

"Just want to make sure we're on the same page as far as legal obligations and rights." She chooses her words carefully and delivers them at a slower-than-normal pace. "I'm okay with you meeting your biological daughter, and if you decide you want to be a part of her life in some capacity, we can discuss that. But I don't want a dime from you. And I want your word that you're not going to sue for custody or anything crazy."

I stifle a laugh at the idea of me palling around the world with a baby in tow. I would never subject a child to my lifestyle, nor would I compromise my lifestyle by adding a kid into the mix.

"Rest assured, Rossi, that custody is the last thing I want from this situation," I say.

"Good. Sounds like we're on the same page then …"

"Same word of the same line of the same paragraph."

Some people visualize their futures and instantly know they want to be a parent. They picture the kids. Make a mental list of names. Envision themselves at baseball games or dance recitals. There's no doubt that's what they want. They don't question it twice. At thirty-seven, I keep waiting for that paternal urge. I find myself glancing at strangers' babies in passing, wondering if or when it'll finally hit me. But that desire never comes. There's never been an itch to scratch there. Never an inkling of longing.

"I'm not trying to be a burden," I tell her. "I've got no plans to disrupt what you have going on. Honestly, I've never wanted children and I'm the first to admit I'd be a terrible father. But knowing I have one out there … I'd be remiss if I didn't use the opportunity to meet her just once, especially if I'm here."

If I didn't, it could haunt me the rest of my life. All I'd have is that five-minute exchange in the parking lot with her beautiful mother. It'd be one of those memories that come at random, that take up residence in the back of my mind. It'd feel like a movie I never finished and never will. An unsettled incompleteness.

"I appreciate this more than you'll ever know," I tell her.

Dragging my hands through my hair, I finger comb it

back into place, ignoring the niggling voice in my head wondering if this is all some kind of extortion ploy. In my earlier, more naïve days, I met a sweet, unassuming Mary Sue type. Shy in a sexy way. She happened to be in my path when I was plastered at a hotel bar after a grueling tournament in London. We screwed for hours like a couple of sex-depraved animals, and I left before the sun came up the following morning to catch a flight. A month later, she'd reached out to my PR rep claiming she had a sex tape of us as well as a handful of compromising photos she was going to leak to the press if I didn't give her half a mil in cash.

I didn't give in to her, and my attorneys were able to get to the bottom of her blackmail scheme, but I learned early on to keep even the nicest people at arm's length. Money tends to draw in the crazies like flies to honey.

"I thought we could do this at my home," Rossi says. "It'd be private, which I'm sure is important to you—it's important to me, too."

It's like we're speaking the same language.

I'd almost go so far as to stamp this as too good to be true.

"Just the three of us," she adds.

"Perfect."

"Is this your cell? I can text you my address. Where are you staying?"

I pace the hotel suite, one hand in my pocket. "In the city. West of downtown."

"So you're about an hour away from me then. Lucia goes to bed around eight. Would six work?"

"Lucia?" I ask. "Is that her name."

I'm met with deafening silence on the other end. Followed by a small, "Yes."

Lucia.

I have a daughter and her name is Lucia.

That one little detail does nothing more than add weight to the gravity of this situation, to make the reality of all of this a little more ... vibrant.

I let it sink in for a few seconds, and then I pull my shit together.

"Six o'clock?" Pulling the phone from my ear, I check the time. It's four thirty now. "I'll make it work."

We hang up and a minute later, my phone chimes with a text containing her address. I copy and paste it into a search window to make sure it's legit—because stranger things have happened—and I'm met with an expired real estate listing for a three-bedroom bungalow. White with a lacquered yellow door, bright like daffodils and sunshine—not quite the electric color of a tennis ball, but close enough. With a deep front porch, hanging ferns, and flower bushes lining the driveway and sidewalk—just like my parents had at my childhood home.

I scroll through fifteen listing pictures. The house was built in the seventies, but the inside has been completely updated. White kitchen. Pale gray walls. Light wood floors. There's a fireplace in the family room and a little covered deck off the dinette. The back yard is encased with a wooden picket fence painted in a shade that matches the fluffy clouds in the blue-sky background.

Clicking away from the movie-scene house, I shoot Taylor a text. I'd brought her along on the trip in case I needed someone to run errands to handle any miscellaneous inconveniences that might've come up, but tonight she's off the clock.

She responds within seconds, asking where I'm going.

Heading to the en-suite bath, I brush my teeth, comb my hair, and freshen up. While we're past the first impression phase, making myself presentable is a part of who I am.

I don't reply to Taylor—where I'm going tonight is a private matter, and since she's off the clock, it's no longer her concern.

Grabbing my keys, I make my way to the elevator, grab my SUV from valet, type her address into the nav and start my journey.

An hour later, I'm pulling into the floral-encased driveway of the same little white house from the pictures—but before I so much as shift into park, I'm overtaken by the very same wild, adrenaline-fueled frenzy that normally fills my chest right before a match. A sensation so strong, it pulls me out of my body for a second, to somewhere else completely.

Strange.

This has never happened outside the court before.

Shoving it down, I kill the engine, put my best game face on, and climb out so I can meet my daughter. The sooner I do, the sooner I can put this entire thing to bed and get back to life as it was always meant to be.

Chapter 7

Rossi

TWO BRIGHT HEADLIGHTS flash into the sidelights of my front door three minutes before six.

"Okay, baby girl. He's here." I don't say Fabian. And I certainly don't say Daddy. Honestly, I don't know what to say, not that she'd understand any of it anyway.

With the baby on my hip, I check my reflection in the mirror above the console table, tucking my hair behind one ear before placing it back.

My heart gallops, inching up the back of my throat before settling in my ears.

"Is it hot in here?" I ask my daughter, despite the fact that she can't answer. A nervous dampness collects at the back of my neck, along my hairline. Sniffing my shirt, I ensure I smell just as lovely as the rose bushes outside, and then I fan my warm cheeks. It's too late to open a window or change from this sweater to a t-shirt. It's also too late to talk myself out of this weird little frenzy because the sexiest man alive is strutting up my walkway.

Six more steps and he'll be ringing my doorbell.

Sucking in a long, cool breath, I close my eyes, gather myself, and let it go.

It's not like I need to impress him …

It's not like it matters that he's the most beautiful human I've ever laid eyes on—second only to my daughter.

Smoothing Lucia's shiny onyx hair aside, I make sure her pink satin bow is straight, and that her outfit is stain-free. As soon as I got off the phone with him earlier, I changed her from the spit-up scented onesie she was wearing into a flower-and-duck covered romper. Nothing frilly or Sunday best-ish, but a serious improvement nonetheless.

He's so close I can hear his footsteps on the other side of the door.

I try to swallow, but I can't.

The doorbell chimes.

Lucia claps in my arms.

I take one last cleansing breath, tell myself this is going to go wonderfully no matter what, and then I reach for the knob.

"Hey," I answer with the feigned confidence of a woman who isn't at all uneasy about this. Stepping aside, I say, "Come on in."

"Hi there." His voice is velvet smooth, and his casual infliction is the kind you'd use with an old friend. His dark eyes lock onto mine, holding them captive for a single, endless second. A heady rush blows through me, a spine-tingling burst of air that came out of nowhere.

"You find us okay?" It's a dumb question to ask, especially given this GPS day and age, but my mind is spinning so fast I can't come up with something better.

"Yeah." He slides off his pristine tennis shoes, placing them perfectly on my door mat alongside three pairs of my own. "Nice neighborhood you've got here. Reminds me of the one I grew up in. Same kind of houses."

"It's adorable, right?" I motion for him to follow me down the hall and to the living room where I've already spread out Lucia's blanket and favorite toys. "You can sit wherever you'd like. I usually hang out on the floor with her …"

His gaze drifts from me to the baby, and his expression straddles the line between intrigue and the way I looked when I used to window shop for rescue cats knowing I was deathly and tragically allergic. There are few things worse than being a cat person but not owning a cat—except for maybe being a baby person and not having a baby.

But I remind myself Fabian isn't a baby person—he's said so himself.

I'm imagining things, and reading into every nuance is going to do me no favors.

Keeping a careful distance, he perches on the center cushion of my gray sofa, elbows resting on his knees as he watches his daughter play with a Baby Einstein radio.

"So," I say with an awkward chuckle. I've never formally introduced a baby to anyone before. "This is Lucia."

"Lucia," he says her name under his breath. "That's a beautiful name."

"I've been holding onto it for years," I say. "Had a hundred names picked out for a boy, but this was the only one that ever felt right for a daughter."

"When you know, you know."

"Exactly." I scoot closer to her, handing off a soft book that she promptly puts in her mouth. "She's cutting some new teeth … everything's a teething toy."

He watches her with intention, hardly moving, studying her like she's some kind of living photograph. Or maybe he's trying to mentally capture this moment so he can lock it away forever, knowing there'll never be another like it.

"I'm not a baby person," he says. "So I apologize if this is awkward."

"I wasn't a baby person before I had her either," I say. "I mean, I love her because she's my own, but I was never one to fawn over other people's babies. It just seems so contrived, you know? Whenever people freak out over other people's kids, it feels forced to me."

"When was she born?"

"Last June."

"My mother was born in June. What day?"

"The seventeenth," I answer."

His lips inch into a sad sort of smile. "Hers was the sixteenth."

Was? Is she no longer living? I don't ask—it's none of my business.

"She passed last year," he volunteers. "About five months after we lost my dad. She would've loved to have been a grandmother, but that never happened."

"No siblings?"

"I have an older sister, but I haven't seen her since I was a kid. Don't even remember her, really. Just that she caused our family a lot of grief."

If his parents have passed and he's estranged from his only sibling, it makes sense why he wanted to meet his child. The tension in my shoulders dissolves a little more as the man before me transforms from an athletic god to a mere mortal.

But only slightly.

He's still very much Fabian Catalano—the man, the myth, the legend.

"I could find her for you." I'm probably—okay definitely—overstepping boundaries here, but I can't help it. "It's kind of what I do for a living. I mean, partially. I'm a genealogist. I help people track long-lost relatives and help create family trees, that sort of thing. I'm really good at locating people …"

His brows knit as if he's considering, but then his mouth presses into a hard line. "Appreciate the offer, but that won't be necessary."

I've rarely heard of someone not wanting to find a long-lost family member, but once again, it's none of my business so I let it go.

Lucia tosses an orange stacking block in Fabian's direction and it rolls to his feet. A second later, she's off to the races, pawing across the living room on all fours until she reaches him. Hoisting herself on his knee with hands covered in slobber, she bounces and grins.

He eyes the wet streaks on his skin, and I toss him a nearby burp rag.

"Sorry, she's teething."

"You'd mentioned that." He cleans up the drool, folds the rag, and places it neatly on the cushion beside him—only to have Lucia grab it and wave it around like a flag. "But it's fine."

"Everything's a toy at this stage …" I say.

He watches her every move, transfixed, as if he's never seen anything like this. And maybe he hasn't. He said so himself, he doesn't want kids and he isn't a baby person. This is probably a trip to Mars for him.

"She seems like a happy kid," he says.

"So happy," I emphasize. "For the first few months of her life, she slept in a bassinet at the side of my bed. I kid you not, starting at about two months, she woke up every single morning with a smile on her face."

The Match

"Maybe she was just happy to see her mom."

I chuckle. "Yeah, maybe."

His cocoa eyes—the ones that match my daughter's speck for speck—divert onto mine for a moment.

"So are you doing this on your own?" He nods toward the baby. "Or is there someone else in the picture."

"Just me. Which is fine. I mean, I obviously knew what I was getting into when I went into this. My younger sister lives about ten minutes away. She's my nanny. And my parents are always a phone call away. And I have the best neighbors. Always willing to help out if I need anything. It's true when they say it takes a village."

He slides to the floor and takes a seat closer to our daughter. It's weird having this rich, famous tennis player in my living room like just another weeknight. Though I've never understood the idolization of people just because they're extremely athletic. I dated a guy once who was obsessed with Tiger Woods. He actually cried when he recalled the time Tiger took a break from golf. He claimed it sent him into an actual depression and called it his own "blue period." He didn't touch a golf club again until Tiger was back.

"Do you have any games coming up?" I ask because I don't know what else to say but this silence is deafening. "Or tournaments? Matches. I don't know what you call them. I literally know nothing about tennis."

He laughs through his nose. "I'm playing the Rosemont Open next week in Atlanta. Going head to head with Xander Fox."

"Never heard of him. Is he good?"

Fabian laughs out loud this time, and his smile is so brilliant it lights his eyes—and the room. This makes him only slightly less intimidating but ten times more gorgeous.

"The media likes to paint us as rivals," he says, "but

we've known each other for years. He's actually a good friend of mine. I was the best man at his wedding two years ago. Of course ESPN didn't mention that."

"Does it bother you? Having no say in the way you're portrayed?" I think of the video of him storming off the interview set.

"It used to."

"I'm going to be honest with you, after I learned you were Lucia's donor, I googled you."

He looks to our daughter, then back to me. "And what'd you find out?"

"Mostly that you have a temper ... and a thing for beautiful women."

"Or maybe beautiful women have a thing for me ..." He winks. "It's hard to meet people. I train most of the year. And when I'm not training, I'm playing. When I'm not playing, I'm fulfilling endorsement deals and other contractual obligations. Half of my relationships have been set up by PR companies. And most of the photos you see, those paparazzi pics of us grabbing coffee or dining outside at some trendy café in New York? Those are staged."

Well, I feel deceived ...

I make a mental note to cancel my US Weekly subscription.

"Why not just try to meet someone the old-fashioned way?" I ask. "And then keep it on the downlow. Plenty of celebrities lead private lives."

"Success—especially in the world of sports—has more to do with relevancy than anything else. If you don't keep people talking about you, if you don't make sure your name is constantly in the news, they'll move onto the next hot thing and forget you exist. At the end of the day, we're all replaceable. There's always going to be someone waiting, ready to take your place."

"Yeah, but aren't you kind of a legend? You've set world records. People aren't going to forget that."

He frowns. "Tennis buffs will remember. I don't know about everyone else. "

"Is that important to you? To be remembered?"

He hands Lucia the block by his feet. "A man's legacy is everything."

"So someday when you're gone, you want to be remembered for breaking records and being really, really good at tennis?"

"When you put it in simple terms like that, it makes it seem so trivial."

"That's not what I meant." I place a palm out. "I'm not trying to downplay everything you've done to get to where you are. It's just ... when I think of legacies, I think of families. Crazy stories being passed down. Reputations being alive and well long past the date on your headstone. Memories. Personal photographs. That sort of thing."

He nods, silent like he's absorbing this.

"I never met my great grandmother on my father's side," I say, "but the way everyone talks about her, I feel like I know her just the same. To me, *that's* a legacy."

"Guess we have different definitions." He swipes the rag off the carpet and folds it once more.

Before I became a mom, I used to be a neat freak. Now I choose my battles. You can only pick up a living room so many times in a row before it becomes a fruitless and epic waste of time.

Abandoning her perch near Fabian, Lucia crawls to me, sidling into my lap and reaching for a strand of my hair like she always does when she's sleepy.

"She's getting tired," I say as she cozies against me and

releases a big yawn. The weight of Fabian's stare anchors us into place. "Is this all you wanted? Just to see her?"

He bites his lip. "Yeah."

"If you want to hold her, you can. I mean, I'm okay with it …"

Fabian shifts in his seat, as if the thought of taking Lucia into his arms makes him uncomfortable.

"You don't have to," I say.

Straightening his shoulders, he says, "No, it's fine. I want to."

Rising, I carry Lucia over and place her in his arms, distracted by the fact that his biceps are the size of her head.

She squirms at first, a flash of panic in her eyes when she realizes she's been handed off, but eventually she settles against him.

"You can sit back and relax, you know." I laugh at his rigid posture. "She's not going to break."

Sliding back against the couch, he cradles her closer, lips skimming up enough to reveal a flash of a dimple in the center of his chiseled cheek. It's a tender, albeit bittersweet, little moment.

I don't know him well enough to know what he's thinking, obviously, but I'd be remiss if I didn't capture this moment for Lucia.

"Hold on." I launch toward the kitchen to grab my phone, and when I return I have my camera cued and ready.

Only the instant he sees my crouching photographer stance, all the sweetness fades from the moment like a deflated balloon.

Lifting a hand, he says, "No pictures."

I don't mean to, but I laugh because I'm positive this is

a joke. I'm not some paparazzo and this isn't a celebrity photo op.

My amusement fades when I realize he's not joking. "Are you serious?"

"I'm sorry." Rising, he hands Lucia back.

Snapping a picture of the two of them was half the reason I agreed to this meeting. I wanted to have something to give to my daughter someday ... a special photograph she could keep whenever she wanted to remember the other half of her DNA.

"O ... okay." I place Lucia over my shoulder, patting her back as she nuzzles her face into the bend of my neck. She's going to be out like a light soon.

"Thanks for letting me meet her. You have a lovely home and you seem like a great mother." His tenderness is gone, replaced with the kind of insincere tone you reserve for a stranger.

I follow him to the door, standing back as he slips his shoes on and readies his car keys.

"I didn't mean to upset you with the picture thing, I just thought it'd be nice to have something to commemorate ... *this*."

"It's just odd to me that not long ago you wanted nothing to do with me," he says. "Then you invite me into your home and want to take pictures."

"I had a change of heart. It happens." I narrow my gaze, trying to comprehend where he's going with this. "Just like you, I'm taking this whole thing minute by minute."

"Why'd you turn down the clinic's offer?"

I wrinkle my nose. Random, but okay. "Because it was laughable."

"So you're gaming for more money."

"I'm not *gaming* for anything—I just want to talk to an attorney first and see what my options are."

"Exactly." He rubs his hand along his chiseled jaw.

"I'm sorry, I'm really confused. We were having a nice conversation and then the second I grabbed my phone …" I think of him storming off the set of that talk show months back. Clearly something triggered him. "Was it something I said?"

Not that it matters at this point, but if I don't get an answer, I'll forever wonder.

The hollow below his cheekbone divots. "I don't know you well enough to know that you wouldn't go selling that picture."

Taking a step back, I almost choke on my spit. "So that's the issue? You think I want to extort you?"

"You said yourself that you're going to talk to an attorney because you think you can get more money."

Sniffing, I say, "Yeah, more than the twenty-five grand the clinic wants to give me."

His expression softens, but his brows are still knit. "That's all they were offering you?"

I nod. "They said because the breach didn't involve my name, they didn't owe me anything, but they wanted to offer that anyway."

Pinching his nose, he blows a hard breath between his lips. "I'm sorry, Rossi. This entire situation is—"

"—insane," I say. "Complex. Life-altering. Bittersweet."

Our eyes catch in my dim foyer.

"I wish this could be simpler for us," his voice is low, his tone apologetic. "For *her*."

"I don't know what it's like to have the weight of the world on my shoulders, to have millions of strangers watching my every move, ready to judge or take advantage of you or accuse or assume at a moment's notice. But at the end of the day, we're only human—and we're both trying to preserve the lives we've worked so hard to create. You have to do what's best for you, and I have to do what's best for us." I bounce Lucia on my hip. "If you don't want a picture, I'm disappointed for my daughter's sake, but I respect that."

We linger in silence, and I get the sense there's something more he wants to say, only those words never come.

"I should get going. Early flight tomorrow." He reaches for the door. I walk him out, following him to the parked Range Rover in the middle of my driveway.

Streetlights glow above sidewalks and I happen to glance over in time to spot Dan pulling into his drive. Climbing out, his attention snaps our way. I give him a wave.

He offers a slow one in return.

"Who's that?" Fabian asks.

"My next door neighbor."

"Why's he staring like that?"

"Probably because he's asked me on a million dates and I told him I'm not ready—wait." Embarrassment flushes my cheeks when I realize I'm giving myself all the credit. "No. I bet he recognizes you. Sorry—I keep forgetting who you are …"

Fabian chuffs. "Can't remember the last time anyone said that to me."

"Is that a good thing?"

He pauses, staring ahead like he's lost in thought. "I don't know."

"What was it like before you were *you*?"

He gazes past my shoulder, staring at my front door.

"Quiet," he says. But before I can ask him to elaborate, he climbs into the driver's seat and starts his engine. A moment later, he rolls the window down, stealing one last glimpse of the raven-haired beauty in my arms.

"Good luck with your ... match, or whatever, next week. Maybe we'll watch. Will it be on ESPN?"

"Should be."

Lucia yawns.

"That's our cue," I say. "Thanks again for ... everything."

Just like that, the world's biggest tennis player (according to Google) and the most breathtaking specimen of man I've ever laid eyes on backs out of my driveway. I watch his red taillights fade to nothing in the distance, and then I carry Lucia inside.

Carina will be pleased as punch tomorrow when I tell her I'm ninety-nine percent sure he doesn't have any custody ulterior motives. He's simply a man curious about his only child. This was simply closure for him, I'm positive.

It'll never be anything more—and it was never meant to be.

I prepare Lucia's bedtime bottle and take her to her room, rocking her in the sea foam green chair by her window and watching as her lids grow heavy and she pushes the bottle away. When she's finally out, I place her gently into her crib.

Lingering, I watch her dream, my sweet little legacy.

When I return to the kitchen, I pour myself a glass of red wine, grab my iPad, and draw a hot bath to wash this strange day off me.

I'm up to my neck in lavender-and-chamomile scented bubbles, ten minutes into the third season finale of *Grey's Anatomy* when my phone lights with a call ...

... from Fabian.

Chapter 8

Fabian

I'M HALFWAY to the hotel when something feels ... off. Like I'm lighter, but not in an emotional sense, in a literal, physical way.

Something is missing.

Shifting in the driver's seat, that's when it hits me. I reach into my back left pocket—and find nothing. My wallet must've fallen out at Rossi's.

Groaning, I lean my head against the headrest and swipe my phone from the console, switching lanes before calling her.

"Hello?" she answers on the third ring.

"Hey. Think I left my wallet at your place," I cut to the chase. "Can you check your couch?"

A whoosh of water fills the background—was she in the bath?

"Um, yeah. Two seconds," she says. More water. The

slap of wet footsteps against tile. A door swinging open. "Checking now ..."

I stop at a red light, glancing up at my reflection in the rearview. A white Audi pulls up next to me, filled to the brim with girls and pumping with dance music. The front passenger rolls her window down, screaming my name. A rear passenger rolls hers down and the entire backseat yells at me. Just before the light changes to green, another passenger rises from the sunroof, flailing her arms.

"Found it," Rossi says.

I acknowledge the girls with a quick wave that sends them screaming, press the gas, hook a right, and turn back around. "I'll be there soon."

Half an hour later, I'm right back where I started, trotting up to the happy yellow door of the pristine white bungalow, only this time the moon glows overhead and the house is a little less illuminated than it was when I left.

Assuming the baby's asleep, I knock lightly. Three times, then I clear my throat and wait. Five seconds later, Rossi answers, her face clean and her curves wrapped in a pink satin robe. A mess of shiny chocolate hair is piled into a bun on the top of her head, and two damp, face-framing tendrils hang near her eyes.

"Come on in, it's in the kitchen," she says.

A glass of wine and an open bottle rest on the island next to my wallet.

"Hope I'm not interrupting anything," I say.

Cinching the lapels of her robe, she laughs through her nose. "I was just unwinding from the day. I'm dressed under here. For the record. I have pajamas on."

"Ah, so you're not trying to seduce me." I give her a wink as her cheeks grow rosy, and I slide my billfold into my pocket. "Glad we cleared that up."

"If I were trying to seduce you, believe me, you'd

know." She reaches for her wine, taking a sip and staining her rosy lips a shade darker. "I'm sorry. This is weird, isn't it? Like we're not flirting but we are? And we shouldn't be. I don't mean to make this awkward. I should probably lay off the fermented grapes …"

She slides her glass away, burying her pretty face in her hand as she leans over the island.

The honesty is refreshing, the awkwardness endearing.

"Maybe we should make it ten times more awkward and have a toast," I say. "To our beautiful masterpiece, Lucia."

"I can totally get down with an awkward toast to Lucia." She retrieves a stemless glass from the cabinet by the sink, dumps the rest of the wine into it, and hands it my way.

Clinking mine against hers, I say, "To Lucia. May she forever stay happy and healthy."

"To Lucia." Her distracting blue gaze melts onto mine. "And to you."

"Me?" I frown.

"Yeah, I'm glad I had a chance to meet you."

"Yeah? Why's that?"

"Because if I'd have spent the rest of my life believing you were some hotheaded zillionaire model chaser, I'd have been secretly disappointed."

On some level, I suppose I *am* a hotheaded zillionaire model chaser—but I'd like to think my other qualities make up for that.

"What made you choose me in the first place?" I sip the sweet wine, letting it linger on my tongue until it turns velvet.

Blowing a tuft of hair from her eyes, she shifts in her spot. "Well. For starters, your moniker was *Ambitious Athlete* —very cute by the way."

"Hm, can't take credit for that. The clinic must've assigned me that name. Either way, it's not wrong."

"My family is laughably unathletic," she says. "Like we tried this family bowling league one year, and none of us had an average above fifty. We literally got last place out of twenty-five teams. So right away, you were bringing something to the table that we didn't have. And your bio said something about being adventurous, placing value on experiences over things."

Ah, yes. I did write that back then—before I had money. When "experiences" were late-night road trips with no destination, hitting up a concert for some band I'd never heard of, and drinking Boone's Farm with my closest friends in some middle-of-nowhere cornfield while a once-in-a-lifetime meteor shower lit the sky.

Those were the good old days—and I'd forgotten all about them until now.

Life was simpler then.

"Also, it said you were half French and half Italian," she says. "Which is what I am. Not that I'm some kind of bloodline elitist or anything, but I took it as a sign. And then of course, we were matched by the clinic. Genetically, psychologically, all that."

Now that she mentions it, I remember having to fill out a fifty-page personality questionnaire and have an evaluation performed by a psychologist who asked everything from my sleeping habits to my earliest childhood memories.

"It's funny though," she continues, "because I don't think we'd have ever matched in real life."

Lowering my glass, I ask, "And why would you think that?"

Licking her lips, she tilts her head, laughing. "Do I really have to answer that?"

"Very much so."

"Because you're *you* … and I'm just a regular girl from the suburbs." She does a quirky little jig with her arm, as if she's trying to lighten her words, but when she catches the weight of my stare, her cheeks turn as pink as her lips. This topic obviously makes her uncomfortable. But the way she squirms under my hot lights gaze is undeniably sexy.

"What qualifies you as *regular*?" I use her words.

Her eyes widen, and her lips begin to move. "I … I don't know … I think I'm pretty average in every aspect. Average height. Average weight. Brown hair. Mid-thirties. I've seen the women you date … plus, I'm all about the quiet, simple life and you're this jet-setting mega athlete who probably doesn't stay in one place for more than a week at a time."

She isn't wrong about that last part, but I disagree with her first statement.

The woman standing before me is anything but average, and I'd hardly call her *regular*.

"Does the self-deprecation schtick always work for you?" I ask.

"Schtick?" Her brows knit.

"When you talk to men, do you usually do the whole *I have no idea how beautiful I actually am* thing?"

"What? I'm not doing any kind of *thing*," she says, jaw hanging slack. "You asked why I said what I said, and I gave you an honest, down to earth answer. We're night and day. If you saw me on the street in jeans and a t-shirt, pushing a baby stroller, you wouldn't think twice. You would *not* be rushing up to me and begging for my number. Which is totally fine. Not trying to be the most beautiful person in the room."

She hides her chuckle with a generous sip of wine.

"That's not true," I say. "When I saw you earlier today outside the clinic, you stopped me in my tracks."

Her ocean eyes roll to the back of her head. "Yeah, because I'd just tripped and I was making a spectacle of myself."

"There's nothing wrong with owning how attractive you are," I say. In LA, women pay a lot of money to look like her—and it never looks natural.

"I think maybe you should slow down on that wine." She nods toward my glass.

"I've had two sips." I take another. "Three. I'm one-hundred percent of sound mind."

She breaks eye contact, gazing toward her cozy, lived-in living room and back.

"Are we flirting? What is this? What are we even doing?" She squints, hooking a hand on the back of her hip. The lapel of her robe falls open, revealing a hint of a lacy black camisole. She's one careless move from spilling out of that thing and I doubt she has a clue.

I restrain my focus and swallow a fourth sip. "Just getting to know the mother of my child while I can."

"How'd you get into tennis?" She changes the subject, straightening her posture.

"My father used to play racquetball at this local club when I was a kid. I started joining him when he needed a partner. Used to love the sound the ball made when it smacked against the wall. So damn satisfying," I say. "As I got older, my father used to bet me a dollar per game. Then I talked him up to five dollars. One summer I made over a hundred bucks beating him. Eventually tried my hand at tennis as I got older—making the state tournament team in high school, which led to a college scholarship, which led to being discovered by my coach my senior year. The rest is history."

She cups her chin in her hand, perched over the island as she studies me. "Did you ever in your wildest dreams think *this* would be your life?"

"I did, actually," I say. "Never felt more at home than I did on the court. This game ... it came more naturally to me than anything I'd ever done—and I played everything as a kid. Baseball. Soccer. Basketball. Football. And don't get me wrong—I wasn't terrible at any of them by any means. But tennis brought out the rock star athlete in me. Kind of think it was always supposed to be this way."

"Okay, so what's with the sperm bank thing? What made you decide to donate?"

I tell her about my senior year of college, needing some quick cash to fix my car. My scholarship was academic only—the rest of my student aid went to cover room, board, and books. My parents sent what they could each month, a hundred bucks or so, but aside from selling every last possession I owned or making minimum wage at a yogurt shop, this seemed like the path of least resistance at the time.

"Twenty-one-year-olds are notorious for having a one-track mind. I was never thinking about the future—unless it involved tennis," I say. "So what about you? What made you want to be a single mom?"

"I've always wanted to be a mom," she says with an indulgent, sugar-sweet sigh and a slightly upturned mouth. "I was actually married in my twenties. Very briefly. To the man I thought would be the father of my kids. It didn't work out—which was a blessing in disguise. But after the divorce, I moved here to be closer to family, and I sort of buried myself in my work and the next thing I know, my mid-thirties were right around the corner. It kind of felt like a now or never sort of thing. One of my friends told me about IUI using a donor, and how someone she knew had a bunch of babies that way and it was cheaper than adoption, so I thought I'd try it … never thought it would work the first time, but thank God it did."

"Think you'll have more?" I ask.

She bites her lip, silent for a beat, and then shakes her head. "There was a time in my life when I wanted five kids—a big, loud, crazy house. But that's not realistic if it's just me. It'll probably always be just the two of us. And I'm fine with that."

The tiniest hint of bittersweet is woven through her words.

"You can plan every aspect of your life down to the finest details, but it doesn't always go the way we think it will," I say. "Sometimes I think that's the whole point."

"Isn't that the truth." She takes a generous gulp of wine, finishing what remained in her glass.

"How boring would this be if we knew exactly what our lives were going to be like in our thirties, our forties, beyond? What would we have to look forward to?"

I let the gravity of my own words sink in, examining them in the context of our current situation. While the last sixteen years have been a wild ride, it'd be disappointing if the next sixteen were nothing more than a continuation of that.

The money, the blinding-lights fame, the all-you-can-eat buffet of sex, the glory of winning tournament after tournament—it's a dream come fucking true.

But there's got to be more.

Only what that "more" is, I've yet to figure out.

"There's always, *always* something to look forward to." She rinses her glass and places it next to the sink, alongside a row of used bottles with pink caps and a handful of pacifiers.

"I know I don't have any say in how you raise Lucia," I say. "But promise me something."

Seriousness colors her expression and her eyes widen. "Okay?"

"Don't let her believe a single thing she reads about me," I say.

Rossi lifts a brow as she spins to face me. "Not even the good stuff?"

I chuff. "She'll have to sift through the bullshit to find an ounce of the good stuff, and even then no one writes about half of it. The charities, the foundations, the youth camps I've held. The kind words I've said about my quote-unquote adversaries. None of that is printed. If she ever looks me up someday, she'll find a highlight reel of my hot-headed meltdowns. A handful of unflattering interviews eternally preserved on YouTube. Some gossip articles chronicling a string of failed relationships with some of the most vapid humans on earth. A collection of all of my stats and winnings. But I don't want her to know me for those things."

"To be fair, Fabian, I don't even know you …" Her pretty face angles to the side. "There's not much I could really tell her other than what's transpired today. But maybe that's enough? It says a lot that you wanted to meet her. You could've walked away completely and pretended she didn't exist, but you didn't. Maybe that's all she needs to know?"

I gather a lungful of the vanilla-blackberry scent of her home and let it go. Would that be enough? I'm sure it's more than most anonymous donors do for their progeny, but now that I've met her, now that I've seen her face and held this beautiful, tiny creature in my arms, now that I know she exists—is it enough?

Enough for her?

Enough for me?

For the rest of my life, a piece of me will be walking around out there in the world, and I'll have no clue if she's safe, if she's okay, if she's being eaten alive by this man's world we live in. While I'm hardly dad material, I can't deny this heavy protectiveness that floods through me when I think of her sweet smile.

"You're quiet," Rossi says. "Everything okay?"

"Yeah," I lie. "Just thinking about how I'll be walking out of here any minute, and I'm never going to see her again. I thought it'd be easier."

"Was it easy the first time?" she asks. "When you did it an hour ago?"

"I didn't really think about it then. Guess it didn't hit me until just now."

"You're not having second thoughts, are you ... about the custody thing?"

"God, no." I speak louder than I meant to, and Rossi shoots a worried glance toward a hallway I assume leads to the nursery. Lowering my voice, I add, "Nothing like that."

The last thing I need is to get embroiled in some legal situation—one involving a child, no less. It'd be yet another PR nightmare keeping me up at night when the only thing I should be worried about is killing it in the next tournament.

"I wish there was a precedent for this kind of thing," she says. "Or some kind of crystal ball, so we could know how this is going to affect her twenty years from now."

"Maybe," I begin to say something I may come to regret. "Maybe we could stay in touch? I wouldn't have rights to her, obviously, but maybe I could be a part of her life? In whatever capacity that makes you comfortable?"

She bites her lower lip and her shoulders fall. "It's a great idea. In theory. But it's also a slippery slope."

"How so?"

"What if everything's great for a while—then you lose interest? When the excitement of all of this passes—"

"—you think this is an excitement thing for me?" I laugh through my nose. "Nothing about this is exciting. Terrifying maybe. Unparalleled. Strange. You think I'm going to get bored with this and ghost her?"

"Anything's possible."

"What can I do to put your mind at ease then? How can I convince you that's not going to happen?"

She shrugs. "Like I said, Fabian, I don't know you. And the only way I can get to know you is if we spend more time together … which is obviously out of the question. So—"

"—wait," I lift a palm. "Why don't I fly the two of you to Atlanta next week? I can get you front row seats at the Rosemont Open. We'd have to be discreet about everything, but now that I've had a glimpse of your life here, this would be a chance for you to have a glimpse of my life."

"A nine-month-old baby at a tennis tournament?" She winces, clearly not a fan of the idea. "And having to sneak around to see you?"

I steeple my hands at my nose.

She has a point.

"When's your next tournament?" she asks.

"Four weeks. Why?"

"Maybe …" She hesitates. "Maybe you could stay here? With us? I have a guest room. And I know this isn't exactly the Ritz Carlton, but you could spend a lot of time with Lucia and I could get to know you a little better? I don't know if that's even an option, but I'd be open to it if you were?"

I'd have to fly my assistant out for a month. Coach too. We'd have to arrange access to a private tennis court for practices, which I doubt would be an issue given this is one of the largest metropolitan areas in the country. It'd take a bit of finessing, but I could make it work.

"Thoughts?" she asks with a slight laugh. "I know it sounds crazy, but we could condense a lot of getting-to-know-you into a short amount of time."

"It's a brilliant idea," I say.

She tries to respond, but chokes on her words instead. Perhaps my enthusiasm caught her off guard.

"That's ... that's great," she finally says. "So, um, I guess when you're done with your match or whatever in Atlanta, you can just plan on staying here for a month? I'll set up the guest room for you, and we can just keep things casual and cordial and ..."

Her voice trails.

"Sorry," she continues. "I don't know why I added the casual and cordial part."

Yes, she does.

She's just as attracted to me as I am to her—she just won't let herself admit it

"Looking forward to this little ... arrangement," I say. "I'll fly in next Friday and we'll go from there. In the meantime, you have my number if you need anything."

I check my back pocket, ensuring my wallet is in the proper place, and then I head to the door. Rossi follows, her bare feet padding against the wood floor as she cinches her robe. In the small confines of her foyer, I can't help but notice the way the top of her head would fit perfectly beneath my chin or the way her subtle lavender scent invades my lungs.

Casual and cordial? I'll try my fucking best.

Chapter 9

Rossi

"SO? HOW'D IT GO?" Carina shrugs out of her khaki jacket the next morning and hangs it on the back of a kitchen chair.

I lift a spoonful of oatmeal to Lucia's lips. "He came over twice last night …"

Squinting, she asks, "Wait, what?"

"He forgot his wallet and had to come back."

"Forgot his wallet," Carina speaks slowly, using air quotes.

"No, I think it was legit."

"Whatever. So the second time, did he just grab his wallet and leave?"

I fill another spoonful with mushy oats. "No. He stayed for a glass of wine and we talked. A lot."

Her dark brows lift sky high. "Mm hm. And what did you two talk about?"

My cheeks warm, but I angle my face so she can't see.

All night I played our conversation in my head, again and again, until I was convinced I didn't actually hallucinate any of it.

"So … he told me I was beautiful," I blurt the words. "And he wants to be a part of Lucia's life—but he doesn't want custody."

"Holy shit." Carina collapses into a nearby chair with a plunk. "He was hitting on you."

"It wasn't like that. He's very … honest. Like no filter. He just says whatever he's thinking and he doesn't mince words. And weirdly enough, I found myself doing the same thing," I say. It's been a long time since I've been around a guy and didn't self-edit every word coming out of my mouth before I said it. "It was nice, actually."

"Okay, let's walk it back." She spins her finger like she's rewinding an old cassette tape. "To the part where he called you beautiful."

I stifle a laugh and roll my eyes. "He wasn't hitting on me. It wasn't like that. It's hard to explain."

She rests her chin on her hand. "Yeah, okay, sure. Whatever you say."

"I need to get started for the day." I rise and hand her the spoon and oatmeal. "And you're officially on the clock, sister."

She takes the bowl, rising. "So that's it? He came over and drank wine with you and told you you were beautiful and then he left? End of story?"

I fight the tug that pulls at the corner of my mouth. "I may have invited him to live with me."

"What?!"

"Just for a few weeks. A temporary, getting-to-know-you kind of thing," I say. "Very casual and cordial. We're not playing house, we're just spending time together. All three of us. If he wants to be a part of Lucia's life, I need to know him better."

"So he's going to completely upend his life, leave his fifteen thousand square foot Malibu mansion ... and move in here?"

I nod. "Yup."

"Rossi ..."

"What?"

"That is *in—sane*."

"This whole thing is insane." I grab my phone off the charger, kiss my daughter's chubby cheeks, and trek toward my office in the front of the house.

"When's he moving in?" she calls.

"Next Friday." Disappearing into my work zone, I close the door, slide in my ear buds, and pull up some study music so I can focus on today's work. This weekend, I'll make a list of all the things I need to do to prepare for his stay—fresh linens on the queen-sized guest bed. Maybe stock up on some of the foods he likes? Plan a few activities the three of us can do that won't draw a crowd.

This entire plan is crazy, but it could work.

Checking my email, I load a message from a prospective client and formulate a quick response letting them know I'm booked out six months. And when I'm finished, I type Fabian's name into a search engine—just to look at his face once more. Not that I need any help in that department given the fact that it was the only thing I could see every time I closed my eyes last night.

This entire thing is surreal.

And almost too good to be true.

But we're doing it.

For four weeks, we'll be one happy little *casual* family.

Chapter 10

Fabian

"ARE YOU INSANE?" Coach screams into the phone. "You met some chick while you were in Chicago and now I have to spend the next four weeks living in a hotel while you get your fucking rocks off? No. I'm not signing off on this."

It was easier to tell him I'd met "some chick" than to let him in on the truth. Not that I don't trust him, but the fewer people who know about this, the better. Not to mention my ex-fiancée just so happens to be his beloved daughter and our break-up predominantly hinged on the fact that I don't want a family.

He wouldn't understand, and the truth would only serve to infuriate him even more.

And if any of this got back to my ex, she'd love nothing more than to make life a living hell for me any way possible. "Hell hath no fury like a woman scorned" is the best way I know to describe Tatum Cartwright.

"You don't have a choice," I remind him. He's under contract, and while he's technically the one who put me on the map, the man works for me now. He's on my payroll. He goes where I go. Same with Taylor, who'll probably shed an ocean's worth of alligator tears when I break the news. God forbid she spends time away from her LA-trash boyfriend, some twenty-four year old douche with bleached hair and neck tattoos who thinks he's going to be the next Machine Gun Kelly. "Anyway, I just got home so I'm going to need you to start calling around for a practice court we can rent for a month out there."

Coach blows a hard breath into the receiver. "You're really something, Fabian. You know that, right? You've done a lot of stupid shit, but this takes the cake."

"I'm bored with Malibu," I lie, sort of. You'd have to be a psychopath to get bored of the mild weather, palm trees, beautiful people, and ocean breezes. "A change of scenery might be good for me. You too."

"Yeah, yeah, yeah. Whatever you have to tell yourself," he sighs before hanging up. He'll get over it. He always does.

I hoist my suitcase onto the foot of my bed and Face-Time with Taylor to break the news—keeping details as vague as possible. And then I task her with arranging accommodations for Coach before informing her she'll remain behind, assisting me remotely for the next four weeks.

She nods, offering a wide smile that hardly contains her excitement, and tells me she's on it.

Less time in my shadow means more time with her cringey boyfriend, but I get it.

I was young, dumb, and in love once, too.

I unpack my things, collapse on my bed, and stare at

the ceiling above. The house is quiet, and should be for the rest of the day. Which normally is a good thing, but today I'm not in the mood to be left alone with my thoughts—which have been all over the place the last twenty-four hours or so.

I wasn't expecting my child's mother to be so easy on the eyes, but it isn't her beauty that keeps me up at night. It's her refreshing honesty. Her lack of desperately trying to impress me by being something she isn't. It's her down-to-earth nature, inherent and genuine. And her unconditional love for the child we created together.

Climbing off the bed, I hit the shower to wash the plane smell off of me. Ordinarily I'd have taken my private jet to Chicago, but I'd loaned it out to a local college team as part of a charity arrangement this week.

Eyes closed, I turn my back to the steaming water, letting it trickle down my body in teasing rivulets as I imagine Rossi's hands palming my sides as she tongues her way down. Taking my throbbing cock in my hands, I bite my lip and go to fucking town.

This is wrong—and I know it.

Rossi made it abundantly clear she wants things to be casual and cordial between us.

But something primal and animalistic stirs inside of me when I think about the fact that she carried *my* child inside of her.

It's sexy as fuck … and I don't know why.

I finish in record time, the proverbial fruits of my labor rinsing down the shower drain.

Soaping off, I rinse, step out, and wrap a white towel around my hips. Only much to my dismay I'm still hard as a rock. Grabbing some gym clothes from my closet, I change up and head down to the lower level to play some racquetball, hoping the satisfying thwack of the ball against the walls will be enough to take my mind off that woman.

It works—but only for a short while.

As soon as I'm done, I'm right back where I started … obsessing over Rossi Bianco.

And wondering if she could ever be mine.

Chapter 11

Rossi

I'VE NEVER WATCHED a tennis match in my life, but watching Fabian grunt and groan on my living room TV, I can't look away. Who'd have thought watching two people hit a ball back and forth could be so ... intense?

Fabian serves, and I'm still trying to figure out this forty-love scoring thing. I don't know why it can't just be one, two, three, four ... but his opponent misses and the crowd claps before returning to silence.

The camera closes in on Fabian's face as he paces his end of the court, and his expression appears angry almost. Or maybe he's hyper-focused. Either way, I wouldn't want to be on the opposite end of anything he's serving.

The doorbell chimes, pulling me out of my moment, and I check the clock before placing Lucia on her blanket and trekking to the foyer.

Shoot.

The Match

Every Wednesday Dan comes over for dinner—and I'd been so busy this week I'd completely forgotten.

"Hey," I answer, shoving my hand on my back pocket. "Come on in. I'm so sorry, I haven't started dinner yet. Been a crazy day …"

And it has been. After busting my hump all morning to finish the Valdez project, I spent the bulk of the afternoon shopping the list Fabian's assistant sent me. I had to go to three different grocers just to find his favorite brand of organic flax seeds, and then I called around to four health stores to find the exact flavor of protein powder he requested. When I got home, there was a delivery at the front door—a set of 1000-thread-count sheets and two expensive-looking pillows.

I only pray this is as high-maintenance as the man gets or I might be regretting each and every one of our twenty-eight days together.

Dan steps inside, a bowl of salad and bottle of wine in hand, and follows me to the kitchen. He helps himself to the drawer with the corkscrew and locates two glasses from the cupboard as I raid the pantry in search of something I can throw together in record time.

I come out with a box of bowtie pasta and a bottle of olive oil, and by the grace of God I find a carton of cherry tomatoes, a bag of unexpired spinach, and a package of feta in the fridge.

"Lucia, Lucia!" He makes his way to the living room and takes a seat by her blanket. "How's my favorite baby doing today? You have a good day with that crazy auntie of yours?"

He throws me a wink. Carina and Dan are strangely two peas in a pod despite being complete opposites in every way. Honestly, I don't know why they haven't dated yet.

No, that's a lie.

I know exactly why.

He has his sights set on me.

I boil a pot of water and rinse and chop tomatoes while he keeps Lucia entertained.

"Since when do you like tennis?" He points to the screen. "Or sports, for that matter?"

I lift a shoulder as I run a colander of spinach under the faucet. "I'm trying it out, seeing if I can get into it."

He laughs. "Really? Because the other day, I could've sworn Fabian Catalano was in your driveway and now he's on your screen. Is there something you're not telling me?"

Busted.

Most of the time Dan lives in his own blissful, ignorant little world where he can easily turn a blind eye to painful realities, but the man can be awfully astute when he wants to be.

"Actually," I say. "That *was* him."

His jaw slacks. "What? I was kidding ... sort of. That was him?"

I nod, turning to salt the water as little bubbles rise to the surface of the pot.

"How do you know him?" Dan asks. "And how did I not know this before?"

"We go back," I say, giving him an extremely abbreviated version of the truth. "Like way back. Just recently connected again."

He hands Lucia a stuffed ballerina, his shoulders deflating. "Ah. Good for you two."

Disappointment colors his tone.

"You like spinach in your pasta, right?" I change the subject.

"Fabian's got quite the ladies' man reputation, doesn't he?" Dan asks, ignoring my question. I don't think he means to. "Didn't he date that supermodel a while back? The one that had that surgery that made her eyes look like a fox?"

I laugh. "Probably."

Just another reason our worlds could never collide. I've got an accounting pining after me and Fabian dates women who look like wildlife.

"I didn't realize you were such a celebrity gossip buff," I say.

"Not me. The ex. She lived for that stuff. I'll never forget the two AM notification she got when Prince Harry announced his engagement to Meghan Markle. Woke me out of a dead sleep. And for what?" He rolls his eyes. "Honestly, I've never understood why people care about the so-called lifestyles of the rich and famous. These people aren't real. I mean they are in a physical sense, but the versions we get are curated by the media."

"This is true." I dump half a box of pasta into the boiling water and give it a stir.

I peek into the living room and catch a glimpse of the game. Fabian is winning. One more point—or whatever—and he'll have the match.

"If you ever want to play tennis, my boss has a membership at the LaGrange Country Club," Dan says. "I could get us on the list for a court."

Chuckling at the idea, I say, "Don't think I've ever touched a tennis racket in my life."

"I could teach you."

It's a kind offer—but the thought of making a fool of myself in front of a bunch of strangers and hating every second of it holds zero appeal.

Nevertheless, I let him down gently. "I'll think about it and let you know."

Tending to the shotgun dinner at hand, I finish making

our meal and set the table while Dan scoops Lucia into his arms and situates her in the high chair at the end of the table. He's always like this, one step ahead of me. Almost as if he's reading my mind.

My ex could've used a page from his book ...

He places a couple of toys on her tray before fetching our wines and taking the seat across from me.

We've been doing this for months now, our little weekly dinners. And I enjoy Dan's company and conversation. Not to mention Lucia adores him. Sometimes I catch myself pretending—in my head—that we're a little family. And I try to envision what it'd be like to be married to him. I think he'd be the kind of husband who helps with laundry *and* irons the sheets. Mows the lawn in a crisscross pattern. Sweeps the garage out on the weekends. Plans family vacations down to the last detail.

And maybe that'd be swell and wonderful.

But without passion or a connection, everything else is moot.

Once I pictured kissing him. Like really imagined it. Eyes shut tight. Lips licked and half-open. His hands in my hair. All that jazz. But I felt nothing. And when it was over, I thought I was going to be sick.

It was like kissing a cousin—unsettling and wrong.

Not that I speak from experience.

"This dish is incredible, Rossi," he says between bites. "I don't know how, but every week you outdo yourself."

For the half hour that follows, I make it a point to enjoy our tedious-yet-sweet little dinner ... because after this Friday, something tells me my life will be quite the opposite.

Chapter 12

Fabian

"WELL, HELLO THERE." A taller, darker-haired, one-off version of Rossi answers her door Friday afternoon. Leaning against the jamb, she scans me from head to toe before flashing an ornery grin. "You must be the baby daddy."

"I'm so sorry." Rossi appears from behind the first woman, gently placing her hands on her shoulders and guiding her out of the way. "Come on in."

Lifting my suitcase over the threshold, I step inside her foyer, inhaling the signature blackberry-vanilla scent I've come to associate with this place.

"This is my sister, Carina, by the way." Rossi points between us. "Carina, this is Fabian."

"Nice to meet you," I say.

"The pleasure is all mine." The sister extends her hand to me. "I'll try not to use my death grip on those mitts—

I'm guessing they're insured for millions. I'd hate to cost you Wimbledon."

Rossi elbows her, leaning in. "You promised you wouldn't make this weird …"

"Think we're a little past weird, don't you?" I intervene. "Pretty sure that ship sailed last week."

Carina's eyes widen. "Yes. Exactly." She turns to me. "See, I like you already."

"Well, that's a relief," I say, deadpanning.

"Carina was just leaving for the day, isn't that right, Carina?" Rossi checks her watch. "Shift ends at four-thirty and it's four-thirty-eight, so …"

"I'm happy to stay if you need me to." Carina bounces on her heels, hands clasped at her hips.

"Do you live here as well?" I ask.

"God, no. I'm just the nanny," Carina says. "Twelve years of sharing a roof with this Type-A Martha Stewart was torture enough."

"Type-A Martha Stewart?" I cock an eyebrow at Rossi.

"I've … relaxed … a bit over the years," she says.

"If it could be color-coded or organized, she would color code it and organize it," Carina says. "Books, CDs, DVDs, sticker collections, nail polish, sweaters, our game cabinet, Mom's yarn basket, the medicine cabinet, cleaning supplies—"

"—I think he gets the point," Rossi interrupts.

"But her floral arrangements are to die for," Carina continues, unfazed. "All of her college friends had her do their weddings because she was cheaper and better than most of the local floral places. Honestly, I don't know why she went into boring genealogy when she could've been hanging out with roses and peonies all day."

That explains the abundance of flora and fauna outside.

Someone gave me a succulent once. Told me it was impossible to kill.

It was dead within a year.

"Carina, would you mind grabbing Lucia? I think I hear her waking from her nap." Rossi clears her throat and nods toward the hall before returning her attention to me. "I can show you around if you'd like. Will take two minutes if that."

"Yeah, of course."

Following her down the foyer, we take a right down a short hallway.

"This first door is my office," she says. "I work from home. This second room is Lucia's."

Peering in, I spot Carina scooping the baby up from a white oak crib. A giant giraffe is propped in the corner, next to a pale pink rocking chair and a gold floor lamp. On the table beside the chair is a stack of books, a pacifier, and a couple of rattles.

"On the left is the hall bath." Rossi reaches into the dark room and flicks on a light. "This is technically Lucia's bathroom, but you'll be using it while you're here." Turning the light out, she ducks back to the opposite side of the hall. "The room next to Lucia's is the guest room. It's probably a little smaller than what you're used to …"

Swinging the door open, she reveals a room easily the size of my walk-in closet—for comparison's sake. A queen bed covered in a million pillows anchors the far wall and a single window with navy curtains offers a view of the front yard.

"I put your sheets and pillows on here," she says. "The ones your assistant sent."

"Thank you." I wheel my suitcase to the foot of the bed, which is a narrow two feet from the dresser. It's tight, that's for sure. But I'm not here to be pampered.

"Someone wanted to see her mama," Carina appears in the doorway, Lucia on her hip.

Rossi reaches for her daughter, a smile engulfing her entire face, one matched only by the one on the child's face.

"Okay, I'm out," Carina says with a wave. "See you next week, baby daddy."

"Can't wait," I tease.

"Look at this bedhead, silly girl," Rossi coos, running her fingers through Lucia's silky dark tendrils. "You had a good nap, didn't you?"

The thought of talking to someone who can't talk back —hell, who can't even understand you, has always struck me as funny and unnecessary. Like people who talk to their pets. Or their plants.

Repositioning the baby toward me, Rossi says, "Look who's here?"

I'm fully prepared to offer an awkward, appeasing semblance of a smile when out of nowhere the baby reaches for me.

Frozen in place, I study her then Rossi.

"She wants you to hold her," Rossi says, nodding and moving closer.

"She remembers me?" I ask.

"She must." Gently, Rossi hands her to me. "Here."

Taking her in my arms, I attempt to make this the least amount of awkward as possible, but I have no fucking clue how to hold a baby. It was different last week when I was already sitting on the sofa and she could just sit on my lap, but now I'm not sure what I'm supposed to be doing or if I'm doing it right.

"Am I supposed to support her head or something?" I ask.

Lucia chuckles. "No, she's past that stage. You're doing great."

The baby squirms, and I can't help but wonder if I'm holding her too tight, so I loosen my grip and relax my stance.

Now what do I do? Rock back and forth? Bounce? Stand here like an idiot?

"You want to go for a walk or something?" Rossi asks, much to my relief. "Get some fresh air? I can give you a tour of the neighborhood …"

"Yeah."

"Awesome." She takes Lucia back, and I grab a ball cap from my luggage along with the pair of sunglasses I'd hooked onto the neckline of my polo.

"Does that really keep people from recognizing you?" she asks when we head out to the garage. A second later, and with Lucia on her hip, she impressively unfolds a black and yellow stroller using only one arm and one foot.

"Sometimes," I say. "If people aren't paying attention, they'll walk right by me."

"Can you hit that garage door button over there?" She points behind where I'm standing.

I get the button and we wait for the door to grind open.

"I've always thought it was funny how movie stars would wear those huge, enormous sunglasses because they wanted to hide," she says. "But all it does is draw more attention to them because normal people don't wear sunglasses that take up half their face, you know?"

"It's a false sense of security," I say.

"Exactly." She punches in the code on the outdoor panel once we hit the driveway, and the door screeches closed behind us. "So this neighborhood is called Magnolia Hills and it was established in the seventies. It's one of the more walkable areas in town. There's a jogging path. A little park with a fishing pond a few blocks that way." She points to the left. "Down this way is a playground. And the elementary school is about four blocks from here. There's a little strip of businesses and restaurants about half a mile away. Sometimes we like to walk to get coffee or dinner or check out the farmers' market in the summertime. It's a very livable area. Great place to raise a family."

"Sounds like it."

"Just about everyone here has young kids, except for a handful of residents. Last year there was a bit of a baby boom, so Lucia should have plenty of little playmates as she gets older," Rossi continues. "Once a month, we try to get the babies together to let them play—and so us moms can socialize with other adults. It's crazy—I thought being a mom ... and a single mom at that ... would've been pretty isolating, but I've met some of my closest new friends because of this little angel."

Up ahead, a green painted sign points us toward the playground Rossi was talking about.

"Lucia loves to swing in the baby swing here—you mind if we make a pit stop?" Rossi asks.

"By all means."

A minute later, she's buckling the baby into some kind of safety swing contraption and giving her a gentle push. Lucia claps, giggles, and bounces.

I wait next to the stroller, hands in my pockets as I take it all in. A small handful of families are here, all of them in other parts of the expansive park. Monkey bars. Tunnels. Slides. Everyone is spread out, running, laughing, not having a care in the world.

If I had to guess, it's been twenty-five years since I last set foot in a park.

"I watched your game the other day," Rossi calls from

the swing. "That grunting thing you do when you hit the ball, is it on purpose or …?"

Chuckling, I say, "It helps with rhythm, helps hit the ball harder. Hard to explain, but there's a science behind it."

I didn't always grunt—it was one of the things Coach taught me in the early days. At first, I refused, telling him I didn't want to sound like a fucking zoo animal. And I couldn't watch other guys do it without busting out laughing. But like all things, a little time, a little maturity, a little bit of pulling my head out of my ass, and I was able to see the light.

Rossi gasps, hand cupped over her mouth as she stares toward the slides. "Oh my god."

"What?" I follow her gaze, searching for something epic based on her reaction. "What is it?"

Ambling toward me, her eyes on whatever prize lingers in the distance, she says, "That's Melanie Saint James … over there. On that bench by the slide." Sucking in a breath again, she adds, "And that's her son, Maddox."

"I've never heard of either of those people …"

"She's a mommy influencer." Rossi keeps her voice low. "Millions of followers. She's a single mom, did IUI like I did. She even wrote a book about it. Huge inspiration to me. You have no idea."

Shrugging, I say, "Go and introduce yourself. I'll stay here with Lucia."

Her brows knit as she turns her focus to me. "You sure? I just … I knew she lived around here, but I've never seen her in person … I'm just … this is … I don't really get starstruck but I—"

"*Go. Say. Hi*," I tell her. Heading toward the baby swing, I take over pushing duties as Rossi makes her way to the woman with blonde waves down to her waist, a preppy striped sweater and tight jeans.

With Rossi's back to me, I have no idea what's being said and have no way of gauging how their little exchange is going—but whatever is said, it doesn't last long. Within seconds, Rossi's returning to our post.

"That didn't last very long," I say. "You should've got a selfie or something."

Swatting her hand, she exhales. "She didn't want to be bothered."

"What do you mean?"

"I told her I was a huge fan, that I followed her on Insta for years and before I could say anything else, she sort of snapped at me and said, *'Can't you see that I'm busy?'* Then she pointed at her kid." Rossi tucks her hair behind her ear and folds her arms across her chest.

I'll admit, I'm not always in the mood to be approached by fans, but if I was a *mommy influencer*—whatever the fuck that means—and another mom came up to me at a park, I'd think it'd be fair game.

It's not like she was at the gyno's office or a goddamned funeral.

"I must've caught her on a bad day," Rossi says. Her voice is light but her eyes are heavy with disappointment—a look I grew to know far too often in my earlier days, when I didn't appreciate the importance of taking three seconds out of my day to give someone a once-in-a-lifetime photo op.

Glancing back at the blonde, I catch her texting on her phone. It's not like she's interacting with her kid. She isn't even watching him for crying out loud.

I push Lucia in the swing, keeping my attention trained on the fake, pseudo-celebrity by the slide, hotness bubbling inside of me with every passing second. It takes all the strength I have to stay planted, to refrain from marching over there and giving her a quick lesson in being a public figure.

"It's going to be dark soon," Rossi says after a few more minutes. "We should head back."

I slide my sunglasses off my face and fold them into my collar as she hoists Lucia from the swing and buckles her back into the stroller. We're halfway down the block, heading back, when the unmistakable sound of sneakers scuffing against sidewalk grows louder behind me.

"Excuse me," a woman's voice calls out.

I keep walking, focusing on Rossi and Lucia.

"Hey, sir, excuse me," she calls louder.

Rossi glances back from the corner of her eyes. "Oh, shoot. It's *her* ..."

Turning around, I'm faced with the blonde in the preppy sweater, her face all smiles as she fixes her hair.

"Oh my god." She jumps, clasping her hands over her perky chest. "It's you. It's actually you." Taking a few steps closer, she adds, "I am *such* a huge fan. You have *no* idea. I was actually at the Rosemont Open last week—third row. I swear we made eye contact at one point ..."

"Doubtful."

Her smile fades, as if she's confused for a fraction of a second.

But still, she prattles on.

"Anyway, I hate to bother you, but would you mind if I got a selfie with you?" Sliding her phone from her skintight pocket, she pulls up her camera, readying it.

"Yes, actually. I would mind." Placing my palm out before she can step any closer, I say, *"Can't you see that I'm busy?"*

She tries to respond, but apparently the cat's got her tongue.

"Fabian," Rossi whispers.

The woman looks to me—then to Rossi, before stepping backwards and nearly tripping on a crack on the sidewalk.

"Oh," she says when she makes the connection. If karma's a bitch, then I'm her faithful sidekick. "I, uh ... I should get ... sorry to bother you ..."

She points back toward the playground.

"Yes, go watch your kid before he hurts himself," I add.

"*Fabian*," Rossi says again, sterner this time.

Turning, the blonde trots away. I can only hope the sting of humiliation haunts her the rest of the night—and I pray the next time one of her loyal fans approaches her, she'll indulge them with a photo and a few kind words.

"You didn't have to do that," Rossi says as we head to her home.

"Yes," I say. "I did."

The mother of *my* child deserves the utmost respect.

Chapter 13

Rossi

I TOSS and turn in bed Friday night, listening to the sounds coming from the guest room across the hall and wondering what the hell Fabian's doing in there. He's probably still on LA time. And maybe he's unpacking. I swear I heard drawers sliding open and close. I think he made a phone call at one point, too. And he gets texts all the time—all those random *dings*.

Sitting up, I switch on my bedside lamp and grab a book from my nightstand in hopes it'll relax—and distract—me. But first, I pluck my phone off the charger, log into IG, and unfollow Melanie Saint James before I forget. Only first, I scan through her photos for old times' sake.

I realize social media is fake. It's all filters and posed photo ops and sponsored ads masquerading as sung praise. But I thought Melanie was different. She reminded me so much of myself. Failed marriage. Mid-thirties. Ambitious and hard-working. Family oriented. Natural, motherly instincts. She made the impossible look like a cakewalk, and she wrote a book about it, too.

In the seconds before I hit the unfollow button, I laugh under my nose thinking about the gobsmacked look on her face when Fabian rejected her request for a selfie *and* fed her her own lines.

I only hope she's kinder to the next person who approaches her.

Flipping my book open to a bookmarked chapter, I read until my eyelids turn to paperweights—and the next thing I know, I wake to the smell of ink on paper and the book splayed out across my face.

Sitting up, I return the book to my nightstand and check the clock ... three AM.

I must've passed out.

A few seconds later, faint whimpers trail from across the hall. Flinging the covers off, I tiptoe to Lucia's room in hopes I can make it before she wakes Fabian. The cries cease the instant I scoop her out of her crib. Making our way to the kitchen, I kiss her cheek before preparing a middle-of-the-night bottle and carrying her back to her room.

We situate in the corner rocking chair, her favorite blanket draped over us, and I rock her as she plays with a strand of my hair, twirling it around her chubby fingers as she eats. A few minutes go by in silence when the creak of the guest room door is followed by the sound of heavy footsteps.

A second later, Fabian's distinct, muscled figure fills the doorway. Leaning against the jamb in low-slung gray sweats and a white V-neck shirt that glows in the dark against his natural bronze tan, he's a sight for sore, tired eyes.

The Match

Dragging a hand through mussed hair, he exhales. "Everything okay?"

He obviously doesn't realize how babies work ...

Which is understandable.

"Yeah, of course," I say. "Sorry if she woke you. She started sleeping through the night around three months, but every once in a while she regresses for a week or two. I think this time it's the teething. Totally normal though."

"You want me to feed her? You can go back to bed if you want." There's a sexy, gravelly quality to his voice, one that makes me feel some kind of way.

"No, it's fine."

"I can't sleep. Might as well make myself useful if I'm up."

Lucia's eyes grow heavy and the bottle is almost empty. I place it on the little table beside me and angle her over my shoulder, patting her back until I get a couple of burps.

"We're about done here anyway," I whisper before placing her back in her bed. When I'm finished, I meet him in the hall, pulling Lucia's door closed. "You can't sleep?"

He combs his fingers through his hair, eyes locked on mine in the dark as his musky, leathery, woodsy scent invades my lungs. It's only now that I realize how close we're standing.

"You want something to help?" I ask. "I have Tylenol PM ... Benadryl ... melatonin ..."

Before he has a chance to answer, I'm shuffling to the kitchen and raiding my meticulously organized medicine cabinet.

"I was thinking," he says as he watches me with a flicker of amusement in his dark eyes. "If you don't mind, maybe I could replace that mattress for you."

Stopping in my tracks, I ponder my response. If I

decline his offer, he'll be forced to sleep on that cheap discount store mattress for the next four weeks. If I accept his offer, he'll probably buy something that costs twenty grand and then I'll feel guilty about it every time I walk by.

"My bed is nicer," I say. A top of the line hybrid, it was a gift to myself when I first bought this place. It's hardly the sort of thing you'd find at a five-star hotel, but it's leaps and bounds nicer than the one in the guest room.

Cocking his jaw, he smirks. "Is that an invitation, Rossi?"

"What? No. I didn't mean it like that. I meant, if you wanted to trade. You can take my room, and I'll take the guest room." Lifting a red and blue bottle of Tylenol PM, I give it a rattle and attempt to change the subject. "This stuff will knock you out in thirty minutes flat."

"Got anything stronger?"

"I might have some Ambien? Though I'm pretty sure it's expired ..." I return to the medicine cabinet, rising on my toes as I work my way to the A section.

"What about whiskey? You have anything like that?" he asks.

"Actually." Abandoning my post, I head to the cabinet above the fridge. "My neighbor, Dan, left some scotch here a few months ago."

"Perfect."

I grab the scotch and a small glass and pour a couple of fingers for Fabian. Dan's going to be tickled when I tell him about this, I'm sure.

"Where's yours?" he asks.

"I've got to get up in four hours ..."

"Never been a fan of drinking alone," he says. "Plus, I'll be up before you anyway. Meeting my coach at seven." Helping himself to the cupboard, he grabs an identical glass and pours me a smaller portion.

"This is a sipping drink," I say.

"It is." He nods. "But you can shoot it if you're feeling brave."

"It's past three AM, I'm feeling exhausted," I say. "And I just want to go back to bed."

"Then bottoms up." He clinks his glass against mine and shoots it without so much as a flinch, blink, or balk.

Crazy, brave, or a little of both?

"Fine." I wince in anticipation, lift the amber liquid to my lips, and toss back what can only be described as fiery gasoline. My stomach recoils, responding with a flash of nausea that quickly subsides—thank goodness.

"Amateur." He winks before rinsing his glass in the sink.

"I can't believe you got me to do that." Heading for the pantry, I grab an emergency pack of Double Stuf Oreos and pop one in my mouth to cancel out the whiskey taste. "Want one?"

I place the package on the counter and peel the top back all the way.

"When Carina and I were kids, we'd have a race and see who could 'do a line' the fastest," I say.

"Do a line?" he asks.

"Yeah. A line of Oreos."

"Let me guess, it was her idea?" he asks.

"One hundred percent." I nudge the cookies towards him. "Come on. I know you eat, like, kale and egg white smoothies and this probably isn't in your dietary guidelines, but don't let me eat these alone or I will eat all of them."

Examining the blue, white, and pink container, he reads the label. "Double ... stuf. One F. That should be your first red flag right there. They can't even spell stuff correctly."

"They're probably trying to be cute."

"Or maybe the FDA wouldn't let them call it 'stuff' because it didn't meet their guidelines? So now they call it stuf with one f so they can get away with it?" he says. "Kind of like the word chocolatey."

Brows narrowed, I say, "What's wrong with chocolatey?"

"If a food says it's chocolatey—with a y—that means there's no real chocolate in it. Just chocolate flavor."

"How do you know so much about this?"

"Years ago, this company wanted me to come out with a line of protein powders and meal replacement bars," he says. "Would've been huge for me. Multi, multi millions of dollars on the line here. But since it would've been *my* name on the label, I started researching the ingredients and realized they were nothing but fillers and chemicals and the kinds of things that have no business going into the human body. It's amazing, really, how they can take a shit product and package it in such a way that you think you're buying something healthy. And then they price gouge you on top of it."

I slide the cookies off the island and into the trash can.

"Thanks for the info, Fabian," I say. "Now I'm going to have trust issues every time I go to the grocery store."

"The more you know …" he winks.

"Maybe while you're here, you can go through my pantry and throw out all the other Frankenfoods I've been deceived into thinking were acceptable to put into my body."

"I'll check the baby foods while I'm at it."

I gasp. "Surely they wouldn't poison babies, would they?"

The warmth of the scotch floods my body, a delayed reaction of sorts, and I brace myself on the island ledge. Without missing a beat, Fabian swoops in to steady me.

The Match

"You okay?" he asks. His hands are warm on my hips, and his body is all but pressed so close to mine I can smell the bleach from his t-shirt.

"Yeah." I steady myself. "That shot just hit me all of a sudden."

"Understandable for a rookie."

"Believe it or not, I wasn't always a rookie."

"I imagine having a baby slows things down a bit."

I realize now he hasn't left my side, still anchored dangerously close to me, his eyes poring over every detail of my face as if he's seeing it for the first time again.

"What's … going on here?" I ask.

"Just looking at your facial features."

"Okay, that's not weird or anything."

The side of his mouth lifts, flashing a dimple. "Just trying to determine which features of Lucia's are yours and which are mine. It's fascinating, these things. Genetics. So random yet so undeniable."

"That's why I went into the field," I say. "It's organized chaos with a paper trail. My favorite projects are the more mysterious ones, the families that aren't super easy to map out. Love a good mystery—especially when it leads to a happy ending."

I think of Fabian's parents, whom he said he lost last year.

And the sister he wants nothing to do with.

"What were your parents like?" I ask, partly because I'm curious but also so I have something to share with Lucia when she's older.

Raking his hand against his stubbled jaw, his gaze grows unfocused for a moment. "They were older when they had me. Early forties. I was a complete surprise, they said. My sister was their only child before that, and she was fifteen when I was born. Honestly, I hardly knew her. She got tangled up in the wrong crowd and was quite a handful from what I was told. I think they overcompensated with me, giving me all of their time and attention and energy, praying to God I didn't turn out like her. Literally praying to God. I'll never forget my mother lighting candles at church and begging the Father, Son, and Holy Ghost to do something magnificent with me. That was the word she used. Magnificent."

"Wow." I lift my brows. "Guess they were listening, huh?"

He chuckles. "That or they knew they'd have to deal with her wrath once she got up there. My mother was no joke. Five foot two and could be terrifying as hell. But no one loved me more than she did."

"What was your dad like?"

"Quiet," he says. "Only really spoke when he felt he had something to say. In a lot of ways, he and my mother cancelled each other out that way. Or complemented each other. However you want to look at it. Worked at the same appliance factory for thirty-five years. Played racquetball when he could. Loved the Cubs. Other than that, he was a simple man."

"Huh," I say.

"What?"

"What'd he think of your anything-but-simple lifestyle?" I ask.

"He hated coming to Malibu. Hated the traffic. And all the people. I usually came home to visit. It was less stressful for him," I say. "But my mother loved to come out. I'd put her up in a five-star hotel in Beverly Hills and she'd spend the weekend getting pampered before packing up and heading to my place to spend a week at the beach. It was her favorite thing in the world. And my staff always got a kick out of her because we could never predict what was going to come out of her mouth."

"Sounds like my dad," I say. "And Carina. They're wildcards."

Fabian hums. "Yeah. She was definitely a wildcard."

"Which means you're half wildcard," I say.

He chuffs. "Yeah. Guess I am."

"Though that would mean you're also half simple man." I lean against the island, examining him. "Which I don't really see …"

"What about your parents? What are they like?"

"My dad is full-blooded Italian and he does this thing with his hands when he gets all worked up." I toss my hand up, demonstrating. "And my mother's name is Suzette, but everyone calls her Suze. She's the quintessential midwestern stay-at-home mom. Volunteers around town, heads up a local book club, makes a melt-in-your-mouth cowboy casserole, and has an unhealthy addiction to Lifetime movies."

"Who doesn't?" Fabian teases.

"They adore Lucia though, to the point of being obsessed sometimes," I say. "She's their whole world. They're already planning her first trip to Disney World, and Mom won't stop knitting blankets for her. At some point, I'm going to run out of closet space. Anyway, she's their only grandkid and probably always will be, so I don't think there's any way to talk them out of spoiling her."

"No bambinos in Carina's future?"

I let out a belly cackle, one that hopefully won't wake the baby. "Never. She loves Lucia, but she has no desire to be a mom. She has her dog and her plants and an extremely robust dating life, and that's all she needs. Granted, she's twenty-nine, so things could change. But it'd be the shock of a century if she flipped that script."

"How'd the two of you turn out so different?"

"How'd you and your sister turn out so different?" I lift a shoulder. "I could deliver an oral thesis on nature versus nurture, but it's a quarter past four and I can barely keep my eyes open and the sun's going to be up in a couple of hours, so …"

He checks the clock on the microwave. "Shit."

Yawning, I cover my mouth so he can't see the Oreo bits stuck in my teeth, bits that officially taste like shame and chemicals. "You sure you don't want my bed?"

"Positive."

I switch the kitchen light off and head for the hallway and Fabian follows.

We stop when we get to the end of the hall. Our doors line up perfectly, one across from the other. And in this still, small, quiet moment when exhaustion gnaws at my bones and whiskey flows through my blood, I know I should be climbing under my covers and chasing sleep like my life depends on it.

But I'm stuck here, my body refusing to move, as if it doesn't want this moment to be over yet.

While it's been a mere twelve hours since Fabian showed up at my door with his suitcase, I'm already enjoying his company more than I thought I would. He's remarkably easy to talk to. My ex and I never stayed up late talking about anything and everything. And I always felt like I had to impress him with every word that came out of my mouth because he was witty and cuttingly sharp and charismatic.

That pressure, for whatever reason, isn't there when I'm with Fabian.

"Thanks for your neighbor's whiskey," he says, eyes searching mine in the dark.

"Thanks for ruining my love of Oreos."

His lips draw up at the corners, painting his face in a lighthearted grin that makes my stomach flip.

"Goodnight, Rossi," he says, gripping his doorknob with his perfect, chiseled, million-dollar hand.

"Goodnight, Fabian."

Disappearing into my room, I all but float to my bed.

One night down, twenty-seven to go.

There's a chance this arrangement might prove to be harder than I expected—in ways I couldn't possibly have anticipated.

Chapter 14

Fabian

I SWIPE the fog on the mirror in the hall bath Saturday, muscles tight from this morning's practice. Today marks a lot of firsts for me—playing on some local real estate billionaire's private court on no sleep being one of them. Second being the shower I just used—the one with shelves lined with yellow baby shampoo and matching rubber ducks.

Securing a thin bath sheet around my hips, I finger comb my hair into place before heading across the hall to grab my clothes. Only the instant I step into the hall—is the same instant Rossi happens to be passing by.

We collide.

My towel slips—though I manage to catch it ... mostly.

I capture her gaze, holding it, testing it, while I secure my towel again. Tighter this time.

"I'm so sorry." Rossi backs into the wall, pointing to Lucia's door. "I was just coming to grab a diaper."

Placing a hand on her shoulder, I wink. "All good. You sleep okay last night?"

She nods, keeping her attention laser focused. "I did. You?"

Wincing, I say, "I hope you don't mind, but I'm having a new mattress delivered this afternoon. Same one I use back home."

Quality sleep has always been a non-negotiable for me. My performance is shit without it. Same with nutrition. And last night was rough. But talking to Rossi in the middle of the night made it slightly less of an inconvenience.

My ex-fiancée used to try to wake me up in the middle of the night when she couldn't sleep. And she'd always ask me the kind of questions that required more brain power than I could muster at 2 AM, like, *"If you could save any endangered animal, which would it be?"* or *"If you could have dinner with anyone—dead or alive—who would you choose and what would you ask them?"*

She never understood my annoyance—or the inconvenience.

I'd usually roll over, fall back asleep, and wake up alone with no covers.

Rossi, on the other hand, offered to trade beds last night.

"Oh?" Rossi's brows rise.

"You can keep it after I leave. It's a Duxiana," I say. "It'll just make things easier for me these next few weeks. I'm a bear if I don't get my sleep."

"No, no, it's fine," she says, injecting a smile in her tone. "Speaking of this afternoon, I was going to see if you wanted to do a picnic? There's a little state park not far from here. They've got a trail and a pond and lots of green space. Trees are starting to fill in and it's going to be in the seventies today—maybe that's cold to you back in LA, but out here it's practically pool weather. Once it hits the forties, it's not unusual to see crazy people walking around in shorts and flipflops."

"I was one of those crazy people once upon a time," I say.

"That's right—I keep forgetting you grew up in the Midwest." Her eyes drop to my chest for a flicker of a second. "Anyway. Picnic? Yea or nay?"

Can't remember the last time I went on a picnic. Probably right around the last time I was running around a playground.

"Let's do it."

WE PARK in the back row of a gravel lot just past the sign for Potter State Park. With impressive efficiency, Rossi climbs out, straps the baby to a carrier on her chest, and I meet her by the trunk to grab the basket and blanket.

Following a dirt path, we find a quiet clearing in the middle of an oaky section of woods and set up camp.

"Okay, are these not the cutest things you've ever seen in your life?" Retrieving a pair of baby-sized sunglasses from her jacket pocket, Rossi slips them over Lucia's face.

I don't melt, but if I did, I'd be a fucking puddle right now.

Lucia giggles, stretching her hands toward the sky and examining them with her new, tinted vision.

"That's ... wow." I'm at a loss for words because "adorable" and "precious" aren't exactly in my day-to-day vernacular.

"You should see her baby Converse," she adds.

"They're a couple of sizes too big right now, but I'm hoping by the time she starts walking …"

"Baby Converse? I didn't know they made such a thing."

Rossi digs into the picnic basket, producing a meticulously arranged tray of artisan crackers, sliced cheeses, green olives, a small bowl of cut fruit, two jars of baby food, a bottle, some white wine, and two goblets.

"I feel like I'm forgetting something …" She examines the spread, her expression pinched.

"You're forgetting to relax." Before I can say another word, my phone rings. Without checking the Caller ID, I silence it.

"If you need to get that, it's fine." Rossi points before popping a red grape in her mouth. It fills the side of her cheek as she chews, but all I can focus on are those rosy lips and how sweet they probably taste. Unscrewing the cap on a jar of pureed prunes, she props Lucia on her lap and loads a tiny scoop onto a rubber spoon.

My phone rings again, but once more I silence it.

I'm here to spend time with Lucia and Rossi—everything else can wait.

"Maybe it's the mattress people?" Rossi asks. "What time did you say they were dropping it off?"

"Between three and four. You want some wine?" I uncork the bottle and pour two generous glasses.

"So what's your schedule going to be like while you're here?" She serves Lucia another mouthful of dark purple mush.

"Practice five mornings a week," I say. "With the occasional Saturday. But afternoons and evenings are for Lucia. And for you."

Getting to know my child's mother is just as important as getting to know my child—in their own regards.

Lucia shoves away the next bite Rossi offers, making a mess of the purple-brown liquid.

"Shoot," she says. "Can you grab me some baby wipes out of the picnic basket?"

A second later, we're wiping up the amazingly large mess that came from the tiny human and the microscopic spoon, and Lucia's relaxing between us on her back, trying to shove a foot in her mouth.

"She's very flexible," I say. "Pretty sure she gets it from me."

Rossi laughs. "One hundred percent."

The sun peeks out from behind a paper-white cloud and thaws the spring chill around us, enveloping the three of us in an otherworldly warmth. Out here, I'm not thinking about my next win. I'm not mentally replaying the last thing they said about me on ESPN. I'm not fielding fans or getting reamed by my coach for having an off day.

I'm simply existing.

I imagine this is the sort of thing people are referring to when they say money can't buy happiness.

Rolling to her side, Lucia reaches for a handful of grass, ripping it at the roots and attempting to shove it into her mouth—until her mother intervenes.

"You're not hungry, but you'll eat dirt and grass?" Rossi brushes the earthen debris out of the baby's fists.

Scooping her up, Rossi lies on her back and holds Lucia over her, making her "fly" as she attempts to make a sound akin to a single engine airplane in distress. Fighting a chuckle, I sip my wine and bask in the carefree moment taking place before me. Rossi doesn't care what I think, she doesn't care how ridiculous this looks—she's simply a mother doing what it takes to put a smile on her child's face.

"Your turn." Sitting up, she offers Lucia my way.

I take my daughter, reluctantly. "I'm really not good at this."

"Play peek-a-boo or something." She shrugs like it's no big deal. But it *is* a big deal. It's like stepping onto foreign land and not knowing an ounce of the customs.

"Okay ..." Clearing my throat, I ignore the fact that Rossi's observing me with an incredibly entertained smirk on her face, and then I hide my eyes with one hand while supporting the baby on my lap. "Peek-a-boo."

"Come on." Rossi tucks her chin against her chest. "You can do better than that."

"What was wrong with my peek-a-boo?"

Laughing, she says, "Everything."

"Fine." Sitting straighter, I try it again, louder this time. "Peek-a-boo!"

Lucia startles, craning her little neck to ensure her mother's still nearby.

"Now you're scaring her," Rossi says, biting her lip as her eyes twinkle.

"I told you, I'm terrible at this."

"You hear this, Luc?" Rossi leans in. "The world's best tennis player is a terrible peek-a-booer."

"Doesn't help that I'm performing in front of the world's toughest crowd."

"Try it one more time," Rossi says. "And I'll look away since you're so sensitive."

"Perfectionistic."

"Same difference," she says, turning away. Though I don't need to see her face to know she's probably holding in the biggest shit-eating grin. Not that I blame her. If I weren't me, I'd find this entire thing ridiculous.

But this is my daughter.

"Peek," I say, pausing and adding a higher inflection in my tone. I'm sure I sound like an idiot, but whatever.

Hiding my eyes behind my palm, I wait a few seconds before the big reveal. "A-boo!"

Lucia's chocolate eyes light and she claps her hands before promptly shoving them in her mouth.

My heart flutters—something it's never done for a *baby* before.

Confidence bubbling, I do it again. "Peek … a-boo!"

God, I'm cringing inside … but I'm also living for this.

Lucia claps again, bouncing in my lap.

With every gummy grin, my body grows lighter, my cares unimportant. And I get it now, why adults make complete and utter fools of themselves for something so frivolous as a laughing baby.

Turning back, Rossi winks. "Told you …"

"Yeah, yeah." I hand Lucia back to her mother, polish off the rest of my wine, and stand to stretch. The last time I sat on the ground to eat was at a Michelin star restaurant in Tokyo several years ago.

"You want to walk the trail?" Rossi asks.

My muscles scream from the brutal training we did today—Coach gave it to me twice as hard since I'd missed a couple days the week before and because he claims I'm not focusing like I should be.

He isn't wrong.

"Yeah," I say, fetching the baby carrier off the blanket.

"Good call." Rossi rises, taking the carrier from my hands before positioning it over my arms, loosening the straps until it fits, then fastening it into place. Next thing I know, she slides the baby into the opening—and I'm officially wearing her.

I'll just tack this onto my growing lists of firsts …

"You don't have to hold onto her," Rossi says, pointing to my hand placement on the carrier—one beneath the baby's behind and the other over her chest. "She's not going to fall."

"You sure?"

She nods. And I let go, taking a few steps until I'm comfortable with the fact that she's securely strapped to my chest and not going to slip and crack her head.

"It's sweet how gentle you are with her," she says. "You're covered in muscles and one of the most agile, coordinated people in the world, but you always hold her like she's a Faberge egg. I like it."

"As opposed to being rough with her?" I tease.

I'll never forget my first pro tournament, how adrenaline coursed through me and made me hypervigilant of every move I made. In some ways, handling Lucia is no different. I've never handled something so fragile, with so many rules.

Packing up our things, we head for the dirt path, the strange little crew that we are, and make our way around the pond. We stop to admire a family of ducks, which elicits a squeal of excitement from Lucia. And Rossi impressively points out various types of trees and shrubs to her daughter. Not that she can understand any of it. Thirty minutes later, we're back where we started, in the little gravel parking lot, loading everything back into Rossi's Subaru.

"You did good today," she says when she slides the baby from the carrier on my chest. I pull the contraption over my head and stick it in the trunk while she buckles Lucia into her car seat. "Not that I doubted you for a minute. I think I've figured you out."

"How so?" I climb into the passenger side.

Rossi gets in beside me, starting the engine. "You're one of those people who are good at everything."

"I'll try not to let that go to my head." Turning my

phone on, I check my voicemail as we pull out of the parking lot. One from Coach. One from my agent. And six from my ex. I delete each one from Tatum, not even bothering to check the transcribed versions because if the past is any indication, they're all likely gibberish because the automatic dictation can never keep up with her screaming fits.

We're almost home when my phone dings with a text.

COACH: Sorry. Tatum found out you're in Chicago with another woman.

My jaw flexes as I tap out a response.

ME: She found out? Or you told her?

COACH: She's a smart girl. You know that. Asked a million questions and read between the lines.

COACH: I'll deal with her though. Just ignore.

"Everything okay?" Rossi asks. "You're breathing kind of heavy over there."

"Everything's fine." I lie. Sort of. Tatum is a spitfire when she wants something, and while we officially ended our engagement months ago—with a press release and joint statement—I know deep down she thought we'd get back together.

I picture her stewing in her West Hollywood penthouse, pacing her expansive walk-in closet and pausing every so often to refresh all of my social media accounts in search of clues.

Sliding my phone out of sight, I lean back into the seat and attempt to forget about the drama for a moment.

"Lucia, it's our song …" Rossi calls out before dialing the volume up a couple of notches and cracking the window a couple of inches. A second later, some catchy, tinkly vintage pop song plays over the radio, and it takes a moment, but I recognize it as *Forever Your Girl* by Paula Abdul. Bopping her head and tapping her fingers on the steering wheel, she sings along—albeit slightly off pitch—as the baby kicks along in the back.

Tatum would've never driven anywhere with the windows remotely down. The only time she'd dance was at a club, after half a bottle of 818 Tequila. And she'd never tap her fingers along to the radio. She was too 'cool' for that. In fact, she'd be the first to make fun of people who drove around LA singing along to the radio as they sped down the freeway.

I may not know Rossi Bianco—yet—but already she's a breath of fresh-fucking-air.

And that puts her miles above any other woman I've ever met.

Maybe I came here for Lucia … but I might have to stay for her mother.

Chapter 15

Rossi

"IS SHE OUT?" I'm perched in the hall Saturday night after assigning Fabian the task of putting the baby to bed. Our time together is limited. If I'm going to be comfortable letting him into our life in some capacity, I want them to have a bond.

"Cold," he says, pulling the door closed with a soft click.

"Proud of you today." I tug the burp rag off his shoulder and take the bottle from his hand. "First peek-a-boo, then the Baby Bjorn. Now bedtime. What's next for you?"

His full lips arch as he readies a response, only he stops. Sniffs. Then glances down at his t-shirt where a very prominent, still moist spit-up stain resides.

"Oh, here—" I'm about to hand him the rag … when he rips off his shirt. My mouth dries and I swallow. "That works too."

"Where's your laundry?"

"It's the door at the end of the hall, between your room and mine," I say, pointing. "You can throw it on top of the washer. I'll take care of it. I've got a whole system for getting formula stains out. The key is to use OxiClean *and* vinegar or you'll never get the smell out."

Fabian drops the shirt off in the laundry room, only instead of making a pit stop in the guest room for a fresh shirt, he returns shirtless.

My skin flushes hot, and it takes everything I have to keep my eyes from roaming the great muscled plains of his chiseled upper body.

I mean, seriously.

How is he real?

And how is he my child's father?

Helping himself to the fridge, he grabs a bottle of water and meets me by the sofa.

"Hope you're not planning on being entertained tonight," I say. "Because this is a typical Saturday night in the Bianco household. Baby's in bed by eight. And I usually spend an hour looking for something to watch on Netflix before giving up and passing out on the couch. It's a glamorous existence we lead. I really hope you'll be able to keep up these next few weeks."

He chuffs, uncapping his water.

"Hold on. Someone's calling." I pull my buzzing phone from my pocket. "It's my sister. Two secs." I press the green button and lift it to my ear. "What's up?"

"I. Fucking. Hate. Men," she groans.

"What happened?" I ask.

"Stood up," she says. "Again."

"I'm so sorry." If I haven't lost count, that's the fourth time this year. Added to the eight times last year. For whatever reason, Carina is a magnet for these types. "Don't let him ruin your night. Go meet up with your friends at The Lounge for a drink or something."

"I'm actually a block away. I thought I could just chill with you tonight?"

"Oh." My gaze flicks across the room to where a very shirtless, very watchful Fabian waits for me to finish my call. "Um."

"Oh, shit. I forgot Baby Daddy is there," she says. "Never mind. I'll go home."

"No, no, it's fine. Stop by."

"You sure?" she asks, followed by the slamming of a car door—which I hear both via the phone and coming from my driveway. A second later, the garage door whines open and my sister blasts through the entrance. "Oh." She stops in her tracks when she spots Fabian. "*Ohhh.*"

"Sorry," I say to him. "I didn't realize my sister was fifty feet away when she said she was a block away."

"I can leave," Carina says.

"She got stood up," I tell Fabian.

"Sorry to hear that." He rises, disappearing into the guest room and returning tragically clothed. Though it's for the best, because my thoughts were starting to take the road less traveled, and who knows where that would've led.

Helping herself to my kitchen, Carina grabs a bottle of green apple vodka, a carton of apple juice from the fridge, and a tall glass.

"I just don't get it," she says, mixing up a poor man's apple martini. "We were texting for months. Had so much in common, more chemistry than I've had with anyone in forever. Like he 'got' my sense of humor—no easy feat as you know. He was even asking me about travel plans for this summer, telling me there's this really great lake we should hit up." She tosses back a mouthful. "So we finally make plans to meet. I show up. Text him to let him know I got us a table in the corner. No response. And then I wait. And I'm waiting, waiting, waiting. And I'm sitting there looking like a loser, you know? So finally after forty minutes, I just left."

"I'm so sorry." I hunch over the island and give her my sad, puppy dog eyes. I don't miss the dating world, and honestly, I'm grateful to be out of it. It's toxic. Terrifying. Unpredictable. Maybe I'll stick my toes back in someday, when my dating pool beckons calm, divorced, established businessmen with grown kids. Until then, I've got Lucia and our perfect little drama-free life.

"Why do you guys do this?" Carina directs her question toward Fabian, who shoots her a deer-in-headlights look.

"I don't think we need to lump Fabian into any of this," I say.

"I've never stood anyone up," he says. "But I know people who have. It always boils down to fear. They're afraid you won't like them in person, they're afraid it'll be awkward, they're afraid you'll see them for who they really are and not for the larger-than-life person they were pretending to be online. It's almost never personal."

Clamping a hand over her chest, my sister practically swoons, head tilted and all.

"Oh my gosh, Fabian," she says. "That's the sweetest thing anyone's ever said to me."

"Really?" I chuckle. "That's the sweetest thing?"

"I'm exaggerating, but you know what I mean," she snaps.

"Anyway, consider yourself lucky," he tells her.

"I feel like I should pay you for that advice," she says. "That was gold. Here. This one's on the house."

Carina mixes Fabian his own poor man's appletini and slides it to the end of the counter.

"You don't have to drink that," I tease.

"Just for that, you get one too." Carina fixes me the same sickly, yellow-green cocktail, placing it in my hands. And for the next two hours, we ensure my sister doesn't have to drink alone.

Prancing off to relieve my bladder, I return to the living room only to find Carina passed out cold in one of my chairs.

"When did this happen?" I motion toward my snoring kid sister.

"About thirty seconds ago," Fabian says. "Kind of disappointed. She's pretty entertaining."

"That's Carina-light," I say. "Just wait until you meet full sugar Carina."

Grabbing a throw blanket from a nearby basket, I attempt to fix her neck so it isn't craned in an unnatural position, and then I cover her up.

"Think she'll be fine sleeping like that?" he asks.

"Where else is she going to sleep? I mean, we can move her to the couch?"

"Put her in my bed. I'll take the couch."

I snort. "Okay, if you hated the mattress I had in there before, you're going to hate the couch even more."

"I insist," he says. "She's your sister and this is your house. Come on. I'll help you move her."

He folds the blanket, places it on the back of the chair, and scoops my sister into his arms. At five foot nine, she's not exactly elfin. But he makes it look like he's carrying a feather. I follow them back to the guest room and help her get situated on top of Fabian's brand new fancy mattress, between his thousand thread count sheets and his expensive pillows.

Sighing, she rolls to her side and cups a hand beneath her cheek like a princess.

She's a pain in my side, but I love her.

"You're a good sister," he says as we turn out the lights and shut the door. "I hope she knows she's lucky to have you."

"What's your sister's name?" I ask as we return to the living room, which now feels a little emptier without Carina's loud presence.

"Francesca," he says.

"That's beautiful."

"But everyone called her Frankie."

"And you two are no longer in touch?" I ask.

He shakes his head. "Unfortunately, no."

"She hasn't tried to reach out to you ... with you being famous and all?"

"Never. And I used to wish she would. Couldn't even get a hold of her last year when my parents passed. Don't know if she's even aware. She sort of ... wrote us off, I guess. Addiction will do that to a person."

He takes one side of the sofa, and I take the other, curling my legs up and getting comfortable—settling in for what I hope will be another getting-to-know-you session. If someone told me last week that I'd be sitting here, curled up on the couch with Fabian Catalano shooting the breeze, I'd have never believed them.

My sister may be a little extra sometimes, but thank goodness for that.

She's the one who talked me into this.

"I meant what I said about helping you find your sister," I say. "And it doesn't take as long as you'd think. Usually when I start a project, I have my clients submit a DNA sample, and I mail it off to this service. Takes about 4-6 weeks to process, but once I get results, I can start putting together a family tree, reach out to distant relatives, that sort of thing."

"If she wrote us off, I doubt she kept in touch with any fourth cousins or second uncles twice removed."

"You'd be surprised. Sometimes people know things …" I shrink my shoulders and tilt my head. "But I won't pressure you. If you ever change your mind, let me know."

"Appreciate it." Rising, he grabs a water from the fridge—and one for me.

"You didn't have to do that."

"I've lived with you less than two days and already all I've seen is how much you take care of everyone else," he says, taking a seat again. "But I'm curious … who takes care of you?"

"No one needs to take care of me," I say with a buzzed scoff. "I'm completely self-sufficient."

"Yes, I know you run your own business and you pay your own bills and you're doing it all and then some," he says, "but what about your other needs? The ones you can't fulfill?"

"If I can't fulfill it myself, I don't need it."

"Ah, so that's how you justify it."

"I'm not justifying anything."

"So what do you do when you have … needs?" He chooses his words carefully.

"I handle them." I sit straighter, cheeks flushing. "How did we go from me being a good sister to talking about my needs? I think we got off on the wrong exit?"

"Sorry." He glances away, the cutest mischievous glint in his dark eyes. "It's just that you're really easy to talk to, Rossi." The way my name melts on his tongue sends a spray of goose bumps down my arms. "It's been a long time since I've been able to talk to someone and feel like I'm talking to the real person and not some version of them. You're not trying to be the person you think I want you to be, and you have no idea how refreshing that is. Guess it makes me forget about boundaries."

I rest my elbow against the back of the sofa, hands knotted through my messy hair as I stare at the gorgeous man mere feet away from me. It only makes sense—he's probably used to everyone putting on airs, trying to come across as perfect and amazing at all times because they want him to like them.

"It probably helps that I'm not trying to impress you …"

Our eyes lock.

"I make a lot of people nervous," he says. "But not you. Why's that?"

"I was nervous the first time you came over."

"Really? I couldn't tell."

"After the Katherine Kingman interview I watched five times in a row? I was borderline terrified of you."

He laughs. "You watched it five times?"

"Maybe six."

"Why?" His eyes shine with bewilderment.

"Curiosity?" I shrug. "Wanting to know what I was getting us into?"

"Fair enough. What else are you curious about? Any other myths I can personally dispel for you?"

"Yeah." I settle in. "What's it like dating other famous people? Do you do normal people things like ordering pizza and sitting around in sweats or do you constantly need to be 'on' and picture perfect? Do you fight or do you have your assistants fight for you?"

His dark brows meet as he snickers at my questions. I hope he finds them more amusing than invasive.

"Everything is off the record and purely for my own nosiness," I say, adding, "Nothing you tell me tonight leaves this house."

I draw an X across my chest.

"Okay." He settles back. "Imagine going out for a fabulous five-course dinner at the hottest restaurant in the city and your date is on a five-hundred-calorie-a-day diet. Or asking if she wants to take a last-minute trip to Fiji but she's still healing from her lip injections and doesn't want to risk being seen with bruised lips. And when you can't get a hold of them, you have to text their stylist, their makeup artist, *and* their personal assistant to figure out where they are. It's exhausting."

"Have you ever just dated a normal girl?"

"Define normal."

"Someone like me. A regular person."

"I thought we already clarified that there's nothing regular about you," he says. "but to answer your question, I've never dated anyone remotely like you."

"Maybe you should," I say. "When you get home, I mean. Someone *not* famous."

"Trust me, if I could find someone like you when I got home, I'd make her mine in a heartbeat. Unfortunately they don't make 'em like you back there."

Speaking of heartbeats, mine is off the charts.

I'm sitting here, perfectly still, only my body is behaving as if I've just finished a twenty-six mile marathon.

I stand to stretch, but the room twirls the second my feet hit the carpet.

Apparently those appletinis are very much still in my system.

With impressive, tennis-pro reflexes, Fabian catches me before I make too much of a fool of myself.

"Take it easy there," he says, breath warm and sweet against the side of my neck. Lowering me to the couch, he says, "What do you need? I'll get it."

"I just wanted to stretch …" I push myself up again, this time retaining my balance—and my humility. Doing a little spin, I make a show of the fact that I'm fine. "I'm just going to check on my sister, maybe make sure she's still breathing …"

A minute later, I return, and Fabian's exactly where I left him.

After last night's 3 AM kitchen party and all the running around we did today, I should be exhausted, but something about being in this man's presence is electrifying, and sleep is the farthest thing from my mind. If I were to call it a night right now, I'm one-hundred percent sure I'd spend the next several hours staring at the ceiling, my body humming with frantic energy. It's almost as if I'm anticipating something … but what?

"How is she?" he asks.

"Out like a light." I take a seat again, closer to him this time. Not on purpose though—but because I'm slightly less coordinated than usual thanks to this massive buzz working through me. "You tired at all?"

"Strangely … no. You?"

Biting my lip, I shake my head.

"Tell me about the last guy you dated," he says, as if it's the most natural question in the world. "You wanted to know about my dating life. I want to know about yours."

"I haven't dated in years … but the last guy, he was an orthopedic surgeon, very much a workaholic—as was I at the time. We liked each other and he was nice, but we couldn't make our schedules work."

"Couldn't or didn't want to?"

"Maybe a little of both? It wasn't like fireworks when we were together, but we were perfect on paper."

"And the guy before him?" he asks.

"The guy before him was an associate professor of

philosophy at Northwestern," I say. "We went to a lot of local indie concerts, drank a lot of craft beer, and went out almost every weekend. But after a few months I realized he just wanted to relive his college days … over and over and over. In an unhealthy sort of way. We were all wrong for each other, but it was fun while it lasted."

"And before him?"

"That would've been the pharmaceutical sales rep that I met at a bar after a Coldplay concert. Extremely handsome, made good money, very generous in every aspect of the word …" I say, "but he traveled a lot and wanted an open relationship, and I'm not really into sharing."

"And before that?" His attention hasn't left me for a second. It's like he's soaking in every last detail.

"If you're trying to piece together whether or not I have a type, I can tell you I don't. If I have chemistry with someone, wonderful. If I don't, I move on. But I've never sought out a certain type of guy because he fits some perfect mold."

"Everyone has a type."

"Oh, yeah? Then what's yours?" I ask.

"Psycho." He takes a sip of water, hiding a smile. "And not by choice. I think I'm just drawn to women who captivate me at the start and then somewhere along the line, they flip a switch. Trying to break out of that though. Anyway, continue on with your history. Who's next?"

"Wow. Okay. So before the pharmaceutical guy would've been my ex-husband. And we were together since high school, so unless you want me to get into my cringey middle school days, I suggest we stop there."

"Do you ever see yourself dating again?" he asks.

"Maybe when Lucia's older? It's not like I can stay out all night, and I'm sure as hell not bringing some date home with me when I have a baby in the next room."

"Good call," he says. "So what do you do when you need a release?"

"Oh, I have Mr. Big for that ..."

"Mr. Big?"

"Yeah. I mean, he's not *big*. He's more medium sized. But I call him Mr. Big. He's always right there when I need him. Always on standby. Doesn't talk back. Eager to please and amazingly efficient at getting the job done."

"You're talking about a sex toy," he doesn't miss a beat.

"Obviously," I say, attempting to play it cool despite the fact that my cheeks are flushing ten shades of cherry red. I don't even talk to my own sister about Mr. Big, and here I am describing my vibrator to Fabian Catalano.

"You don't miss the real thing?"

"Of course I do. And kudos on the smooth transition from my dating life to my present-day sex life."

"You're the one that brought up your dildo ... *by name*, I'd like to point out."

"He's not a dildo. He's a vibrator. There's a difference."

Lifting a shoulder, he presses his full, flawless lips together. "I wouldn't know. I've never needed to use one on anyone before."

I try to swallow, but I can't.

The tension between is so ripe I could pluck it.

So much for any of this being low-key.

Fanning myself, I say, "This is, like, 10th date conversation and we're not even dating."

"Is it making you uncomfortable?"

"No, it's just ... not exactly what I had in mind when I said we should keep things casual ..."

"This *is* casual, isn't it? We're having an open and honest conversation, Rossi. That's kind of what we do ... Besides, if I were hitting on you, you'd know."

"Would I though? Because I'm really good at imagining things … too good, actually."

"If I were hitting on you …." He leans in, narrowing the space between us. Lifting his hand to my chin, he runs his thumb along my bottom lip. "… I'd kiss you right *here*."

My heart gallops, irregular little trots that make me want to check my pulse, but I'm too frozen to move an inch.

His touch abandons my mouth, leaving a cold sensation in its place.

And I'm officially more confused than before.

"Okay," I say. "Glad we cleared that up. But for the record, if I were hitting on you, I'd probably do this." Reaching for his forehead, I brush a strand of silky dark hair from his brow before tracing my finger down his steel cut jaw. "And I'd do this." Leaning in, I bring my lips inches from his mouth, until his sweet breath mixes with mine—and then I pull away. "Because I always want to make the first move, but then I chicken out at the last minute."

"Ah," he says, eyes examining mine. "So then if that were the case, I'd probably do this …" Without warning, the tall, dark, and handsome Adonis pulls me into his lap, his hands gripping my hips and his gaze commanding mine. Next, his hand slides up my neck, his thumb stopping at the bend beneath my jaw.

I don't know what he's serving up here, but it's officially my turn to return it.

Anticipatory creeps between my legs as his hands travel the outer sides of my thighs before grabbing a handful of my ass. My full, soft ass. The one that hasn't seen a man—or sunlight—in years.

It's funny—we can sit here and talk about anything and

everything, but the second shit gets real, it becomes a chess match.

"I want to kiss you," he says, his voice a graveled whisper as he tucks a strand of hair behind my ear.

His words force my heart to skip a beat. Literally. I almost ask him to repeat his declaration so I can enjoy it this time …

Tracing his fingers along my partially-opened mouth, he adds, "I've been thinking about this all day. What it would feel like. What it would taste like. What I would do to it …"

I force myself to swallow while my mind runs laps, conjuring up images of this powerful man driving himself inside of me … juxtaposed with images of this entire thing blowing up in our faces.

With his hand along the side of my face and his fingers curling around the nape of my neck, he guides my lips to his and claims them so hard my thoughts stop spinning and my body melts against his. A second later, his tongue dances with mine. With each gentle rhythm of my hips against his lap, his hardness grows and my worries take a backseat.

Fabian smells like the woods, tastes like green apples, and lights my entire body on fire. The sensory overload alone is enough to drive me mad with want.

I've officially boarded a runaway train.

Tugging at the hem of his shirt, I pull it over his head before running my hands down every ripple of his chest before tracing his eight-pack. It's like touching marble. Smooth yet veined, cut to perfection.

Our mouths crash once more, his kisses growing greedier by the second as he works the buttons of my blouse and shoves it off my shoulders like a man with zero patience. With a single fluid move, I find myself in his place on the sofa. His fingers work the fly of my jeans before shoving them down and going back for my panties, all but ripping them off to get them out of the way. Within seconds, the insatiable man is making a meal of me—kissing his way up my inner thighs before stopping at the center to drag his tongue up and down my seam.

My sex pulses, offering miniature orgasmic previews in response to his flicking and circling. And after a few minutes, he inserts a finger, curling it against my g-spot until every nerve ending I have is firing on all cylinders.

Clamping my mouth, I muffle the sounds attempting to escape.

It's been years since anything *wet* and organic has been down there.

Honestly, I'd forgotten how amazing it feels …

Biting my lip, I grip a nearby sofa pillow with one hand and reach for a fistful of Fabian's hair with the other as he buries his tongue deeper, harder inside of me.

Every wave grows more intense, and I try to stave off the inevitable for as long as I can because if it were up to me, this would go on indefinitely—but my body will have no part of it. As if they've got a mind of their own, my hips buck in response to the thrashing of his tongue and my breathing hardens. Eyes squeezed tight, I give it one last fight before letting it go and riding the longest wave I've ever ridden in my entire life.

Only when it's over, Fabian remains planted between my thighs, devouring my arousal, his tongue flicking faster than before, soft moans vibrating against my sensitive flesh.

Before I have a chance to protest, to tell him it isn't necessary to keep going—I'm hit with another electric shock of pleasure.

I've never come twice in a row …

Wasn't even sure I could.

Mouth agape and unable to form a complete sentence, I gawk at the man with the golden tongue—and the extremely large bulge. Falling to my knees, I reach for his sweats and shove them down his muscled thighs along with his boxer briefs. Taking the base of his cock in my hand, I pump the length before bringing my tongue to the tip.

A moment later, I take the first few inches of him into my mouth, opting to take it slow because this is no Mr. Big I'm dealing with—this is Mr. Huge.

With his fingers tangled in my hair, he guides himself deeper into me, until the taste of pre-cum hits the back of my throat. Swallowing his length again and again, I pump the base of his cock, stopping every so often to drag my tongue along the underside.

Fabian groans as he fucks my mouth, the pace quickening as his breathing comes in short breaths. Tugging fistfuls of my hair, he releases a muffled groan before his veined cock spurts hot streams of cum down the back of my throat.

I swallow, wiping my lips and rising to meet him.

Everything happened so fast, so unexpectedly.

And my body is still reeling ... weak knees, tingles everywhere, confusion. The aftereffects of a mind-blowing sexual exchange with Fabian Catalano are suspiciously similar to those of a mild concussion.

"So—" I attempt to fill the silent space between us with a witty quip, something to make light of the insanity that just took place.

Only Fabian silences me with a tender kiss.

And maybe I should, but I don't protest.

Scooping me up, he carries me to my bed, climbs in beside me, and pulls me into his arms.

A million words come to mind, but before I have a

chance to utter a single one, his eyelids drift shut, his breathing slows, and his hold around me relaxes.

While the double orgasms are definitely ones for the history books and the man's hot, sweet kisses alone are enough to silence even the loudest of thoughts, this was a one-time occurrence.

Doing this again would be reckless and irresponsible.

And I'll tell him that first thing tomorrow. Maybe I'll casually work it in after breakfast, dropping it like a "no biggie" kind of thing before nonchalantly moving on to the day's itinerary.

If we don't make a big deal about it, it won't become a big deal.

Naked, our legs intertwined, I stare at the ceiling and listen to him breathe. A minute later, I roll to my side, perched up on my elbow, and watch him sleep. I study his features, matching them up with Lucia's, marveling at their perfection. The symmetry alone is remarkable.

Yawning, I stop gawking and settle in for the night.

If I fall asleep now, I'll get a solid six hours before Lucia's up.

But before I close my eyes one last time on this insane day, I steal a final glimpse at the painfully gorgeous man in my bed, the one who threw my "casual and cordial" rules out the window without so much as a second thought—but now that I think about it, what good are rules to a man who's never had to follow them off the courts?

Chapter 16

Fabian

MY HEAD PULSATES as I shuffle down the hallway Sunday morning. The house is quiet—save for Lucia's faint cries. Rossi looked so peaceful this morning sleeping next to me, her dark hair splayed out on her pillow and her lips slightly swollen from last night ...

I didn't want to wake her, so I crept out the instant I heard the baby.

Only now that I'm standing outside Lucia's door, I don't know what the hell I'm supposed to do.

"Lucia," I whisper when I step in. "*Shhhhh.*"

Her eyes widen—fear? Shock? Impossible to know. I'm sure she was expecting her mother, but I'll have to suffice.

"It's okay," I say, scooping her up and carrying her to the kitchen.

Placing her in her high chair the way I watched Rossi do several times yesterday, I buckle her in and head to the fridge. I distinctly remember Lucia eating yogurt at one point yesterday—a yellow container, laughably small and covered in cartoon bananas. I manage to find one, as well as a baby spoon from a drawer, and take a seat across from her.

She pounds on the high chair tray, eyeing her breakfast and licking her lips.

"I feel like we're missing something …" I scan the surroundings. "But I have no idea what that would be."

My daughter giggles, reaching as I peel off the yogurt top and load her first bite.

Only the instant the yellow goop slides down her face and lands on her pink pajamas, I realize exactly what I'd forgotten: a bib.

Hopping up, I make my way around the kitchen in search of the bib stash—locating a slew of them in the drawer beside the sink.

A minute later, we're back in business.

I load up another bite, this one smaller, and I move her hands aside as I spoon it into her mouth.

"I know," I say, "food is exciting. But when *you* reach for it, it tends to go flying and I'm going to be the one stuck picking up the mess, so …"

She bounces in her seat as I load up the next one.

It's weird, talking to a baby.

And I'd never be caught dead using one of those vocally fried baby voices.

But I'd be lying if I said I wasn't thoroughly enjoying this one-on-one time. Not that Rossi makes me feel judged, but there's more pressure when she's around. This is one of the rare scenarios in my life where I'm the amateur being watched by the professional.

The sound of heavy, shuffling footsteps signals that our alone time is officially over.

"*Morninggggg*, Baby Daddy." A froggy, pseudo-whining

voice says. I don't have to turn around to know it's Carina. A cabinet opens and slams shut. "Thanks for letting me sleep in your room last night. Hope the couch didn't suck."

"Slept like a dream," I say, giving Lucia her last bites before chucking the container in the trash and rinsing the spoon in the sink.

"Whoa, whoa, whoa." Rossi lumbers into the kitchen in her pink satin robe, her hair a tangled mess. "Is everyone hanging out without me? In my own house?"

"Thought I'd let you sleep in," I say.

Rossi keeps a careful distance, planting herself at the opposite end of the kitchen island.

"You didn't have to do that," Rossi says.

"Oh my god!" Carina shrieks and Rossi clutches at her robe.

My stomach drops. "What?"

"The guy from last night." Carina slides her phone toward Rossi. "He texted when I was passed out. Look at this—he posted a picture from the restaurant and he asked if I was still coming. And then he texted me ten times before he finally left. He says he was running late and he couldn't tell me because his phone died. He had to borrow a charger from the bartender. By the time he could text me, I'd already left. I wonder if he was there the whole time?"

Rossi folds her arms. "Do you believe him?"

Biting her lip, Carina says, "I want to? I don't know. I need to talk to him again. See if he's full of you know what."

Within seconds, Rossi's kid sister flits around the kitchen, gathering her phone, purse, and keys before locating her shoes by the back door.

"I'll see you chickens on Monday," she says, stopping

briefly to kiss Lucia on top of the head. "This little chicky too."

With that, she's gone.

Arrived on a breeze, left on one too.

Rossi makes her way to the high chair, pulling up the seat beside Lucia before leaning in to kiss her cheek.

"Good morning, sweet girl," she says in a tone fit for a Disney princess.

"I fed her some yogurt … not sure what else she eats for breakfast … or if that's enough …" I say.

"I can't believe I didn't hear her this morning …"

"You slept pretty hard," I say, adding, "Must've needed it."

"You really didn't have to do that."

"Just say thank you." I give her a wink. I get the sense she's not used to asking for help. She'd mentioned before that it "takes a village" and that she's got friendly neighbors and parents a phone call away, but other than her sister helping out, this woman does it all.

Crossing her legs, her attention migrates from Lucia to me. "Last night was … fun."

"To say the least."

Her lips inch into a two-second flash of a smile. "But I think we got a little carried away. For Lucia's sake—and for the sake of making sure these next few weeks go smoothly—I think we should promise each other it won't happen again."

Frowning, I stay quiet. I'm not in the habit of making promises I can't keep.

Rossi Bianco is the perfect woman. She's all curves and honesty, tender and selfless, independent, successful, and down to earth.

The mother of my child …

"So you didn't enjoy it?" I ask.

"Of course I did." She rights her posture, tucking her robe tighter as if it could possibly keep me from undressing her with my eyes.

I've seen what lies beneath all of that and it's fucking magnificent.

"Good, that's all that matters," I say. "Go grab a shower, I've got this."

"What? What are you doing now? What is this?"

"I'm taking care of you." I wipe Lucia's mouth with the corner of her terrycloth bib.

"Why?"

"Because someone should. And as long as I'm here, that someone should be me."

She tries to speak again, but I silence her with the swipe of my hand before pointing toward the hall.

"I don't want to see you for at least an hour," I tease.

Without a word she rises from the chair, pours a cup of coffee, and shuffles out of sight. Only three seconds later, she pops her head around the corner and says, "You should probably change her diaper. And maybe give her some mashed banana."

Chuckling, I wave her away. "I've got this."

Can't say I've ever changed a diaper before, but that's what Google is for.

Not like it's rocket science.

"I can do it really quick if you'd—"

"—go," I cut her off.

Her pretty lips lift up at the side as her blue eyes flash in the morning sun. Our gazes hold for an endless second, as if we're each attempting to capture this image for the rest of our days, and then she's gone.

I honestly don't know what's happening between us, but I've never felt more at ease—or at home—with anyone in my entire life.

Lucia kicks in her high chair, arms stretching out for me to lift her. Unfastening the buckles, I pick her up and carry her to the window overlooking the backyard, where a couple of robins are building a nest in the tree off the patio.

For some reason, I think of my house back in Malibu. Statuesque and grand, sitting empty next to the ocean shore. Filled with trophies, memorabilia, Italian sports cars, and a handful of priceless art works, but also filled with things that don't matter.

A rare two-point-six acres of ultra-private, ultra-exclusive water frontage.

Cedar ceilings, granite walls, and automated glass partitions.

A chef's kitchen personally designed by Alain Ducasse.

An infinity-edge pool, state-of-the-art tennis court, and grotto spa.

An architectural triumph with which I have no one to share.

Things you can't take with you in the end.

Maybe it's human nature to complicate things, to constantly wish for the next best, brightest, shiniest, newest thing. My entire life I've been grinding toward various goals, convinced that the second I got there I'd finally get to rest, and I'd finally get to be happy.

But standing here, watching these robins build their nest one branch at a time, my infant daughter in my arms and her mother in the next room—I'm flooded with a peace I've never known before.

Could it be *this* is the happiness I've been chasing all this time?

Chapter 17

Rossi

"OKAY, I'M CONFUSED," Dan says over lunch Tuesday. At the last minute, he invited me out to this new café walking distance from our neighborhood, and since Carina has the baby all day and Fabian was at practice then an afternoon of meetings, I figured I might as well.

Only I'm certain the invitation had less to do with the fanfare about this place and more to do with Dan's curiosity over my current situation.

"So you know Fabian Catalano from a long time ago," he says. "And you recently reconnected."

I nod, taking a swig of still water. "Basically."

"And he's in town," Dan continues, "but instead of staying at some fancy hotel downtown … he's living with you?"

"Exactly." I spread the white linen napkin over my lap before folding it in half. A black Range Rover passes, stealing my attention, only it isn't him.

Ever since we messed around Saturday night, things have been ... interesting.

He's been keeping his hands to himself—and his gorgeous lips too—but I've lost count of how many times I've caught him staring at me, either lost in thought or lingering on a part of my body he knows he can't touch.

"How is he with Lucia?" Dan asks.

"They adore each other. Two peas in a pod," I say.

"Nice." His tone is flat. He wants to be happy for me, I'm sure. But this has to be difficult for him.

Our server drops off a fresh bread basket. "Your food will be out shortly. Here's a little something to tide you over."

"Thank you," I say, diving in.

"What kinds of food does Fabian eat?" Dan asks.

"What?" I chuckle.

"What does a world-famous athlete eat on a daily basis? I've always wondered. I know they do those magazine interviews sometimes, but I've never believed them. They always seemed too perfect."

"He's pretty disciplined," I say. "Lots of protein shakes and superfood smoothies. Lots of fish and chicken."

Granted, it's only been less than a week since he moved in ...

Though it feels longer.

It's the strangest thing—he's been in my life less than two weeks, but I swear I've known him my whole life, that's how comfortable I am with him.

"You're glowing," Dan says.

I swallow a hard lump if bread. "Glowing? How?"

"I don't know, you just seem radiant or something. Did you change your hair?"

I shake my head. "No?"

"You're smiling more ..."

The Match

Frowning, I say, "No, I'm not."

"Every time a black SUV goes by, you glance out the window," Dan adds.

"What are you getting at?" I grab another slice of bread while it's still warm.

He hasn't touched a single one.

"I think there's more going on between you than you're letting on." Disappointment colors his face, and my chest squeezes.

I hate keeping secrets from Dan when he's become such a good friend to me, but I also don't want to hurt him. And if the truth behind Fabian's visit ever got out, it would hurt both Fabian and Lucia.

"I can assure you it's nothing," I say.

And that's the truth.

Sure my heart flip-flops every time he walks in the room. Sure I pass the hall bath after his daily shower just to catch a whiff of his intoxicating body wash. And maybe I replay last Saturday in my head more times than I should. But it's still nothing.

We got carried away after a few of Carina's appletinis—and after the stressful week we'd each had, we needed a release.

I'm not falling for him.

And he's simply trying to show that he's worthy enough to stay in Lucia's life, that's why he's being so helpful and accommodating.

"Anyway, how's your new supervisor?" I change the subject. "What was her name? Janet?"

Dan's wide shoulders loosen as he tells me about the woman who replaced the last woman who replaced the guy who knocked up his secretary who was half his age …

And meanwhile, I make a mental note to call around this afternoon to find a good medical malpractice attorney, someone who can review the settlement the clinic offered. I'd be stupid to walk away from free money, but I want to make sure they're not trying to pull one over on me. I'd be remiss not to ensure I'm getting the best possible deal for Lucia's future.

After lunch, we head to the alley parking lot, stopping at my car. Since Dan was working from his actual office today, we drove separate, though he offered to swing by and pick me up. Typical Dan—always going out of the way for people.

"You know you can't lie to me," he says as I unlock my door. "I can see through all of it."

"What are you talking about?"

"You and Fabian." He speaks softly and lifts a hand in protest. "And I get it. You don't have to confirm or deny it. You're allowed to be with whoever you want, and it's none of my business. But someone like him, Rossi? That's heartbreak waiting to happen. And not just yours, but Lucia's, too. And it isn't a matter of if, but when."

"Seriously, Dan, it's not like that between us." The words taste bitter on my tongue, as if my head and my heart are at odds over the statement.

"Maybe not yet," he says. "But think about it. He's got this big, fancy life back in California and he packed it all up to live with you for a month? He's trying to sweep you off your feet."

I stifle a laugh, wishing he could know it has nothing to do with me.

"He might say the right things and promise you the world," he says, "but at the end of the day, people like that … people like him … are always going to be looking for the next new thing."

I take a step back, digesting his words, tucking them in my pocket should I lose my footing with Fabian again.

"If you ever want to talk to me about anything," he says. "I'm your man."

Without hesitation, I throw my arms around him and wrap him in a hug. Never mind that he's a whole foot taller than me and I have to rise on my toes just to reach his shoulders. When I pull away, he's smiling, though it's a tight, sad sort of smile. I'm sure the gesture meant more to him than I could possibly know. He's lonely, and the one person he wants is giving all of their time and attention to someone else.

It has to hurt.

"You're an amazing friend," I tell him. "Know that."

Heading home, I turn the corner to my street, and my stomach sinks at the sight of my empty driveway. Pulling into my garage, I snap myself out of it. I have no business being excited about Fabian's company in any capacity, and allowing myself to entertain that path is a reckless, slippery slope.

He's my child's donor.

He'll never be more.

He'll never be less.

I press the garage remote on my visor, and climb out. Only the second I shut the driver's side door, I catch a glimpse of Fabian's blacked out Range Rover pulling up.

Without an ounce of permission, my stomach somersaults.

Chapter 18

Fabian

"ANY UPDATES?" I park in Rossi's driveway Tuesday after practice, taking a minute to check in with Steen and Farber before heading inside.

"We're getting close," Steen says. "They're dragging their feet, but they know we have the upper hand here. Hoping we reach an agreement by the end of the week, next week at the latest. But I'll keep you posted."

Hanging up, I kill the engine.

My phone dings with a text from Tatum, the tenth one today. Swiping across the screen, I delete the group of messages without reading a single one. And then I waste zero time calling Coach.

"Tatum needs to back off," I say when he answers.

Not that the man has an ounce of control over his spitfire spawn.

The two have a complex relationship. Coach was never

around when she was growing up, mostly traveling and touring with me or the hopefuls who came before me. And when he wasn't elbow deep in the pro tennis circuit, he was chasing the bottom of a whiskey bottle. It wasn't until a few years ago I realized the man had a serious problem. I'd found him lying face down in an alley outside a bar in Dublin, having been mugged and then beaten an inch within his life. In an ironic twist of fate, the near-death experience was exactly the wakeup call the man needed to find a newfound appreciation for sober living, and it was during his early days in AA when he reached out to his estranged daughter to apologize for his absence and attempt to make amends.

Her presence in his life was intense at first. She wanted to go everywhere with him, watch everything he did, jet-set with us around the world. The girl clearly had daddy issues. But she was also fun. Frivolous. The life of the party in a way that I never could be. Raised by a former Hollywood A-list actress and a stepdad producer, Tatum was practically royalty and she owned it.

In retrospect, we had no business being together.

But she intrigued me with her fascinating brand of crazy, and she was one of the only women I'd ever met who understood the kind of pressure I was under *and* who could keep up with me between the sheets.

Looking back, I was blinded by lust.

Hindsight is twenty-twenty.

But everything's crystal-fucking-clear.

"Just keep ignoring her," Coach says. "She'll calm down if you don't feed into it. It's like a dog, you can't reinforce bad behavior or they'll just keep doing it."

I choke on a laugh. He did *not* just compare his daughter to a dog ...

Although there are compelling similarities between

Tatum and a yappy, palm-sized West Hollywood chihuahua.

"Been ignoring her for days." I head toward the front door. "Anyway, if you could talk to her again, I'd appreciate it."

Another message comes through—followed by a phone call.

I ignore both.

He groans. "I'll try."

"You'll *try*?" I chuff. "Imagine if I said that to you on the court. You'd cut my fucking balls off with net string."

He laughs. "Yeah, yeah, yeah. I'll see if I can't reason with her."

Inside Rossi's house, I pass the living room, where Carina and Lucia are spread out on the floor while Sesame Street plays on the TV.

"Hi, Baby Daddy," she calls.

"Not sure if you were aware, but my name's actually Fabian …" I tease before making my way to Rossi's office and rapping on the door.

"Come in," she calls.

"You're still working?" I check the time.

"Just finishing up." Her raspberry-colored nails clack on the keyboard. "Just finished one of the most complicated family trees I think I've ever done. Want to see?"

I take the seat in her guest chair and she turns her rose gold MacBook to face me.

"Look at this. This woman married this guy. He died after a year, so then she married his brother. Only it turns out it was his half-brother because his mother had an affair with the neighbor. And then the half-brother died, so the mom married a cousin. But the cousin was actually adopted into this huge family with, like, thirteen kids, so if you look here, I've got his bio parents and his adopted parents."

I'm lost. But I nod like it all makes sense.

"Isn't that crazy?" she asks. "All of this because a handful of relatives took DNA tests and submitted them to this database. That coupled with archived public records and I was able to make all of those connections. Insane, right?"

"Yeah, actually." I scratch my temple, quietly grateful for my simple roots. A mom, a dad, a sister. A handful of aunts and uncles. Nothing crazy or complicated.

"You know, even if you didn't want to find your sister, I could help you put together your family tree. I could potentially trace it back hundreds of years—depending on records, obviously. But I've had clients I was able to trace back to 15th century London."

With my parents being in their forties when they had me, most of my aunts and uncles are getting up there in age, and some are no longer with us. Once they pass, they'll take the family history with them. Not that I've ever given it much thought. I tend to focus on the future more than the past, and I always have. But once they're gone, so, too, will be my opportunity to know about any cracks or interesting branches in the family lineage.

"All right," I say. "Let's do it."

"The DNA testing? Really?" She rises halfway, hovering over her desk.

"Yeah."

Within seconds she's digging some kit out of a drawer, unwrapping swabs and tubes and laying everything out on top of her desk. Snapping on a pair of gloves, she grins.

"You really love this stuff, don't you?" I laugh.

"Obsessed with it." She lifts a swab. "Now open wide."

I try to picture my family tree now, the little dash beneath my name for Lucia. A dash I never would've even known about if it weren't for the clinic's error. While my parents are no longer with us, a part of them lives on in my daughter.

"Okay, all done." Placing the swabs in a tube, she seals everything up in a biohazard bag before placing it carefully in a pre-labeled mailing envelope. "They should get this in two days, and then it could take a week or two to process. I know some people though, so I might be able to speed that up …"

"You said you could find Frankie?"

"I can definitely try. You want me to?"

"My parents died without ever knowing if she was okay … if it's this easy, I think I'd like to know."

"It isn't always easy—or fast—but I'll do everything I can to find her." Rossi places a hand over her heart, her blue eyes shimmering in the afternoon sun that bakes through her office window, warming her skin. The faint scent of vanilla and peonies lingers between us, soft and sweet. Strong yet delicate.

Like her.

"I want to take you out tomorrow night," I say.

Toying with the diamond heart pendant at her neck she examines me. "Out? Like … on a date?"

"Yes. Like on a date."

Her brows knit.

"You said you haven't been on one in years," I say.

"Yeah, but it's not like I'm missing out on much …"

"Don't you ever go stir crazy? Sitting in this house seven nights a week?"

"I'm sorry my life seems dull to you, but—"

"—that's not what I'm saying." I cup her face and drag my thumb along her bottom lip until it turns from a frown into a sly smile. "You're a mother, not a martyr. It's okay to

The Match

do things that are solely for you. And you need balance or you're going to burn out. Believe me, I know."

She exhales, gaze focused on mine.

"I'll see if Carina can watch the baby tomorrow night—she owes me for stealing my bed last weekend." Sliding my hands to her hips, I pull Rossi closer, breathing her into the deepest parts of me because I can't fucking get enough. "I've got a friend in downtown Chicago who owns this Italian place. He's got a backdoor entrance and a private dining room we can use."

"What are we doing?" Her words are slow and laced in reluctance, but her body remains melted against me.

"I don't know what *you're* doing, but *I'm* enjoying myself," I say. "Maybe you should join me?"

"I'm not worried about enjoying myself, Fabian. I'm worried about the aftermath of enjoying myself."

Slinking away, she places a careful distance between us, perching behind her desk.

"By the way, my neighbor is coming over for dinner tomorrow night," she changes the subject. "It's our Wednesday tradition. Just wanted to give you a heads' up in case you didn't want to be here ..."

"Your next door neighbor? The one who's deeply and madly in love with you?"

She laughs through her nose. "Yes. He's a good friend of mine, and I know he'd love to meet you, but I completely understand if you—"

"—I'm in," I say.

Because someone's got to make sure this neighbor knows his place.

Chapter 19

Rossi

"I'VE BEEN TRYING to get Rossi and Lucia to come out to my parents' farm in Wisconsin with me," Dan says over dinner Wednesday night.

Fabian stabs a forkful of field greens, watching Dan like a hawk as he teases Lucia with a toy lamb.

"You want to see the real thing, don't you, Lucia?" Dan asks.

"At this age, would she even know the difference between a real one and a stuffed one?" Fabian breaks his silence.

"Only one way to find out," Dan answers Fabian, but looks at me.

He's been doing that all night, avoiding Fabian's watchful gaze, directing his comments my way. It's not like Dan to be so cold. I spent all day talking him up to Fabian, telling him how much he'd love him. Now he's made a liar out of me.

"One of these days we'll make our way up there." I reach for my wine and shoot Dan a calming smile. A second later, Fabian's fingertips brush against the top of my knee under the table. "You like your salad?"

"So, Dan, what do you do again?" Fabian ignores my question.

"Accountant for a Fortune 500 Company," Dan answers, sitting straighter. "Not nearly as exciting as your job though. I'd much rather be jet setting around the world than working in a stuffy office all day. Unfortunately, my strength lies up here instead of here." Dan points to his head before squeezing his average-sized biceps.

Shots fired.

"Dan." I clear my throat and shoot him a look. "Tell Fabian about your family's farm."

We need to keep this neutral.

Rising from the table, I grab the lasagna from the oven while Dan tells Fabian about the homestead that's been in his family for generations. I'm sure it bores Fabian to death to hear about how they raise sheep and alternate beans and corn every planting season, but I pray it neutralizes the energy between them, if only for a few minutes.

"This is extremely hot …" I plate their food and top off their wine before taking the seat next to Fabian and straightening the napkin in my lap.

"So how did the two of you meet again?" Dan points his fork across the table, waving it side to side. "Rossi never really went into detail."

Fabian and I exchange looks.

"We were introduced by a mutual acquaintance," Fabian answers, leaving out the fact that the mutual acquaintance was a fertility clinic. Close enough.

"And then you just … randomly … reconnected?" Dan asks.

"Pretty much." I take a drink.

"It's just weird that all this time we've been friends, you never mentioned that you knew one of the world's biggest athletes," Dan says, a curious glint in his eye as he examines Fabian. "If it were me, I'd work it into every conversation I ever had."

"Yeah, well, Rossi's not like that," Fabian says, turning to me. "Which is one of my favorite things about her."

Dan clears his throat.

"So where'd you go?" he asks.

"Pardon?" Fabian coughs.

"If you knew her before and you recently reconnected, why was there a disconnect? Did you stop talking to her? Disappear from her life? I guess I'm just trying to paint a picture here," Dan says. "I don't do well with ambiguity."

"Fabian's a busy guy," I say. "And I'm a busy girl. Our paths crossed again at the perfect time."

Dan slices a corner of lasagna with his knife before loading it into his fork. Frowning, he doesn't take a bite. He simply continues to study Fabian.

At least he's actually looking at him now—which was more than I could say twenty minutes ago.

Lucia squeals, tossing a sticky handful of yogurt melts on the floor before knocking her sippy cup aside. Pushing away from her tray, she winces.

"She's been in there a while." I hop up to unfasten her. "I'm sure she wants to stretch."

"I've got it." Dan swats me away, retrieving Lucia before I have a chance. She offers him a drooly grin, which he promptly cleans up with her bib before placing her on his lap. With one arm holding my squirmy daughter, he finishes his dinner.

For the next several minutes, Fabian's stare is heavy, his jaw is set, and his lasagna goes cold.

"You don't like it?" I ask, though it's a silly question because he hasn't even tried it. "I used that organic sauce you were telling me about ..."

Forcing a breath through flared nostrils, he digs into his food, but he doesn't take his eyes off Dan and Lucia.

Tossing back the rest of my wine, I sit in awkward limbo as Dan bounces my baby on his knee and makes silly sounds that send her into roaring giggles—all the while Fabian shoots daggers his way.

Is he jealous?

Protective?

Rising, I casually make my way to the other side of the table, scoop my daughter into my arms, and carry her to the kitchen. With Lucia on my hip, I begin cleaning up. Maybe I shouldn't leave those two to their own devices over there, but I couldn't stand another second of whatever the hell they're doing.

"Oh, Rossi, let me help you." Dan meets me by the island, stacking plates and silverware, washing utensils and placing everything back into its rightful spot—the way he's done a hundred times before.

For the next ten minutes, no one says a word.

On a normal Wednesday, we'd eat dinner, clean up, play with Lucia for a bit, then we'd watch a movie or a couple shows after putting the baby to bed.

But something tells me that's not going to happen tonight.

"Thanks for stopping by, Dan." Fabian grips the back of Dan's left shoulder, giving it a tight squeeze. "Think I can take it from here."

Elevens form between Dan's brows. "I'm confused."

Only I know he isn't confused. He knows exactly what Fabian's implying.

"I'll walk you out?" I offer, before things get worse.

Dan shuts off the faucet, dries his hands, and exhales.

I follow him to the front door, Lucia on my hip.

"Well, that was interesting," Dan says, voice low. His eyes scan past my shoulder, toward the kitchen where Fabian is finishing what he started.

I debate apologizing—but I stop myself.

I didn't do anything wrong.

I didn't participate in the pissing match.

As far as I'm concerned, they both owe each other some kind words.

"Call me tomorrow," he says, a distinct air of concernment in his tone. "I'm worried about this ... situation."

"Stop." I roll my eyes and swat his chest. "Have a good night, okay?"

I close up behind him, carry Lucia to the living room, then return to the kitchen, perching at the island where Fabian waits for me.

"So?" I ask. "What do you have to say for yourself?"

"That guy's a fucking creep," he blurts before eyeing Lucia and wincing. "I'm sorry, Rossi. But something's off about him."

"He's just lonely," I say. "And protective of us."

"Protective?" he asks. "*Protective*? Rossi, that man wants to wear your *skin*."

I laugh so hard I snort. "Dan? No. He might be a little socially awkward, but he's no Buffalo Bill. This is not a *Silence of the Lambs* situation."

"It's weird how much he likes Lucia." Fabian's expression sours. "That's not normal. Grown men parading around babies like that."

"Believe it or not, there are guys out there who love babies and who are naturals with them," I counter. "He and his ex-wife really wanted to have a family, but it never happened. I think he sees Lucia as the daughter he never had."

Fabian slaps his hands on the quartz counter. "Yeah, well she doesn't need another daddy."

Lifting a brow, I cock my head. "Fabian Catalano, I believe I'm sensing some extreme jealousy here."

Shoulders arched, he exhales. "The man's a creep, Rossi. And watching him with Lucia ..." His voice trails. "It made me feel something I've never felt before."

"Like what?"

"I don't know ... like I wanted to dive across the table like a goddamned tiger and rip his face off?"

My jaw falls. "Really? That intense?"

Fabian comes around the island, placing his arms around my waist and steering me into his arms. I press my cheek against his chest, sensing the steady, swift thrum of his heart.

"Promise me something," he says.

"What?"

"Promise you'll never date that freak."

Laughing, I wrap my arms around his lower back and breathe him in. "I promise. But only if you promise to stop calling him names. We're not in middle school."

"Fair enough." He cups my face, angling my chin until our mouths align. "But if he ever looks at you like that—like he wants to eat you alive—it's game over."

"Glad to know you're watching out for us."

Pressing his wine-flavored mouth against mine, I accept his kiss—and his fingers in my hair and the butterfly frenzy in my chest and the lightness under my feet. They're here to stay. Unlike Fabian. His time here is limited; sand through the hourglass.

"I should put the baby to bed." I slink away, and his hands trail down my arms until his fingers intertwine with mine. Our eyes hold and matching smiles paint our lips. He wears the look of a man who wants to eat me alive—in a *different* way.

Whatever's happening between us is as terrifying as it is magical.

And I'm here for it.

But only for the next three weeks.

After that, it's back to reality.

Chapter 20

Fabian

I'M CHANGING in my room Thursday, hair damp from the shower, when I hear a set of unfamiliar voices coming from down the hall.

A man and a woman.

Peeking my head out, I'm met with Rossi flouncing down the hall, hands waving. "My parents are here."

"O .. okay."

"They were in the area and just decided to stop by." She bites her lip.

"Do they know ... about me?"

"They do now. I had to give them the bridged version so my Dad doesn't have a heart attack, but I think they handled it okay. Carina's keeping them entertained right now, but they want to meet you." She takes my hand in hers. "I'm so sorry to put this on you. They're really nice though, I promise."

"You said the same thing about Dan ..." Leaning in, I steal a kiss before flashing a smile. "But no worries. I've got this."

Following the sound of laughter and conversation, I find the three of them—plus Lucia—seated at the kitchen table.

The instant I step into the light, the room goes silent, as if someone pressed a 'mute' button.

"Mr. Bianco," I say, giving him a nod before turning my attention to his lovely wife—an older carbon copy of Rossi. "Mrs. Bianco."

"Mom, Dad, this is Fabian." Rossi places her hand on the small of my back.

Her father rises, coming at me with an extended hand but a face that means business. "Fabian, good to meet you. Our daughter just, uh, filled us in. It's quite the, uh, story."

With a hand clasped over her décolletage, Rossi's mother's eyes glisten as she makes her way to me.

"Can I give you a hug?" she asks. "You're practically family. I mean, you're Lucia's ..." Her voice trails, as if she can't decide on a word.

Daddy?

Donor?

Opening my arms, I accept Mrs. Bianco's hug, breathing in her lilac shampoo and the motherly warmth she exudes.

"This is just *crazy*," she says, her blue eyes sparkling when she pulls away.

"Remember," Rossi says. "This needs to stay strictly between all of us."

"Yeah," Carina chimes in from the table, bouncing Lucia on her lap. "So don't go telling Aunt Peg or the entire family will know by Sunday."

Their mother swats. "My daughters think I'm a gossip or something, but I promise, my lips are sealed."

Her father studies me, jaw jutted forward ever so, laying the scrutinizing stare on thick as honey but hardly as sweet.

"So what are your plans with my grandchild?" he asks. "Going forward?"

"We're still figuring things out, but that would be up to your daughter," I say. "That's why I'm here."

"Fabian lives here," Carina says, shooting me a wink. "Until the end of the month."

Her mother's expression fades. "Oh? So you just ... moved in?"

"I'm staying in the guest room," I say, enunciating every syllable. "But yes. We thought it'd be easier to get to know each other if we ... immersed ourselves in this situation."

"And what would you like to see come from this?" Her father asks. "Do you want to be a father or do you want to remain an anonymous fixture in our granddaughter's life?"

"Don't mind my father, he tends to go straight for the jugular," Carina says.

"*Dad.*" Rossi clears her throat. "Fabian and I are still figuring things out. Can we save the hardball questions for another time?"

"That's an excellent idea, Rossi." Her mother slides her hand into her father's elbow and leads him back to the table. "We were just out running errands and wanted to stop by for a quick visit and to see our little doll baby." Shuffling to the other side of the table, she takes Lucia from Carina, smothering her chubby cheeks with kisses, leaving smudges of red lipstick. "Though I will say, Rossi, I thought it was strange we hadn't heard from you in the past week ..."

"As you can see, things have been a little crazy …" Rossi says. "Was waiting for a good time to share all of this with you, but anyway."

"You're hogging her, Suze." Mr. Bianco reaches toward Lucia, who reaches back at him with a drooly grin the size of Neptune. "There's my favorite baby girl."

"Hey," Carina says.

"Oh, stop." Suze paws at the air, chuckling. "You're *all* his favorite."

"Your mom made some of those Madeleines," Mr. Bianco points to a white plate wrapped in clear plastic. "I told her she's got to stop making those. I'm supposed to be on a keto diet or whatever."

"His A1C is up." Suze rolls her eyes.

"They told me I'm supposed to eat seventy-five percent fats or something," Mr. Bianco says, "But I can't eat cake or ice cream. How the hell does a guy do that?"

"Fabian's actually really good with nutrition," Rossi nudges my arm. "I bet he could put together some lists for you?"

Her father's bushy gray-black brows knit. "You think you could do that?"

"I'm certainly no nutritionist, but I know a thing or two about macros."

"See, what the hell is a macro? They gave me all these pamphlets at the doctor's office, but it's like reading Latin."

Chuckling, I nod, "I'd be happy to break it down for you sometime, sir."

"Sir." He points across the table. "I like that. You hear that, Suze? Biggest athlete in the world and he calls *me* 'sir.'"

Suze glances up from playing with Lucia and offers a warm, sweet smile.

Rossi's dad checks his watch before tossing his hands in the air. "Just got a text from our accountant. Wants to know if we can meet a half hour earlier to sign our taxes, otherwise we'll have to reschedule for next week."

"Well, that's unfortunate," Suze says with a pout as Lucia tugs on her necklace. "I was looking forward to getting to know a little more about Rossi's new friend."

New friend.

That's one way to put it.

I fight a smirk.

"I need to get back to work anyway," Rossi says. "And Fabian probably has some phone calls to make …"

Carina takes the baby and Mr. Bianco helps his wife up, not that she needs it. But he strikes me as the old-fashioned type. Reminds me a lot of my father, actually.

"I'll walk you out." Rossi disappears with her parents outside for a few minutes, and when she returns, I catch her by the office.

"Everything good?"

"Yeah …" She squints. "They kind of … really like you."

"And you're surprised?"

"No. I mean, yeah. It's a lot for them to take in at one time. And you couldn't tell, but I know my dad was freaking out on the inside. He's not an avid tennis fan, but he knows who you are in a way that non-golfers know who Tiger Woods is. I bet he low-key wanted to fangirl a bit."

"Really? Because he came with those questions like …"

She laughs through her nose. "He was trying to play it cool, and I think he overcompensated by being ice cold."

Pulling her against me, I kiss her smiling face. "Oh, yeah? Is that was he was doing?"

"Seriously though, they think you're pretty great. And

they think what you're doing is great," she says. "Even though I don't think *you* even know what you're doing …"

"Psh." I scoff. "I know exactly what I'm doing."

"And what's that?"

"Falling for my baby mama …"

Chapter 21

Rossi

"WHAT ARE you thinking about right now?" Fabian asks late Thursday night. We're snuggled under a blanket on the couch, watching some newly released documentary on some basketball player he knows and I'm trying to pay attention out of politeness, but sports have never held my attention before. Doubt they're magically going to start now.

"I'm thinking that my dad is probably sitting in his leather recliner—his thinking chair, as he calls it—staring at the fireplace and analyzing everything from earlier today," I say, fighting a laugh. "And my mom is probably nagging at him to come to bed because she can never sleep alone. She says the bed gets too cold, but who knows. While she waits for him, she'll probably put on an extra layer of Oil of Olay and mentally go over all the questions she's going to ask me the next time we're alone."

"Your parents are definitely … interesting."

"They're a handful sometimes, but it's a wholesome handful, so it's all right."

"You're lucky to have them around," he says. "I never really had the quintessential grandparent experience. Mine were all gone by the time I was barely out of diapers. I'm glad Lucia has them."

"Yeah." I sigh. "They're pretty great. Still crazy in love after forty years of marriage. You know, they almost didn't happen. She was engaged to another guy when they met. But my dad was relentless."

"Imagine that."

"He worked at my grandfather's electronics store on the weekends, sweet-talked him into letting him do a few things around the house. Mowing and cleaning the gutters. But he just wanted to see my mom. Anyway, long story short, she left her fiancé and married my dad. Thank goodness for cold feet."

"And persistent Italians," he adds.

"She almost didn't though. She was scared she was going to choose the wrong guy."

"My dad once told me any time you make a decision from a place of fear, ninety-nine percent of the time it's the wrong one," he says.

"Ooh. That's a good little nugget. I'll remember that. Got any other ones?"

He pauses the documentary. "Yeah. Actually. There's a rule in tennis, that if you hold the racket too tight, you lose control. I think relationships are that way too, so I've always made a point to hold people closely, but not too tight."

"Damnnnn. I had no idea you went this deep." I rest my elbow on the back of the couch, angle my body toward him, and rest my cheek against my hand. "You should write a book or something."

"I'm working on one actually," he says. "Or I should say a ghostwriter is. This publisher wants me to do an autobiography … never mind that I haven't even lived half of my life yet …"

"Yeah, but you've done more living in thirty-seven years than most people do in eighty," I say. "I bet you have all kinds of good stories. And think of all the aspiring tennis players who want to be you when they grow up."

A wave of exhaustion washes over me, sinking into my marrow. I could stare at this beautiful creature all night, if only my eyes would let me.

Thank goodness for pictures.

In an unexpected yet endearing moment earlier tonight, Fabian told me to snap a few pictures of him and Lucia with my phone. And he made me swear up, down, sideways, and to Heaven and back not to share them with anyone. He said they were only for her and only so she had something to remember him by, come what may. I wasted no time grabbing my phone, and I snapped no less than fifteen images—images I'll treasure and keep safe the rest of my days. He also told me not to send them off to get printed, that he'd buy me a photo printer to use. I teased him, telling him he was being paranoid, but he told me it wasn't about him … it was about Lucia.

Her privacy, *her* safety, *her* future.

"I'm going to head to bed," I say, yawning.

"Here." Fabian pulls me into him, situating me into the cozy bend of his shoulder and readjusting the blanket over our laps. "I'll carry you to bed when this is over."

He presses play on the remote and settles back, arms wrapped around me tight.

With my ear pressed against his warm chest, I fall asleep to the steady drum of his heartbeat.

A girl could get used to this.

Even if she shouldn't.

Chapter 22

Fabian

"WHAT ARE YOU THINKING ABOUT?" I ask Rossi after dinner Friday night. The warm flicker of candlelight makes her eyes shimmer in the dark.

I haven't taken my eyes off of her since the moment she emerged from her room earlier tonight. She teetered, unsteady, in sky high black stilettos as she tugged at a little black dress that hugged her curves in all the right places and left nothing to the imagination. Speechless, I bit my fist as I visually devoured her from head to toe, and she muttered something about not having worn any of this since before the pregnancy.

I immediately silenced that fucking nonsense with a punishing kiss and a squeeze of her perfect, peach-shaped ass.

"If I tell you I'm thinking about the baby, you're going to lecture me ..." she says.

"Damn right I will."

She rolls her eyes. "This is the first night I've spent away from her since she was born."

The city skyline twinkles outside our private dining room.

"And I promise, I'll make it worth every second." I toss my napkin over my plate, retrieve my wallet, and place a few large bills to cover the tab since our server went MIA.

Dabbing her mouth, she folds her napkin, places it aside, and rises from her chair, her breasts all but spilling out of her skintight ensemble. My cock strains against the inside of my slacks.

With my hand on the small of her back, I press my lips against the side of her neck and whisper, "I don't know if I can wait another second. I have to fucking have you."

"Unless you want a quickie in the stairwell, you don't have a choice."

That's what she thinks …

Slipping my hand into hers, I lead her out the private exit, to a reserved parking space behind the building. Pressing her against the passenger door, I slide my hand against her soft cheek and claim her Aperol-tasting mouth before working my way down the side of her neck and stopping above her ample cleavage. Dragging my fingertips down her outer thigh, I tug at the hem of her dress, inching it higher and higher until I find the lace trim of her panties.

"Are you crazy?" she whispers, breathless. Her eyes are bright in the dark. "Right here? Right now?"

"It's going to take at forty minutes to get home. Another twenty until Carina gets out the door. By my count, it's at least another hour before you're screaming my name, and honestly, I don't know if I can wait that long."

I graze my lips against hers, which arch up at the sides.

"For the record, I'm not a name screamer," she says. "And you're going to have to wait because I'm not trying to get arrested for public indecency."

Reaching for the rear passenger door, the locks click open.

"Get in," I say.

"What?"

Sliding across the buttery leather, I pull her into my lap and slam the door shut. "The windows are tinted dark enough no one will see us, and as long as the car isn't bouncing like a seventies van, we should be fine."

"Here?" Her eyes widen as I tease my finger along the inside of her leg, stopping to shove her panties aside. Rossi bites her lip, tossing her head back as she grinds against me.

"You're so fucking wet …"

With her hands on my shoulders, she steadies herself, rocking against me until we settle into a playful rhythm.

"Slow down," I whisper against her warm skin.

"But it feels so damn good." She winces, exhaling hard.

Guiding her lips to mine, I claim her mouth before tasting her tongue. A second later, her fingers are working my zipper and her palm is wrapped around my shaft. Moaning, I sink back into the leather as she pumps my length.

"Did you bring a condom?" she whispers. "I'm not on anything …"

Fortunately, I'm nothing if not prepared for these things.

This thing, in particular.

I'd actually stopped at a pharmacy earlier today in preparation.

A second later, I'm ripping a gold foil packet between my teeth before unrolling it over my throbbing cock. Rossi straddles me, impaling herself with my hardness one torturing inch at a time.

"Oh my god," she exhales when I'm all in. "I forgot how good this feels …"

"After this, you'll never forget again." Gripping her ass, I pull her taut against me as I thrust into her.

Gasping, she rocks back and forth.

"Slower," I whisper into her ear as she buries her head against my neck. The rocking steadies, but the car is still bouncing. Anyone walking by with half a brain cell will know exactly what's going on.

"I don't know if I can …"

"Yeah, you can … like this." I guide her hips into a circular, grinding motion. "Take your time, enjoy it. You deserve this.." Tugging the top of her dress down, I take a nipple in my mouth, gently sucking the soft bud. And for the endless hour that follows, slow and steady wins the race.

Chasing off the inevitable, we lose ourselves in sweet anticipation.

She isn't *just* a mother.

I'm not a world famous athlete.

In this moment, she is mine—and I am hers.

"I can't hold off any longer," she whispers, grinding harder against me. My cock strains, my balls tighten and I let go, my explosion meeting hers until we collapse against each other with stolen breaths and dizzied heads.

"Good God, woman." I cup her face, holding her pretty eyes captive in the dark. "I could do this all night and it still wouldn't be enough."

Swatting my chest, she climbs off and adjusts her dress into place. "We should get home before it gets too late."

Home.

That word on those lips makes me feel some kind of way.

And I'm here for it.

Chapter 23

Rossi

I WAKE with a sweet soreness between my thighs, the smell of fresh coffee in the air, and the opposite side of my bed made. My bedroom door is cracked a few inches and the sound of Saturday morning cartoons trails from down the hall.

Last night was nothing short of insane—for a myriad of reasons. One of which being I'm pretty sure I set a world record for most amount of orgasms in one night.

Grabbing my robe off the hook in the bathroom, I slip it over my shoulders, cinch the tie around my waist, and head to the kitchen.

"Good morning." I shove my hair from my face and grin at the handsome shirtless man covered in baby food and the squirmy, happy baby in the high chair.

"We had a bit of an incident," he says, dabbing at his rippled abs with a burp rag. "But I've got it under control."

"Yes, I see that." Pouring a mug of coffee, I stand back and watch this moment unfold in real time.

It's crazy how this man blew into my life like a hurricane, but he's settled in so peacefully.

It's almost too good to be true.

"Oh, hey, would you mind grabbing my phone? It's on the charger in the guest room," he asks as he loads a baby spoon full of Hawaiian Delight.

"On it."

I mean … we don't make the worst team.

And if something happened to come of this, it's not like crazier things haven't happened.

Shaking my head, I quiet my inner narrative before she gets too ahead of herself, and I shuffle down the hall, coffee mug in hand, to retrieve his phone. Only the second I pull it from the plug, the screen comes to life and a message appears.

TATUM: I miss you and love you so much, baby. And I absolutely cannot wait to see you next week. XO

My stomach sinks. Rock hard. Like an anvil going over a cliff in a Warner Brothers' cartoon, only far more painful because this is real life.

If Fabian's ex-fiancée is texting him that she loves and misses him and can't wait to see him, there's got to be some sort of conversation happening between them.

People don't send things like that out of the blue for no reason.

My mouth turns dry, but I manage a painful swallow before taking a deep breath. I wait until the nausea subsides before heading out to face him. And with each step, I contemplate confronting him about this. For the past week and a half, he's been kissing me, wooing me, taking care of me. And last night we screwed so many times I stopped counting.

Tears cloud my vision, but I wipe them away before they have a chance to fall.

We're not dating. He doesn't owe me anything. And I knew from the moment he first kissed me that this was a bad idea.

Honestly, it serves me right.

If I'd have stuck to my guns, held steadfast to my original plan, I wouldn't be standing here right now, in the dark of my own home, feeling like the world's biggest fool.

Sucking in a deep breath, I put on a brave face and stride to the kitchen, his phone in hand.

"Here you go." I keep my tone light and place it face down on the island.

"You're the best." He kisses the side of my forehead.

Only this time, my insides fill with knots instead of butterflies.

"Oh, forgot to tell you," he says. "I have to go to California for a few days to take care of some things. Leaving first thing in the morning, hoping to be back mid-week."

With my back to him, I nod and swallow the dry lump in my throat so my voice doesn't break.

"Okay," I say. "Sounds good."

Visions of last night stop dancing in my head, and I promise myself that someday I'll forget the way he looked at me when I was dressed up, the way he worshipped my curves and whispered all the right things into my ear at all the right moments.

Fabian is hot like fire.

I'm sure I'm not the first girl he's ever burned, and I certainly won't be the last.

It was fun while it lasted …

Chapter 24

Fabian

I ZIP my suitcase Sunday and wheel it to the door before heading to the living room to see my girls one last time before I head home for a few days. In the midst of everything going on, I'd forgotten I had a photoshoot scheduled for some fitness magazine for this week, and I figured while I'm home I might as well have a come-to-Jesus meeting with Tatum because the barrage of texts and phone calls hasn't stopped. I'd block her number, but knowing her, she'll just get a new one, and changing the number I've had for over a decade will be more hassle than it's worth.

"Hey," I say to Rossi. "Going to head out, so …"

Focused on the baby, she doesn't so much as bother to look up. "Have a good flight."

"I should be back Wednesday," I say.

"Okay." Her tone is flat. Different. Unreadable. Which describes how she's been the past twenty-four hours.

Everything between us was amazing … until I

mentioned going back home yesterday, then something changed. The warmhearted, jovial woman left and an ice queen showed up in her place. Only she isn't cruel and heartless—Rossi Bianco could never be those things. This version of her is simply distant, less receptive.

Flinching at my touch, lips stiffening at my kiss.

Cordial and casual.

"Can I steal you away for a second?" I ask, nodding toward the baby. I can't leave on this note.

She finally glances my way.

I motion for her to come closer. I refuse to have a conversation like this from across the room.

She hands Lucia a stuffed elephant and pushes herself up, slowly making her way across the room.

Arms folded, she asks, "What's up?"

"Are you upset that I'm leaving?"

She frowns. "No. Why would I be?"

I rake my hand along my jaw, studying her, attempting to read between any and all lines—only she's not giving me much to work with.

"I just … we were getting along so well … and Friday night was amazing … and then yesterday something changed," I say.

Folding her arms, she shrugs. "I just think we're moving too fast."

True. We're moving at the speed of light.

"This whole thing between us," I say. "It's not exactly conventional. And it's not like there's some timeline we're supposed to be following. We can slow it down, if that'll make you more comfortable, but if you're into this, Rossi, like I am. For the love of God, don't pull back. I'm having the time of my life with you. With Lucia too. This is all new for me, but I'm loving every crazy, confusing second of it."

Her lips press together and her attention skims past my shoulder. "You always know exactly what to say, but sometimes the things you say are too perfect, you know?"

"Sorry?" I smirk. "I didn't realize that was a bad thing?"

"If I hardly know you, how can I know that what you're saying is genuine?"

"You can't know. These things happen with time. You just have to trust me, and meanwhile, we'll keep getting to know each other." I go to reach for her and stop myself. She's clearly not receptive to being touched right now. "Are you scared? Because it's okay if you are." Swallowing, I add, "We're in this together—whatever *this* is."

Her eyes catch on mine, lids heavy with exhaustion. I slept in her bed last night, but rather than curl up in my arms and fall asleep with her cheek against my chest, she stayed on her side, tossing and turning until the covers were a twisted heap on the floor.

"What are you afraid of?" I ask.

Clearing her throat, she says, "I just think we're being selfish about this. For Lucia's sake, I mean. We shouldn't be doing this because if it blows up in our faces, it's only going to hurt her in the end."

My jaw tenses.

I see what she's doing.

"If you want to use Lucia as your excuse to do—or not do—things that scare you for the rest of your life, that's your prerogative," I say.

"I'm not using her as an excuse," her expression twists and her words cut sharp. "It's a valid concern. I don't want her to get hurt if things get strained between us."

"Why would they become strained?"

"Because I don't know what you're doing and what you expect from this," she says. "And in a few weeks, you're going back to California, back to your actual life. And I'll still be here, thinking about the gorgeous man who waltzed into my life and said all the perfect things and made me feel things I had no business feeling and made me hope for things I had no business hoping for."

I scratch my temple, chin tucked as I wrap my head around this. "You honestly think I'm just going to walk out of here three weeks from now and act like none of this happened?"

"As opposed to the alternative, yes," she says. "I'm trying to be realistic here. Your life is in Malibu. Your coach, your assistant, your friends, your business deals, everything."

"My *life* can be anywhere I want it to be," I say. Fuck it. I grip her waist and pull her against me before tipping her pointed chin upwards. "If you really think I can walk away from the two of you after this, then you have me all wrong."

I drag my lips against hers, teasing the promise of a kiss that I won't fulfill.

If I'm going to make my runway time, I've got to go.

"When I get back," I say, inhaling her vanilla-sweet scent. "I'll show you just how wrong you are."

Chapter 25

Rossi

"MS. BIANCO, IT'S HAROLD," the malpractice attorney I'd contacted last week calls me late Monday morning. "Just spoke to the clinic's counsel, and I have good news."

I sit up in my desk chair. "Okay?"

"They're currently putting together a settlement package for you at the request of your donor," he says. "He waived all rights to his settlement and asked them to give it to you instead. I don't have any of the details yet, but they said it's significantly more than the original one they offered you a few weeks back. They said they'd send over preliminaries this afternoon, so I'll get back to you when I have more. Just wanted to let you know the good news."

"Thank you so much." I end the call and sit motionless at my desk for a timeless eternity, lost in a sea of thoughts, mind drifting this way and that—as it has been the past couple of days.

Fabian left yesterday morning to go back to California for a few days.

I thought the time apart might help clear my head, but the only noticeable change around here is that the house is a little quieter. A handful of times, I've caught my stomach flipping when I pass the guest room door. And I even wandered in there the other day, curious to see if he'd left anything behind.

He had.

A diamond Rolex on the nightstand.

Drawers full of clothes.

A bottle of cologne—which I shamefully sprayed for some insane reason.

I've decided it's okay to miss the illusion of what we had, but it doesn't mean I have to miss *him*. Sometimes I wonder if it'd have been better to live out the rest of the month in ignorant bliss for the sake of a few more magical weeks feeling like a suburban single mom fairytale princess.

But like my Nonna used to say, everything happens for a reason.

There's a reason I saw that text when I did.

Dragging in a long hard breath, I make the short trek to the kitchen for a glass of water. Glancing out the window over the sink, I spot Carina and Lucia in the back, lying on a blanket in the afternoon sun.

I'm not sure how things will be after this month is up. How often he'll visit or how big of a role he'll want to play in my daughter's life. I'm fine with keeping that door open —but the door to my heart is officially deadbolted.

Chapter 26

Fabian

"HEY, BABY!" Tatum all but squeals when I approach her table at LaGrange 71 on Melrose. "I ordered you a Sazerac. For old times' sake."

The drink I had on our first official date …

"I won't be drinking today." I take a seat across from her. "In fact, I won't be staying more than a few minutes."

After several failed attempts on Coach's part to stop her incessant harassment, I figured it was time to take matters into my own hands. Arranging a meeting at one of the trendiest Beverly Hills restaurants seemed like the safest bet. She's not going to cause a scene here because she knows people, and they know her.

Animals don't shit where they eat.

Outside, a man walks by with a black Canon camera around his neck, chin tucked as he paces the sidewalk waiting for a shot. Someone must have tipped him off.

Across the street are two more. It's like fucking ants at a picnic.

"I just came to tell you to your face," I begin, "that we're over. We've been over. And you need to stop contacting me. I've moved on and you should too."

I expect tears. A crestfallen face. A sorrowful protest.

Only the psychopath smiles wide, ear to ear.

And then she dips her manicured little hand into her limited edition Birkin bag, retrieving a small black and white photo, which she places between us.

"What's this?" I ask.

"An ultrasound, silly." She swats the air. "We're having a baby!"

Studying the image, I can't breathe.

"Anyway, it's a good thing you came back when you did because my PR team wants to make the announcement tomorrow. Figured you should get a heads' up on that." She pours some San Pellegrino into a stemless wine glass and takes a sip.

"Who's the father?" I finally manage to formulate a sentence.

Choking on her water, she says, "Oh my *gawwwd*, Fabian. Do you even have to ask that?"

"Yes," I say. "I haven't fucking touched you in months."

"Yeah, and I'm several months along," she says without hesitation. "I didn't know I was pregnant until I realized I hadn't had a period in months." Pressing her lips together, she tucks her chin. "You know I never paid attention to that stuff."

And that part is true. Once a year, she got a birth control shot in her arm and never looked back. While I never paid much attention to her cycle unless she was on a hormonal rampage and it directly affected me, I do recall hearing her mention a handful of times that things were irregular.

None of what's happening is entirely implausible.

Rising, she smooths her hand along the front of her dress until the fabric showcases a very undeniable bump. And with her slight stature, it won't be long before she's looking like she swallowed a basketball.

"I'm starting to show already," she says. "Which is why we thought we should announce sooner than later. Need to get ahead of the rumors."

Stepping closer, she grabs my hand, placing it over her swollen middle—only before I have a chance to yank it back, a bright flash from outside the window captures this moment forever.

"God damn it." I jerk my hand away.

"I know it's a bit of a shock," she says. "And I'd wanted to tell you this privately, but I've been trying to reach you for weeks …"

Another flash follows.

And another.

Soon a half dozen paparazzo are gathered outside our window.

"You called them, didn't you?" I ask through gritted teeth.

Within seconds, the restaurant manager dashes outside in her Chanel suit, shooing them away. But it's too late. They're going to sell that image of my hand on Tatum's belly and it's going to be all over social media this time tomorrow.

"I know how you feel about children, so I don't expect you to be a doting dad or anything. But I do expect full financial support." She takes a seat, and all I can think about is the life growing inside of her with half of my DNA.

Another branch in the Catalano family tree.

A half-sibling for Lucia.

While I never wanted to be a father in the traditional sense, I especially never wanted to be a father with Tatum. It never made sense why someone as self-centered as her would want to be responsible for another human life—until I met her mother.

Tatum was brought up *with* unlimited wealth and privilege and raised *by* nannies. Plural. She was an only child, but there was an entire team of people dedicated to ensuring she had everything she needed around the clock. They even had a night nanny on staff until the day she graduated from high school. If she woke up in the middle of the night, parched, she'd ring that nanny for a glass of sparkling water. Another nanny was actually a cosmetologist by trade, hired on part-time to do Tatum's hair and makeup before school each day and for occasional special events.

Tatum was nothing more than a shiny doll on a shelf for her mother. A prized possession she could bring out at parties and show off to her friends. I'm convinced Tatum's entire existence was based on bolstering her mother's ego and reputation.

Tatum wouldn't even know the first thing about raising a child.

She's never kept a plant alive or owned a pet.

This woman couldn't even raise a Cabbage Patch Kid if she tried.

"Do you want to go somewhere so we can discuss this alone?" Tatum asks.

Rising, I clench my jaw. "That won't be necessary."

I check my watch. I'm supposed to be in Culver City in an hour for a photoshoot, and even if my entire schedule was clear, I wouldn't be caught dead alone with Tatum.

"We'll let our lawyers sort this out." I force a breath through flared nostrils.

"Wait." She wraps her hand around my wrist. "You're just going to leave?"

"What did you think would happen today? That I'd cry tears of joy and ask you to marry me again so we could be a family?" I chuff, freeing my wrist from her pathetic grip.

I'll do everything in my power to ensure that child—if it even *is* my child—has a decent upbringing.

But right now, all I can think about is breaking the news to Rossi before she finds out on social media. If she was having doubts about me before, seeing a picture of me with my pregnant ex when I told her I was going home to take care of some business … is only going to compound her misgivings tenfold.

I can only imagine how Tatum's PR team is going to paint this scenario, and within minutes of the "breaking news" going viral, there'll be rumors of us getting back together as well as a plethora of fake blind items and gossip articles.

I get my silver Maybach from valet and head to the studio, assembling my thoughts and dreading the phone call I'm about to make with every passing second.

Chapter 27

Rossi

MY PHONE BUZZES on my desk Monday afternoon, but the last name I'm expecting to see flashing across it is Fabian.

He hasn't called since he's been home, though he texted me to let me know he landed yesterday. I was in the middle of feeding the baby, so I sent him a thumb's up emoji in response. When I didn't hear back after that, I figured he was just giving me space.

But it's strange that he's calling.

With a tightness in my throat, I press the green button and press the phone to my ear.

"Hey," I say, neutral.

"Rossi, hi." My name on his lips still sends a thrill down my spine, though it's slightly less intense than it was a few days ago. With time, I'm hoping that little sensation fades altogether. "Do you have a minute to talk?"

My stomach hardens.

Those words are almost always a precursor to bad news in all forms.

"Yeah, what's up?" I rise, perching next to the window. Outside, Dan washes his Lexus in his driveway sans shirt. He must've taken the afternoon off? I should ask him to wash my car when he's done …

"So, you know how I told you I had to take care of a few things?"

"Yep."

"One of those things," he says, "was my ex-fiancée."

My head fills with an image of the text on his screen Saturday morning. I can still see it crystal clear. In fact, every time I close my eyes, it's there. The human mind can be cruel and persistent.

"Ever since she found out I was in Illinois … with someone new … she started blowing up my phone, sending me texts about how much she loves and misses me, begging to get back together," he says. "Calls me twenty times a day sometimes."

To be fair, his phone is constantly going off.

But half the time it's on silent. And a quarter of the time he places it in the next room altogether. Given his line of work and his celebrity status, I assumed it was par for the course, and I never questioned it—until Saturday.

"I've tried to have her father reason with her, but she won't listen," he says. "And I could block her number, but she'll just call me from a new one. I figured since I was going to be in town for that shoot anyway, I might as well meet with her in person …"

My insides swirl with nausea, and my stomach fires a sour-hot warning shot up the back of my throat.

He's calling to tell me he's getting back with her. That has to be it. I'm already playing their reunion up in my mind, conversation and all. I bet she dressed to the nines in his favorite outfit, threw her arms around him, and told him she knew exactly where they went wrong. I bet she promised to change, convincing him it could still work, that they could still have their happily ever after.

If he loved her once, he could love her again.

That's how these things happen.

People break up and get back together every day.

Absence makes the heart grow fonder, and all of that.

And maybe all the time he's spent with a "normal" woman in a boring suburban house without a pool and a butler and a tennis court or any of life's finest luxuries made him realize just how perfect he and Tatum truly were for each other.

"Rossi, did you hear what I said?" he asks. "You're quiet. What are you thinking about?"

Shit.

I completely tuned him out while I was lost in my anxiety-ridden nightmare of a daydream.

"I think you cut out," I lie, wincing. "Can you say it all again? I got the part where you said you wanted to meet with her in person, but not the rest."

He blows a breath into his receiver, pausing. "I said Tatum is pregnant."

My legs turn numb and I lean against the nearest wall before they give out completely.

"Did you hear what I said?" he asks.

"Y—yeah," I stammer. "I heard."

"Wow." My lip trembles. Even with all the barriers I'd put up around my heart these last two days, the tiniest crack remained. When he left on Sunday, he told me I had him all wrong. He said he was going to prove that when he came back. A miniscule, feather-sized piece of me wanted to believe him.

Now it doesn't matter what he said, if he was genuine

or not. He's having a baby with a woman he was once going to marry. He's not going to walk away from that to woo someone he's only known three weeks.

I have my naïve moments, but I'm not an idiot.

"Congratulations," I force a smile into my tone despite the throbbing ache in my chest. "That's great news, Fabian. You're going to be an amazing father. And hey, you'll get to experience all the firsts now."

"This isn't going to change anything between us," he says. "And it doesn't change the way I feel about you."

I swipe a thick tear from the corner of my eye. "Of course it does."

"I want to be with *you*."

"But you're having a baby with someone else," I say.

"It complicates things," he says. "But it doesn't make them impossible. We can figure this out."

"You're not being realistic. You have a life in California. You're jet setting all over the world for tournaments and photo shoots and appearances and interviews. And then you want to date some random woman you barely know in Illinois while also being there for your ex as she carries your baby?" I scoff. "That's a little ambitious, don't you think? Even for you."

"First of all, you're not some random woman in Illinois. And secondly, it's extremely ambitious. But I've never been someone to walk away from something because it seemed too hard," he says. "So you can push me away if you want, Rossi, but it's not going to change how I feel about you."

Once again, he says all the perfect things.

And once again, a glass-shard-sized piece of my shattered heart wants to believe him.

"I have to go in now," he says. "They're waiting on me. Just ... think about what I said. And maybe stay off social media for the next few days. We'll talk more when I get back."

I scrape myself off the wall, toss my phone on my desk, and shut my laptop lid.

I could barely concentrate today as it was—now the rest of the day is shot.

Shuffling to the kitchen, I pull up a seat at the table where Carina and Lucia are eating lunch, and I stare at my beautiful daughter, reminding myself she's all I ever wanted and all I'll ever need.

"What's wrong? You look sad." Carina says. "Like sadder than this morning. And you looked pretty freaking miserable then."

"Fabian's ex is pregnant," I say, monotone.

Carina drops her spoon into her cereal bowl. It lands with a splash, splattering milk over the sides. "Um, excuse me, what?"

"He just called," I say. I hadn't filled her in on the text thing yet, mostly because I didn't feel like rehashing it since I'd already re-lived it a million times in my mind. "Apparently she'd been harassing him since she found out he was here with someone else. He claims he went back home to take care of a few things and decided to have a face-to-face talk with her while he was there to get her to back off." I pick at a hangnail until it bleeds. "Which is when she informed him she's pregnant with his child."

Carina claps a hand over her open mouth. "*No.*"

"Yep."

"So what's he going to do?"

I pick at a loose thread on a nearby placemat. "He says we'll talk about it when he gets back. But I don't know what there is to talk about. That's his ex. I'm basically a stranger. He doesn't owe it to us to stick around. He should be there with them. That's where his life is anyway."

"Is that what you're telling yourself so you don't get hurt?" Carina asks.

I don't tell her we're way past that.

"Just trying to be rational about it." I rise and push the chair in. "Going to go for a walk, try to clear my head."

A minute later, my sneakers are laced up and my ear buds are playing Funky Town, which normally puts me into a good mood, but for some reason today the song grates under my skin. I tap the right bud to shuffle to a new song and within seconds Ann Wilson is crooning in my ear, a depressing eighties ballad about a woman who has a one-night stand with a handsome stranger for the sole purpose of having a baby.

Next …

By the time I get to the sidewalk between my house and Dan's, I settle on Prince's Little Red Corvette.

"Hey!" Dan waves the instant he spots me, bending to place his giant soapy sponge into the five gallon bucket by his trunk. I swear he's been washing his car for an hour now, but it doesn't surprise me because meticulous is the man's middle name.

I pause my music and trot toward him.

"Haven't heard from you in a while," he says. "I thought maybe you were upset with me about the other night."

"No, sorry." I'd almost forgotten about that fiasco. "Just been really busy."

Sliding his hands in his pockets, he rocks back on his heels. "You mind some company on your walk? Such a gorgeous day—I'll use any excuse I can to stay outside."

"Sure."

We hit the pavement, taking our usual route down Berkshire Street, then north on 17th, around the cul-de-sac on Preston Circle …

"Haven't seen your friend around the last couple days," Dan says after killing the first few minutes of our walk with mundane small talk.

"He's back in California, taking care of a few things," I say as we turn back toward our street.

"You don't sound too thrilled …"

From the corner of my eye, I feel the weight of his stare.

"Trouble in paradise?" he asks as we cross at a four-way stop.

"Can trouble even be *in* paradise when there never was a paradise to begin with?"

He chuckles. "You're a terrible liar, Rossi. You two couldn't keep your hands off each other at dinner last week. I saw all the looks and the nudges and the way you two looked at each other. Reminded me of teenage love or something. And you two thought you were being sly … that's the funniest part."

"There's definitely some attraction between us," I say.

"Clearly. Because neither of you are blind."

"But I think we got ahead of ourselves for a while," I continue. "And I'm not looking for a boyfriend or any kind of commitment at the moment. I had to give him the just friends spiel the other day."

"Not going to lie. Feels good knowing a famous, handsome multi-millionaire got the same line I did," he teases, nudging my arm.

"Can I ask you something?"

"Anything."

"So you know I had Lucia with an anonymous sperm donor, right?"

He nods, brows knitting.

"Actually, never mind." I was going to ask him a "hypothetical" question about sperm donors and fatherhood and boundaries and all of that because I'm curious as to what a man in that position might deem fair or appropriate, but Dan's not an idiot. He'll easily piece it together. Not to mention, Lucia already suspiciously resembles Fabian.

"Were you thinking of having another baby?" he asks. "Are you looking for another donor?"

"Um …" I start to answer before realizing my only option here is to tell a little white lie—not that I'm proud of it, but at least it won't hurt him. "Yeah, maybe. But the original sperm donor I used is no longer available. I was just thinking out loud, I guess. You know how random I can be sometimes …"

I try to pass it off with a chuckle, making a crazy face at him as I stick my tongue out.

"I mean … if you need someone …" He lifts his hands and lets them fall against his sides. "I don't know how I'd feel about simply being a donor, per se. But I'd be open to figuring something out."

Oh, god.

That's not where I wanted to go with this.

"Appreciate the offer, Dan. I think I'm probably an only-child kind of mom," I say. "Don't want to bite off more than I can chew."

We're halfway down our street when Dan's pace slows, as if he's stalling the inevitable.

"Oh, hey." He points to his house. "I just had some new living room furniture delivered yesterday, but I can't quite nail down the best arrangement. If you have a couple minutes to spare, I'd love to pick your brain."

I eye my house.

While I should be holed off in my office the rest of the afternoon trying to salvage the time I've lost today, I'm also far from the right headspace.

"Sure. I can spare a few minutes."

I follow him up to his driveway, where he punches in a code that gets us in, and then we head through his kitchen, past his dining room, and into his formal living room.

"Why'd you get rid of the old stuff?" I ask. "Wasn't it pretty new?"

"I got it in the divorce settlement. Wanted something that was all mine," he says. "Anyway. I tried putting the sofa here, but I feel like it blocks the window. And when I put the armchairs along that wall, it sort of divides the room in half."

"For a numbers guy, I'm shocked you didn't measure all of this out ahead of time …"

He laughs. "You and me both. Guess it was an impulse buy. Got a hell of a deal on this set."

Walking around the room, I visualize a handful of other configurations, but the L-shape of the space really limits us.

"I'd put your sofa there," I point. "Then the two chairs to the left and the love seat to the right. Sort of like a U-shape right in front of the fireplace. If you get a rug, it'll ground the space and tie it all together. And I'd get a different coffee table. The one you have is very mid-century modern, but your new stuff is very traditional."

Pinching his upper lip between two fingers, he squints at the space, likely picturing the new layout.

"I can help you move these around really quick if you want?" I offer.

Five minutes later, we're only slightly winded, but his living room looks five times bigger and ten times more functional.

"Maybe you can help me pick out a coffee table this weekend?" he asks, disappearing into the kitchen and returning with two bottled waters.

"Fabian's coming back on Wednesday …"

"Ah." He takes a swig. "I see."

"I can look online later and see if I can't find something you can just order," I offer.

"Well, that takes half the fun out of it ... was looking forward to strangers complimenting us on our cute baby at the mall," he winks, though I know he's serious. It never fails, we always get approached any time the three of us are together and Dan always gets a kick out of playing along. "We still on for Wednesday night?"

"Oh, um ..." After last week's dinner, I don't think it's wise to put Dan and Fabian in the same room again.

It'd be like putting two male betta fish in the same tank.

"I think we should put a hold on those for the next couple of weeks," I say.

His lower lip juts forward into a makeshift pout as his eyes rest unfocused on the fireplace mantel. "I understand."

"I should head back." I point in the general direction of my house. "Good walk and talk though. Thanks for the company."

Rising on my toes, I give him a hug—the way I always do when we part ways.

Only to have him kiss me.

It happened so fast, I thought it was an accident at first.

And it was over before I had a chance to process it.

"What was that?" I ask, laughing to lighten the awkwardness.

"Sorry, for some reason I thought you were going in for a kiss?" His cheeks turn a deep and undeniable shade of beet red. "I'm so sorry, Rossi ..."

I pat his chest. "Don't sweat it ..."

Showing myself out before anything gets any weirder between us, I trek home—replaying that innocent but awkward little peck in my head a few times. There's no way he thought I was going in for a kiss. We weren't flirting. We weren't talking about anything remotely romantic. Nothing about our exchange would've remotely implied that I wanted to kiss him …

Did he do that on purpose?

But he seemed embarrassed …

Kicking off my shoes, I leave my ear buds on the foyer table and attempt to work for the next two hours so I don't have to think about what just happened.

I'm two minutes from logging off when an email pings my inbox from my contact at the DNA site. I'd overnighted Fabian's sample last week and sent the loveliest email to her, asking if she could expedite the processing. Normally I wouldn't ask for favors, but since he's only here a short time, I wanted to see if I couldn't speed things up.

I click on the subject line.

Dear Rossi—

As requested, I was able to rush the processing of your friend's submission. For privacy purposes, I've entered him into the system as USER82765. You can access his results via your account when you're ready.

Best of luck!

Caitlyn Morrow

Founder and CEO of AncestryFinder

THESE KINDS of emails are the "Christmas morning" part of my job. The rush of excitement. The promise of what's inside. The mystery. I live for these emails and they never get old.

Logging into my account, I pull up Fabian's information and feast my eyes on all of the connections that propagate the page. There must be at least twenty-five 2nd-3rd cousins and fifty 4-5th cousins. An excellent start.

For the hour that follows, I copy and paste the same message to every last one of his genetic connections. It's a spammy shot in the dark, but this is always step one.

Hello!

My name is Rossi Bianco, and I'm a genealogist in High Valley, Illinois. I'm currently searching for Francesca Catalano on behalf of a private client who has been matched to your genetic profile. If you have any information as to how or where I could find Francesca (who also goes by the name Frankie), that would be greatly appreciated.

Respectfully,
Rossi Bianco, BCG
Bianco Genealogy

Logging out, I shut my laptop and call it a day.

And what a day it has been ...

Chapter 28

Fabian

IT'S BEEN over twenty-four hours since I last spoke to Rossi. Despite the two thousand miles that separate us, she's been dancing circles in my head since the second my jet went wheels-up over Chicago.

Lying in bed, I pull up my phone and tap out a text: LANDING TOMORROW MORNING … CAN'T WAIT TO SEE MY GIRLS.

I hit send and watch the read receipt stay on 'read' for the following hour.

Sitting up, I fling the covers off and pace my room. A room that's ridiculously, laughably large. One fit for royalty or Silicon Valley billionaires who ran out of stupid shit to blow their money on. This entire house is ostentatious and showy, the kind of thing a man buys when his ego is so gaping and empty he needs to shove something inside it to feel something.

The pool below reflects the moon above, and beyond

that the ocean tide rolls gentle. It's a multi-million dollar view, no question. Four years ago I got into a nasty bidding war over this property. It was one of the only beachfront estates with room for a full tennis court. Ended up paying twenty percent more than what it was worth, but with the market the way it is lately, I could sell it for a lot more than that.

Regardless, what good is a man's money if he has no one to spend it on?

A man could shove his soul full of thousand dollar bills and still feel that gnawing emptiness at the end of the day.

I make a mental note to call my attorneys tomorrow and have them draft up a new will. Everything I own, everything I'll ever own—I want it to go to my daughter when I'm gone. And if the child Tatum is carrying turns out to be mine, they'll get their share as well.

Still, all the money in the world couldn't buy me the one thing I want—Rossi.

Pulling up her number, I press the green button. With the first ring, my heart hammers in my ears, whooshing with adrenaline and anticipation. With the second ring, I bite my thumbnail. With the third, I hold my breath. After the fourth, I'm met with her voice—but not her.

"Hi," her greeting says. "You've reached Rossi Bianco with Bianco Genealogy. Please leave a message, and I'll return your call as soon as possible."

It's eleven o'clock here, which means it's 1 AM there. She's probably sleeping, which means at least she isn't blatantly ignoring me.

Head pressed against the window, I wait for the beep.

"Rossi, it's me," I say. "Just wanted to hear your voice … guess I'll settle for your voicemail." I chuckle. "Anyway, I miss you. I've been running around here like crazy the last couple of days, but I haven't stopped thinking about you once. And all the things you said on Sunday. I know you're scared, Rossi. But we can take this slow. And the stuff with Tatum—that's not going to change anything. I know I probably sound like a broken record and I'm not telling you anything I haven't already told you … but maybe it wouldn't hurt for you to hear it again." I laugh through my nose—I've never done the whole lovesick puppy thing. I've never had to beg or grovel or prove that I was worthy to be the apple of anyone's eye. "First time I ever saw you, I forgot to breathe. Second time we met, I realized you were a woman who didn't need me, didn't want a damn thing from me, and not only that, but you were genuine and honest. You weren't trying to impress me, but you did it anyway. Without even trying. And your lips, Rossi … I live for those lips, the way they turn bright pink and swollen when I kiss you. And watching you with Lucia …" I gather a breath. "Couldn't ask for a better mother. Your love for—"

"*If you'd like to hear your message, please press one,*" an automated voice cuts me off.

God damn it.

I hang up, pray it went through, and hit the sheets.

I've got an early flight to catch, and the sooner I close my eyes, the sooner I'll see my girls.

I SETTLE into my seat on my jet Wednesday morning when my publicist calls.

"Fabian, I'm so glad you answered." She's breathless and her voice echoes.

"Take me off speaker, Phoebe. You know I fucking hate that shit."

Two seconds later, she says, "Fine. Better?"

"What's going on? We're about to take off."

"So there are these pictures that are going out in the next couple of days. Someone's been shopping them around," she says.

"Yes, the one of Tatum and I at LaGrange. We already discussed this yesterday, and —"

"—no," she interrupts. "These are different pictures. Nothing to do with Tatum."

I can't imagine what other pictures someone would have of me that would put me in any sort of scandalous positions, but I hear her out.

"So it's you and a baby," she says.

With those six words, my blood turns to ice, cracking in my veins. "The fuck are you talking about, Phoebe?"

"There's some woman in Illinois claiming you're the father of her baby girl," she says. "She's got pictures of the two of you together, and Fabian, before you say anything, they aren't photoshopped. I had my guy verify that. Also this baby is the spitting image of you. Two secs and I'll forward the screenshots to you."

Jaw clenched, I wait for my phone to vibrate, and then I check the images.

Sure enough, they're the ones Rossi took of Lucia and me last week—after I made her swear on her life she'd never share them.

"Fabian, you still with me?" Phoebe asks.

"Mr. Catalano, we'll be taking off momentarily." My flight attendant delivers a flute of organic orange juice and Cristal along with an egg white omelet destined to go cold because I'm about to be sick.

"There's been a lot of interest in these pics," Phoebe continues. "All the magazines want it. I heard one of them wants to run a cover story with some headline about your secret love child. Please tell me this is a niece or something?"

I wish I could.

"You've been in Chicago the last couple of weeks—this woman is from Chicago," she says, spacing out her words as if she's piecing it all together. "Please tell me you didn't get pussy whipped by some Midwestern con-artist …"

Leaning back, I pinch my nose and breathe out.

"I'm going to need some kind of statement," she says. "So you're going to have to give me something to work with. How are you involved with this woman and this baby?"

While Phoebe is an utmost professional, heads one of the top publicist firms in the world, and signed an ironclad NDA, I wasn't exactly prepared to have to share this with her.

Or anyone.

Ever.

"They're trying to get her to do an interview," Phoebe adds. "But so far it's just pictures. Which actually is kind of worse because then the articles can say whatever they want and they're going to print shock value shit, whatever's going to move more copies."

My head throbs as my jet taxies to the runway.

"You need to make a decision, Fabian." She breathes into the phone. "Sounds like they're pushing seven-figure offers and it's only a matter of time before this hits newsstands. I can deny this of course. And I can see if we can't delay it a bit to buy more time. We need a statement at the very least."

"Give me a few hours to think about this."

"So it's true—this is the woman you've been hanging out with all month? Jesus, Fabian."

"I'll call you when I land."

The plane lunges forward, faster and faster until the nose tips up. Within seconds we're airborne, en route to Chicago.

I don't understand why Rossi would do this ...

If she were anyone else, it would make sense. This would be a phenomenal way to exact revenge on me—but the woman I've come to know would never jeopardize her child's privacy for petty retaliation and some quick cash.

Still, Rossi took those photos.

She was the only one with access to them.

And now they're being shopped around the biggest tabloid magazines in the country.

I don't want to believe ...

But if it wasn't her, then who was it?

Chapter 29

Rossi

I'M HALFWAY through my to-do list for the afternoon when an email notification pops up—a reply from one of the many Catalano cousins I'd contacted yesterday. I must have sent close to one hundred messages, but so far I've had four responses—none of whom know the whereabouts of Francesca Catalano.

Rossi—

Saw your message. Frankie is a third cousin of mine. We lost touch years ago, but last I heard she occasionally keeps in touch with another cousin of ours. Was able to get the last known number and address for Frankie, but sounds like no one's talked to her in years. Hope this helps and good luck with your search!

Maureen Catalano

I scroll beneath her message to find an Iowa address and phone number. A quick Google search tells me she's only two hours from here. Despite everything going on with Fabian, I can't wait to give him this information.

The front door opens and closes—likely Carina grabbing a package from the Prime delivery man who usually comes this time of day. But I stay planted in front of my computer, seeing if I can't dig up anything else connected to that name and number. A reverse number search tells me it's a prepaid cell number, and a quick search on an assessor's site tells me the house is registered to A-Plus Rentals, Inc.

There's no guarantee we'll find her at the end of this rainbow, but my fingers are crossed.

Three raps at the door pull me out of my frenzy.

"Come in," I call to my sister, clicking on the next result.

Only it isn't my sister standing in the doorway—it's Fabian.

"Oh." I sit back. "Hi. I didn't know you were here."

He closes the door behind him, but stays on that side of the room. Worry lines spread across his forehead, and his eyes are squinted, pinched almost. Nothing about this suggests he's happy to see me, which is odd because he left me a rambling two-minute voicemail last night that indicated he couldn't wait to see me again.

While I'd never admit this to anyone, I must have listened to that thing fifty times—mostly because I was convinced if I listened closely enough, I'd be able to tell if he was being sincere or not. Unfortunately, it turns out I'm not a human lie detector and results were inconclusive.

"Just got here," he says. His eyes are darker than usual and his hands are hooked on his narrow hips.

"I got your message," I say. "But it's been a crazy morning. Carina had to run to a dentist appointment, so I had Lucia and it's just been one thing after another since my feet hit the ground ... anyway, you actually have perfect timing."

I tear the paper with Frankie's info from my notebook, only before I get the chance to hand it over, he lifts a palm to silence me and stop me in my tracks.

"Rossi," he says. The indentation above his jaw divots, pulsing in and out, and the faint bulge of a vein across his forehead forms.

"Y … yes?"

His nostrils flare and his eyes flash. "How could you?"

"What?"

"You sold her out," he says. "You sold *us* out."

Rising, I fold my arms. "Care to elaborate? Because I'm really confused …"

"I honestly thought you were different." He shakes his head, digging into his back pocket to produce his phone. A few swipes later and he turns it to face me. An image of Fabian with Lucia fills the screen—one of the fifteen images I took last week when it was just the three of us.

"How … what … okay, this makes no sense." I cover my mouth with my hand, breathing in through my fingers. "I don't understand."

"I don't either," he says with a cruel huff before shoving the phone away. "What'd you get for those, huh? Heard offers were hitting seven figures."

Despite the fact that this situation is hardly hilarious, I manage a laugh. "Seven figures?"

"Is that all this was worth to you?"

"Wait, someone is selling that image for a million dollars?" I point. "Can … can you do that?"

He drags a hand through his hair, which is already mussed from his flight, and groans. "You can drop the act, Rossi. I know it was you."

"It absolutely was not me." I march across the room, invading his space, hands on my hips. "I would *never*."

"Then explain how *that* image went from *your* phone

and into the hands of tabloids all over the country," he says.

"I can't explain it." I toss my hands in the air the way my father does when he's trying to fix a sink leak and keeps dropping the wrench. "Maybe I got hacked?"

"Really? Some random person just happened to randomly hack into your phone, go through your pictures, find these specific images, lift them, then—"

"—yes!" I yell. "That's exactly what I'm saying because there's no other explanation. Why would I jeopardize my daughter's privacy?"

"That's what I've been asking myself all day.'"

"I didn't do this, Fabian." I step closer to him.

He steps away. "I was going to ask you to move in with me. You and Lucia. Because you're the one that I want, Rossi. And maybe we were moving too fast, but I wanted to see where this would lead. And you were right. Jetting back and forth, it isn't realistic. But I was prepared to do whatever it took to make it work … and then you pulled this. You betrayed my trust—you used me."

"I didn't *pull* anything." I run my fingers through my hair and tug a fistful. "And I never *used* you, Fabian. I certainly didn't *sell you out*. I don't know how this happened, but I swear to you, it wasn't me."

Swiping my phone off my desk, I pull up my settings.

"All of my images are backed up to my iCloud, which is connected to my Apple ID. My password is encrypted and I have two-factor on everything." Pulling up my iCloud, I whiz through a few menu items before pulling up log-in and user activity. "Look at my most recent log ins. They've all been here, same IP address. No one's accessed my phone except for me. And I didn't send those pictures."

"Who else has access to your phone during the day?" he asks.

I begin to answer, then stop.

"If you're suggesting my sister did this, you're out of your mind. She would *never*."

"How are you so sure?" he asks. "If it wasn't you and she's the only one who had access to your phone ..."

I take a seat on the edge of my desk. There's no way Carina would do something like that. She's my sister. My best friend. Family. Lucia's the closest thing to a daughter she'll ever have. She wouldn't throw all of us under the bus for five minutes of fame.

"I'll ask her." I keep my voice low. "But I'm one hundred percent sure she wouldn't do that."

He points to the door. "What are you waiting for?"

Condescension colors his voice.

Fabian has never used that tone with me.

"She's watching the baby right now—I'm not going to bother her with this," I return the favor, snipping my words at him just the same.

Chin tucked, he rubs his eyes with his thumb and index finger, chest filling with hard, heavy breaths.

"My daughter's image is going to be plastered all over social media and every news outlet this time tomorrow," he says. "So unless you come clean about this—and put a stop to it immediately—"

Grabbing fistfuls of air, I groan. "*I'm not coming clean about something I didn't do.*"

We lock eyes in a feverish stare down.

"Why would I do anything like that?" I ask. "I don't need money, and I made that clear from the first time we spoke. And my daughter's privacy is my first priority. Another thing I've made abundantly clear."

"I don't know, Rossi." His lips press into a hard line and his fingers dig into his hips as he shifts. "All I know is last weekend, you became cold and distant when I told you

The Match

I was going home for a few days. And when I told you the news about my ex, you congratulated me and told me I had no obligation to be with you and Lucia. Then magically these pictures are being shopped around, pictures from your phone that you took."

"So you think I'm jealous that your ex is pregnant and I did all of this out of spite? Is that what you think?" My vision narrows.

I realize he hardly knows me, but for the love of God, he knows me better than that.

"All right. I'm done with this conversation." Turning, I grab Frankie's info from my desk. "This is for you. Best of luck."

With squinted eyes, he scans the scribbled address and number. "What's this?"

"I may have found your sister," I say.

His gaze holds mine for a fraction of forever, but we don't exchange another word.

The room hangs heavy with the weight of everything we aren't saying. Everything we could say, would say, and will never have a chance to say again.

Once he calms down and comes to his senses, we can talk about moving forward, but I will not put up with him storming into my house accusing me of doing something so deplorable to my own daughter.

Folding the paper, he jams it in his jeans pocket, gives me a parting glance I couldn't read if I tried.

And then he's gone.

Chapter 30

Fabian

I STOP at a four-way intersection a few blocks away from Rossi's, retrieve the torn paper from my pocket, and scan the handwriting.

Frankie Catalano
746 County Line Road
Unit 1
Spearville, IA
309-555-8829

My headache whooshes and my skin is still flushed hot from that infuriating exchange with Rossi, but I type the number into my phone and press the green button.

"The number you have reached is no longer in service …" greets me. I hang up. It's not like I knew what I was going to say if she answered anyway.

Typing the address into my GPS, the screen shows an arrival time of two hours. It's still early enough in the day that if I showed up, it wouldn't be too late.

Assuming she even lives there.

There's a chance I could drive one hundred and twenty miles for nothing.

Either way, it's not like I have anything better to do.

Until I figure out what happened with those photos, everything's in limbo. A dark gray void where nothing makes sense and everything that was once sweet is now sour.

I press the "go" button on the navigation system and follow the guided prompts until I hit an open stretch of highway outside of town.

Knuckles tight around the steering wheel, I head toward Spearville with a head full of doubt and body full of white-hot adrenaline.

Even if Frankie turns me away, it's not like this day could get any worse.

Chapter 31

Rossi

"WHAT THE HECK WAS THAT ABOUT?" Carina shuffles into my office as Fabian tears out of the driveway. "Just put Lucia down for a nap and then I heard the front door slam."

The wild look in his eyes, his fingers digging into his hips, the cutting tone, the harsh words, the slamming of the door—I've officially experienced Fabian's famous hotheaded temper. Only something tells me that was the diet version ...

"I'm going to ask you something, and I don't want you to get offended," I say, softening my words.

"You know you literally cannot offend me, right?" She laughs.

"Just wait ..."

She pulls up a chair to the other side of my desk, crossing her legs and shrugging. "What's up?"

"So apparently some photos were leaked," I say. "Of Fabian and Lucia."

I pause to read her expression. I've known my sister for three decades and half the time I know her better than she knows herself. Any time she's ever told a lie, her nose twitches and she gets this weird curl to her upper lip, like she's trying not to laugh.

"These pictures were on my phone," I continue. "And somehow, someone accessed them and now they're shopping them around to tabloids for a lot of money …"

Carina's jaw falls and her brows knit. "Oh my god. You guys think *I* did it?"

Lifting my palms, I say, "No one is saying you did it. We're just trying to narrow down the possibilities."

"But I'm a suspect." She frowns, sitting up. "Rossi, I would never, *ever*, in a hundred *billion* years do anything like that. Not to mention your phone is Fort Knox. You have fifty million passwords on everything, and you have to log in with your face. How could I access your pictures? And why would I sell them knowing I would get caught?"

There's no movement in her nose, no curl in her lip.

No tell-tale salesman tenor in her voice, like she's trying to sell a lie.

"I believe you," I say.

The room turns silent. She chews on her lip and I pick at a hangnail, both of us lost in thought.

"Okay, so this is really disturbing. We have to figure this out," she says. "Who else would've had access to your phone?"

The idea of my daughter's face being plastered all over social media is nothing short of upsetting, but the upside is babies change so drastically from month to month. An image of her at nine months will hardly resemble an image of her six months from now. This is less than ideal, of course. An extreme invasion of privacy, to say the least. But it could be worse.

"Did anyone stop by the last couple of days after work?" she asks. "Or did you go shopping and set your phone down somewhere?"

"We went to the grocery store Sunday night …" my voice trails as I mentally rewind everything we've done since Fabian left town. "And we stopped at the hardware store for bird seed after that. I didn't take my phone out either time though."

"Okay …"

"Oh my god." My hand flies to my chest. "Dan stopped over last night …"

Carina rolls her eyes. "If I can't access your phone, Dan sure as hell can't either—unless you did something stupid and gave him your passcode."

"No." I cover my mouth. "Monday night he came by around dinner to drop off some mail of mine that had gotten mixed in with his." And also to apologize for that awkward kiss, but I don't mention that part to my sister because it's neither here nor there. "I invited him in since I was in the middle of cleaning up Lucia's mess … most of which was in her hair. Anyway, I told him to hang on quick while I gave her a bath. I left my phone on the counter. I was maybe gone for less than ten minutes."

"How could he get into your phone though without the code?"

"I'd been texting with Mom right before he showed up. It's set to automatically lock after five minutes, but it'd only been a minute or two." I suck in a sharp breath. "Oh my god, Carina. It had to have been him."

She shakes. "I just got the chills. I always had a weird feeling about that guy. Like he was borderline obsessed with you, and not in a cute way."

"Fabian noticed that too," my voice lowers. "But why would he do this? We were friends?"

"He never wanted your friendship, Rossi." She tilts her head. "He wanted you. And if he couldn't have you, maybe he wanted to make sure Fabian couldn't either?"

"That conniving …" I mutter under my breath, shoving my chair out from my desk and flinging the door open.

"Where are you going?" She chases after me.

"Next door to confront that bastard." I step into my sneakers, nearly stumbling into the wall in the process.

"You're not going anywhere." Carina steadies me, her hand on my shoulder. "Anyone who does something like this? They're mentally unstable. Do *not* go over there. I *forbid* you. I will literally handcuff you to this console table if you take another freaking step."

I jerk my shoulder out from under her.

"Let the police deal with him," she says.

"Is this even something the police can deal with?" I ask, envisioning a police officer laughing in my face when I explain the situation. "This is the sort of thing that involves attorneys and court orders and the way Fabian made it sound, this is going public tomorrow."

"Then let Fabian deal with him."

Charging into my office, I fetch my phone and dial Fabian.

He doesn't answer.

Chapter 32

Fabian

"YOUR DESTINATION IS ON THE RIGHT," the GPS guide announces. I slow to a crawl outside a brown duplex.

Parking by a broken concrete curb filled with weeds, I double check the address. A sun-faded red Grand Am is parked in the driveway, which is nothing more than two strips of gravel divided by patchy grass. No garage. No landscaping. No sign of life other than an empty terracotta planter by the front door of the left unit.

Heading up the drive, I notice the front windows of the duplex are cracked a few inches, emitting the scent of stale cigarette smoke and the sound of canned laughter coming from a TV.

There's a chance the person living here isn't Frankie.

There's also chance the person living here is Frankie—and that she'll slam the door in my face.

Before my parents' respective deaths, they were adamant that if my sister wanted to be found, she'd come out of hiding. And that's how they always described it. She was "hiding." Though occasionally they'd say she was "on the run from her troubles." They made her sound lost and unstable, hopeless, and they warned me to "leave her be."

Now that I have a daughter of my own, I can't imagine turning my back on her in her worst time of need. I imagine my parents thought they were doing what was best for me, but at what cost?

My father once said Frankie was beyond saving.

My mother kept a scrapbook of pictures and newspaper clippings of my sister, all of which stopped around the age of fourteen. Before she became "precocious." It's as if they wrote her off after that, and for reasons they never quite explained in any detail.

Standing at the front door, I knock three times.

A large-sounding dog barks from the neighboring unit.

"Hello?" I call out. "Anyone home?"

The TV goes silent, replaced with the sound of footsteps as a dark-haired woman steps into view.

"Are you Frankie?" I ask.

She stops in her tracks, studying me, silent. "Fabian?"

It's her.

On the drive here, I was certain this day couldn't get any worse.

But I wasn't expecting that it could actually get *better*.

The woman steps closer, and I catch a glimpse of the wiry grays streaking her dark hair and the deep lines embedded in her forehead, painting a picture of a hard fifty-two years.

"My god. I can't believe it's you." She gets the door, ushering me in. "Well, don't just stand there. Come on in."

I step into a small living space with green shag carpet, wood paneled walls, and sagging furniture. To the right is a small kitchen table with three chairs, and on the back of one hangs a black waitress' apron bearing the name FRANKIE C. in bold blue embroidery.

"I have to go to work soon." She points to her apron. "But I've got a few minutes. If I'd have known you were coming, maybe I could've found someone to cover for me."

"Sorry to show up unannounced. I tried calling a number I had for you, but it was disconnected."

She swats a hand and ambles to the living room, the slightest limp in her gait. Mom had the same thing in her older years, chalked it up to a bad knee, but she refused to get it looked at. The thought of having surgery and being unable to walk for any period of time terrified her, so she chose to live with the pain and suffering.

"We can have a seat in there," she nods toward the living room, which is a handful of steps away. I take a seat in a sunken-in La-Z-Boy, next to a coffee table littered with TV guides, overflowing ash trays, and empty cans of Diet Wild Cherry Pepsi. "Sorry the place is a mess. I'm ... remodeling."

It's a lie, I'm sure.

But I'm not here to judge.

She takes a seat on the couch. "You want something to drink?"

I offer a polite smile. "I'm good, Frankie. Just wanted to come by and see if you were okay, if you needed anything."

She laughs, raspy and wheezy and tinged with a smoker's cough, and when she smiles, I spot a missing canine on the left side. "Haven't bothered you for money yet, have I?"

No. No she hasn't.

In this day and age, it wouldn't be hard for someone to contact me through my email, website, agent, publicist, or one of my various social media channels.

But Frankie's kept her distance.

The Match

My father always said it was for the best, and he made me promise that if she ever came around asking for money, I wouldn't indulge her because it would only feed her demons. My whole life, my parents painted Frankie as something just short of terrifying, but the woman in front of me has kind brown eyes that match mine fleck-by-fleck and a face that softens when she smiles, despite her imperfections.

A basket of clothes rests unfolded on the edge of the couch and an old dinner plate lies abandoned on a side table. Reminds me of the way I used to keep my room as a teenager.

I don't see a lost cause here.

I see a woman who maybe never quite grew up all the way.

"Frankie, I'm not sure if you're aware, but Mom and Dad passed last year. January and July," I say.

Reaching for a pack of Marlboros, she taps one out and slips it between her fingertips. "You mind?"

"It's your home."

With the flick of a Bic lighter, she inhales until the tip glows orange-red, and then she blows a cloudy ring of smoke between wrinkled lips.

"I heard," she says. "About Mom and Dad, I mean."

She stares ahead at the muted TV, taking another drag.

"Was hoping I'd see you at their funerals," I say. "Always looked for you at the burials. I was sure you were standing back, hiding behind a tree or something."

She takes another drag before tapping the ashes into a jade-green tray. "They didn't want me around when they were alive, why would they want me there when they're dead?"

"I think they always hoped you'd come back around," I say. "Mom kept a scrapbook of you. And every year, she'd bake brownies on your birthday. With rainbow sprinkles. It wasn't until I got older that I figured out why. They missed you."

She blows a ring of smoke through the side of her mouth. "Bullshit."

"Mom prayed for you every night," I say. "I always heard her from the next room. She'd get on her knees at the foot of her bed, ask God to watch over you—"

"—and what about Dad? Did he pray for me too?"

"You know how he was," I say, head cocked. "But he worried, in his own way."

She taps her cigarette once more before reaching for a soda can, swirling it around and taking a sip.

"You make them sound so sweet," she says. "Almost makes up for the fact that they disowned me and left me out on the streets. Literally."

"What?" The word *disowned* was never a part of our household vocabulary.

"I'm sure there's a lot they didn't tell you," she says, pointing her cigarette at me. "You were their second chance."

That much I've always known.

"As soon as you came along, I was chopped liver," she says with a bittersweet smile. "But damn, you were cute. Those big brown eyes, full head of hair. Really wanted to keep you."

I wrinkle my nose. "You wanted to keep me?"

"I was fifteen. No way I could've done it on my own. Dad wanted me to give you up. Closed adoption style. But Mom wouldn't have any of that. She wanted to raise you—"

"—wait." My head pounds as I process this information.

"Oh my god. You didn't know?" She stubs out her half-smoked Marlboro before angling toward me. "They didn't *tell* you?"

"Let me get this straight ... you're my biological mother?" I ask. "And the people who raised me ... were my grandparents?"

Her dark eyes dart from left to right, and then she nods. "Uh, yeah."

Hunched over, elbows on my knees, I steeple my fingers over my nose and breathe in a lungful of nicotine air.

"Jesus, Fab. I had no idea you never knew." Her mouth twitches to one side, the way Mom's always did when she was holding something back. "No wonder they were so hell bent on keeping me away. I tried to come home once. You must have been three or four. And it was your birthday. I'd been working part-time as a hotel clerk and I saved enough to buy you one of those little foam baseball bats and a pack of whiffle balls. Your dad—your biological dad—was really into sports, so I assumed maybe you would be too. Anyway, I showed up that morning, and Dad told me I was no longer welcome under their roof. I peeked in the window and saw you eating pancakes at the table with Mom. She was singing some Etta James song and you were grinning, covered in syrup, and you looked so happy, Fabian. So content."

"Wait, they wouldn't let you see me?"

"In their defense, I was probably strung out at the time. Things are kind of foggy when I think that far back," she scratches the back of her neck. "My mind isn't what it used to be. But I'll never forget that smile of yours as you looked at Mom like she hung the moon. And she was pretty great. As far as moms go, I mean. She tried with me. She did her best. I wasn't easy. I gave them a run for their money."

My face tightens. "Yeah, but they shouldn't have abandoned you just because they got a second chance."

"What are we going to do about it now, huh?" She shrugs, flashing a crooked, bittersweet smile. "They're six feet under, and it's not like we can undo three decades' worth of damage. Regardless, I think you turned out okay, don't you think?"

I drag my hand along my jaw, shaking my head.

It still isn't right.

And while I'll forever love my parents and be grateful for everything they did for me, it's going to be a while before I can forgive them for taking this secret to the grave.

"You had a good life, kid," she says. "I think I made the right call, leaving you with them and staying out of the way."

We sit in silence, the TV flickering, soundless on the other side of the room.

Mom was forty-four when I was born, which was why she said I was such a surprise. They weren't "expecting" me—which makes sense now because Frankie was the one doing the "expecting." They'd always told me I was an unplanned surprise. Guess they weren't lying.

"I'm sorry you had to go through all of that," I say.

"And I'm sorry you had to find out this way." Standing, her knees pop and she takes the last swig from her soda can. "You okay?"

"I will be. I just need time to digest all of this."

She chuffs. "I'm sure you do. Anyway, I'd love to hang out and catch up a little more, but my new boss is a dick and if I'm late one more time—"

I rise. "No, it's fine. But if you don't mind, I'd like to continue this conversation sometime?"

A million questions linger unspoken—the identity of my biological father, for starters.

She studies me. "Yeah, all right. Sure."

Sliding my phone out, I create a new contact for her. "What's the best way to reach you?"

She rattles off ten digits. "I don't have texting though."

"Noted." I walk to the door, turning back to add, "You don't have to stay away anymore, Frankie. I want you to know that."

"Not sure what I could add to your life at this point, kid."

I stare into the strange-yet-familiar eyes of a woman who was conditioned to believe her own son would be better off without her.

But it ends today.

With me.

"You're family, Frankie," I say, still attempting to comprehend that the woman standing before me is the very woman who brought me into this world. For that reason alone, she'll never have to want for anything for the rest of her days. If she needs any kind of help at all—I won't hesitate to arrange it. But one thing at a time. "Let's make this right. Let's fix this."

She swipes her apron off the chair and ties it around her narrow waist before grabbing a rattan purse off the counter and a set of keys dangling with a car dealership worth of keychains.

Walking out together, she locks up behind us.

"I'd give you a hug or something, but I'm not a touchy-feely person," she says as she shuffles across the grass to her Grand Am.

"Same," I sniff. "I'll call you."

Unlocking her car, she gives me a casual wave. I take it she's not one for emotions or sentiment. Maybe it's a Catalano thing. For the most part, we're doers not feelers. A second later, her engine hums to life, muffler coughing as she backs out of the gravel drive and heads west.

On my drive back to Rossi's, I think of my daughter. I think of her twenty years from now. Thirty. Fifty. Anonymous donor or not, I'm a part of her. And the idea of Lucia growing up without knowing everything weighs heavy on my mind.

As her mother, Rossi gets to choose what Lucia knows and when she knows it. But as her biological father, I need to make it unquestionably clear that I want to know my daughter and be there for her in every moment of this rollercoaster we call life.

I don't want Lucia to wake up on her 52nd birthday and wonder if her life could've been different if only a piece of it wasn't missing.

I've spent the last week falling hard for Lucia's mother, but not once have we sat down to figure out my role in Lucia's life going forward.

For the next two hours, I replay my last exchange with Rossi, the cruel accusations I hurled at her without giving her a moment to explain. The hatred in my voice. The arrogance in my stance. The clench in my jaw. She was adamant that she didn't do it. And while I wanted to believe her, I was so worked up, I couldn't fucking see straight let alone think straight.

I lost my cool.

I hope I didn't lose her too.

Chapter 33

Rossi

I SWITCH off Lucia's lamp and place her in her crib when two headlights flash across my driveway. For hours, I tried calling Fabian to tell him about Dan, only his phone went to voicemail every time. For a moment, I wondered if he'd blocked me. And by the end of the night, I was convinced he'd written me off completely, which only made me stew over this entire thing even more.

All night as I cared for my daughter, I went through the motions, forced smiles and did my best "mom voice," but our little exchange was running circles through my head. And not only that, but I kept tapping out furious texts to Dan—only to delete them before they could be sent.

Carina was right—Fabian needs to deal with this.

He has the means and the connections.

And I need to maintain a safe distance from Dan … just in case.

I meet Fabian at the door a minute later, swinging it open before he has a chance to knock.

"Look who came back." I lean against the jamb, arms folded. "Been trying to call you all night."

"I turned my phone off … went to see Frankie."

I lift a brow, despite the fact that I'm beyond upset with him right now, I'm a sucker for a long-lost family reunion story. "How'd it go?"

"You mind if I come in so we can talk?" he asks.

Stepping back, I nod. "I just put Lucia down, so as long as you refrain from raising your voice at me this time …"

His shoulders sag and he exhales, eyes softening. "I'm sorry, Rossi. I shouldn't have spoken to you like that."

"No," I say. "You shouldn't have."

"I got that call this morning, and I just … I blacked out. I saw red. I went for the jugular," he says. "I don't give a damn what the press writes about me. I'm used to that shit. But Lucia's privacy and safety is paramount. That's why I was so upset. And I'm still upset, but I've had some time to calm down, to think about our next step, and—"

"—it was Dan," I interrupt.

His dark brows come together. "The neighbor?"

I nod.

"Are you sure?"

"Not one hundred percent," I say. "Carina wouldn't let me confront him in case he does something crazy, but I'm ninety-nine percent sure."

"I knew that guy was a fucking creep." Fabian shakes his head, fingers digging into his hips. "How'd he do it?"

"He came over last night when I was cleaning Lucia up after dinner … I ran off to give her a bath and left my phone on the counter. It was unlocked. I was gone for maybe ten minutes," I say. "I'm assuming he Air Dropped the photos to his phone. I don't have proof, but it's the only thing that makes sense. And he's the only one who'd have a good reason to do this."

"I thought he was your friend? Why would he jeopardize that?"

Biting my lip, my gaze flicks to his pristine loafers. "He's very jealous of you—of your new place in my life, I guess you could say. And the other day, he kissed me."

Fabian's jaw sets, his hands ball into white-knuckled fists, and the same livid flicker that colored his eyes earlier today returns.

"I'm going to fucking *murder* him." Fabian turns to reach for the doorknob, but I hook my hand into his elbow and steer him back.

"Stop," I say.

"I told you he was a creep, did I not?" Hard breaths flare his nostrils.

I lift a hand to his angled jaw and trace my fingertips down the side of his face, and with a soothing, motherly tone, I say, "Calm down, okay? Getting worked up isn't going to fix this. And you're not going away for murder. You're too pretty for prison."

I manage to crack a smile out of him, but it fades just the same. "So what do you propose we do?"

"Confronting him isn't going to do much. He'll just deny it. And the police aren't going to do anything. They'll say it's a matter for the courts. We're going to need a court order to stop this."

Within seconds, Fabian is speed-dialing someone named Phoebe, and then he disappears into my office to make another call. Ten minutes later, he steps out, one hand hooked on the back of his neck as he blows a breath through his full lips.

"They're on it," he says. "But it doesn't make me want to kill the fucker any less."

"Will they be able to stop this from going through?"

He winces. "That's the plan, but no guarantees. They'll call with any updates."

We remain in my foyer. Other than the phone call in my office, I haven't technically invited him beyond this point. And I don't intend to.

"I can't stop thinking about earlier." He studies my face. "I wish I could take it back, the way I spoke to you."

"You apologized. It's over." I shrug.

He leans in, cupping my face. "I'll make it up to you, I swear. I'll never doubt you again."

I brush his hand aside. "You should probably go to your hotel—or wherever you're staying tonight."

Squinting, he chuffs. "Really? So that's what it's come to? Rossi, I made a mistake and I'm owning it. It doesn't mean we should throw in the towel."

"It's not about that," I say. "I mean, it is. That's part of it. But you're having a baby, Fabian. With a woman you were going to marry. That's big. You should be there—with her. Having a baby is a beautiful thing and it's always worth it in the end, but believe me when I tell you, it sucks to do it alone. She's going to need you."

"I'll be there for her, and for the child—but I want to be *with* you," he says. "Tatum and I—we're over. There's no future for us. But you, Rossi? And Lucia?"

"You've known us, what? Three weeks?"

"Long enough." He dips his chin, gathering his thoughts. "I want to be a part of Lucia's life. I want her to know me, and I want to be there for her. And I want to get to know you, *all* of you."

Stepping closer, he hooks his hands around my waist and pulls me in.

"You're welcome to be in Lucia's life," I say. "But I think it's best that we keep things platonic between us."

He exhales, his breath hot on the top of my head. "What are you so afraid of?"

Everything …

The way he makes me feel when we're together, like everything is glimmering and new, strange and familiar, impeccably suited for each other. Fabian and I are like that optical illusion where two shapes, when separate, look different, but when you place them over top of one another, they line up perfectly.

But mostly I'm scared of the way he makes me feel when we're apart … like half of my heart is empty and hollow and I'm permanently holding my breath.

That's no way to live.

"You promised me things would be casual if I let you stay here," I say. "And maybe I'm just as guilty as you for getting caught up, but this is where it ends. I've got a child to raise and you've got a mountain of responsibility waiting for you two thousand miles away."

"I knew from the first time we kissed things were never going to be casual between us," he says. "And watching you with Lucia, my daughter, spending time with the two of you in this home you've created—it put a lot of things into perspective for me. Made me realize I had my priorities all wrong."

"Fabian …" My voice trails into nothing. Half of me hurts for him. The other half of me aches for myself and the whirlwind rollercoaster of the past several days. The text message. The pregnancy bombshell. The accusations. "I love my simple life. I don't want to give up what I've worked so hard for because some gorgeous, rich guy—who happens to be my daughter's sperm donor—has stars in his eyes every time he looks at me. I don't want to be just another name on a list. And I don't want to worry about what you're up to every time you fly home. You should've told me you were seeing your ex before, not after."

His lips flatten. "I'm terrible at communication. The worst. But I'll work on that … for *you*. We'll get it right. And in the meantime, it may not be perfect, but we'll get there."

Once again, he says all the perfect things at just the right moments.

"Rossi, please." He presses his lips against mine, his fingers laced in the hair at the back of my neck. "I don't want to leave here and always wonder if we could've been something more." He swallows, releasing his tender hold on me. "I'm falling for you."

Tears sting my vision in the dark foyer, but I blink them away before he notices.

"Don't make this harder than it already is." I step back, keeping my attention trained on the rug by the door because if I lose myself in his capturing gaze one more time, I might lose my nerve and change my mind.

It'd be so easy to get caught up with him again.

But it'd also be reckless.

I have a child to support, a business to run, a family who needs me, and a heart that can only break so many times before it shatters completely.

He might be the athlete, but I have more skin in this game.

Chapter 34

Fabian

I PUNCH the steering wheel of my rental SUV, staring at the front of Rossi's garage.

Meeting her was like finding something I never knew was lost. It was like drawing a line and forgetting everything that ever existed before her.

Before them.

I can't go back.

Not now.

For thirty-seven years, I've been addicted to the thrill of the next big thing. The attentions. The glory. The accolades. I've spent so much time building myself into a household name, a fucking empire.

And for what?

So I can go home to my empty mansion, to an empty bed, staring at a lifeless ceiling in a house so quiet you can hear a pin drop?

I think of Rossi inside, warm in her bed, the way her

dark hair splays across her silk pillowcase when she sleeps. The way her lips would twist into a bashful half-smile in the mornings. The sound of Lucia's giggles. The sweet scent of the fabric softener Rossi used on Lucia's blankets. Hell, even the taste of Gerber apricots.

I didn't sign up for this, but good God, I've never wanted anything more than I want this.

I'll trade the Maybach for lazy Sundays, the mansion in Malibu for cartoons and pancakes, and every last tournament trophy for stuffed bunnies and jogging strollers if it means forever with these two.

I need this brown-eyed baby girl who looks at me like I hung the moon—and the baby mama who checks me out when she thinks I'm not watching and has never been afraid to put me in my place.

I didn't sign up for this, but give me a contract and I'll sign the rest of my life to them.

My perfect little family.

Rossi's porch light goes dark, but I'm not leaving. I'll sleep here all night if I have to. I can promise that woman the world, but at the end of the day, words are just words. She needs to see I'm not going anywhere. And when she wakes tomorrow morning, she'll see just that.

My phone buzzes from the cupholder, sending a start to my chest.

"Phoebe," I answer.

"Good news," she says. "Radar Online bought the photos—however, I have an in over there and I was able to make a phone call and explain the situation and the impending legal entanglements they'll face if they publish, and they were willing to call off the hounds."

Exhaling, I say, "Thank god."

"They did, however, make a small request," she says.

"Which is?"

"They want an exclusive statement from you regarding Tatum Cartwright's pregnancy announcement."

"Of-fucking-course they do."

"Honestly, it's the lesser of two evils in my opinion," Phoebe says. "I'll work on putting a few options together and we can go over them in the morning. Anyway, you can breathe a little easier tonight."

I stare up at Rossi's dark house. "Yeah. Guess so."

We end the call, and I recline back in my seat, glaring at Dan's house in all its well-lit glory. The thing is practically a beacon in the night, a siren song calling me over to give the bastard a piece of my mind. And if he's lucky, that's all I'll give him.

Cracking my knuckles, I glance at the steering wheel, then to the neighbor's house and back.

I shouldn't do this ...

But he fucked with the wrong family.

Climbing out, I march next door, punch the doorbell six or seven times, and wait for the sorry asshat to meet his fate.

A second later, the door swings open—slow and careful. But before the plaid pajama-wearing coward has a chance to process my presence, I gift him with a sucker punch to the gut, and when he's hobbled in half, I throw in a knee to the face because I'm nothing if not generous.

A stifled, animalistic grunt escapes his thin mouth as he falls to his stoop with a sickening thud, writhing as he curls into a ball. His knees are tucked against his chest, a protective stance. Not that it could possibly save him from anything else I might see fit to do to this ass hat.

While it would bring me great pleasure to take things a step further, I'm pretty sure I've made my point.

With that, I return to Rossi's driveway and settle in for

the long night in the driver's seat of my rental. And when she wakes in the morning, I'll be here.

Waiting.

I'll wait for her forever if I have to.

And eventually she'll realize, I'm hers forever too.

Chapter 35

Rossi

SHUFFLING past the foyer the next morning in a half-asleep stupor, I nearly drop my coffee mug when I spot the black Range Rover in my driveway.

It's six AM ...

Did he sleep there all night?

Moving closer to the window, I take a better look. Sure enough, my knight in shining armor is fast asleep behind the wheel, his seat reclined and his arms folded across his steel barrel chest.

Trekking to my room, I grab my robe and throw it on before stepping into house slippers. And I make a pitstop in the kitchen to pour him a coffee before heading out.

I knock on his window, three gentle taps, and wait for him to stir awake. Sitting up, he presses a button by the steering wheel before rolling down the driver's side window.

"Good morning, sunshine." I pass him the coffee mug. "No vacancy at the Ritz-Carlton?"

He takes a sip, his dark, dreamy eyes focused on me. "Something like that."

"Why'd you stay, Fabian?" I cut to the chase.

"I have my reasons." His eyes scan past my shoulders, landing on Dan's house for a handful of seconds. "Wanted to make sure your creepy friend didn't pull any more stunts, for starters." Dragging his gaze back to me, he adds, "Was also hoping a good night's rest would help you come to your senses."

I roll my eyes. "Wishful thinking. And I slept like shit, for the record."

"You should've called me. I would've come inside and we could've slept like shit together."

I fight a smile, hiding my amusement. "Honestly, I feel bad. If I'd have known you were going to be this pig-headed, I'd have caved and given you the guest room."

"Sweetheart, you haven't seen pig-headed yet." He sips his coffee, gifting me a glinting wink.

"Seriously though, what's your plan?" I ask. "You just going to camp out in my driveway every night until your next tournament?"

"No," he says. "Just until you admit you're wrong about *us*."

Waving my head, I head toward the front walk and motion for him to follow. I'm sure he needs a shower and a decent breakfast, and since he's here, he might as well spend some time with his daughter.

"You can come in for a bit," I say. "But you can't stay long."

Chapter 36

Fabian

I HIT THE SHOWER, freshen up, and change into clean clothes before joining the girls in the kitchen. Taking a seat next to Lucia's high chair, I hand her a chunk of mushy banana from her tray while stealing a glance at Rossi in her pink satin robe. With messy hair piled on her head, she hums some eighties melody while she keeps a watchful eye on the egg white omelets she's making for the two of us.

She told me I couldn't stay long.

But this is progress.

And I'll fucking take it.

"You never told me how it went with Frankie yesterday," she says, back toward me.

I was going to, but the conversation took an abrupt left turn before I had the chance …

"The number didn't work, but the address was hers," I say. "She was pretty … shocked … I'd say. We didn't have much time to talk because she was on her way out the door, but I learned something new about her."

Rossi flips an omelet, twisting back to look at me. "What's that?"

"Frankie is actually my birth mother." Those words on my lips for the first time makes the room tilt sideways for a moment.

"What?" She sits the pan aside, turning back to face me, arms folded.

"Turns out she had me when she was fifteen," I say. "And my parents—who are actually my grandparents—raised me as their own."

"And you had no idea?" She wipes her hands on a dish towel.

"Not a clue."

"No one ever told you? Not even a cousin or aunt or something?"

I shake my head.

Rossi makes her way to my side of the table, draping her arms around me. "That must have been a lot to take in yesterday—on top of everything else."

"To say the least." I give my daughter another hunk of banana, which she promptly tosses on the floor.

"How are you feeling?" she asks, standing back and examining me with sympathy in her serene blue gaze.

"Little bit of everything."

"Naturally."

"Just trying to understand how two people could give me the world—and turn their back on their own daughter." I chuff. "I think what hurts the most, is they both took that secret to the grave."

Rossi pulls up the chair beside me, placing her hand over mine. "I obviously didn't know your parents, but I'm sure they had their reasons. Maybe they were trying to protect you?"

I think of Frankie's words yesterday, the story about showing up on my birthday, seeing me so content and thinking I'd be better off without her anyway.

"The important thing is it's not too late for the two of you to reconnect, to get to know each other …" she says. "You exchanged numbers, right?"

"Right."

"Okay, so there's your silver lining in all of this." She removes her soft palm from the top of my hand. "Did she say who your biological father was or anything else like that?"

"We didn't get to that part. She had to go to work."

Rossi heads to the other side of the kitchen, plating the omelets, grabbing forks, and carrying everything back before taking the chair across from me.

"Rossi, I want to be in Lucia's life," I say. "Whatever happens—or doesn't happen—between us, I want to be here for her. I know I'm her donor, but I want to be her father too."

She swallows a bite, gaze averted.

"So you want custody? Is that what you're saying?" Her tone is icy, but that's just the fear talking.

"I promised you I'd never ask for that," I say. "But what I am asking is for the two of you to move west."

She coughs, eyes widening.

"After talking to Frankie yesterday, realizing everything we've missed out on by not knowing each other, feeling like half of me is suddenly this riddle to be solved … I don't want Lucia to ever have to go through any of that."

"Plenty of donor children turn out fine," she says. "And plenty of single parents do an amazing job …"

"I'm not discrediting any of that."

"You're saying she needs a father figure in her life to feel complete."

"I'm saying she needs me," I say. "Maybe not now. But she'll need me eventually. And I don't want her to ever look back and wonder why I wasn't there. And damn it, Rossi. I know you don't need me, but you want me. Even if you refuse to admit it out loud."

She pushes her omelet aside, silent.

"Hear me out," I say. "Because I spent all night figuring how this is going to work. I have to be on the West Coast. You can work anywhere in the world—"

She lifts a palm. "Okay, I know where you're going with this, and before you continue, I have family here. Our entire life is here—our doctors and our play groups and our friends. My parents. I can't just up and leave."

"Which is why I was about to propose that you bring your sister and your parents with you ... they're retired, yes?"

She nods.

"I've got a three bedroom casita on my property that they can use until they find a place of their own—which I'd be happy to assist with since the cost of living is a little higher out there," I say. "I'll do whatever it takes to make this work, Rossi. I can't leave this state and not take the two of you with me. All I'm asking is that you give this a chance, that you meet me halfway."

Rossi gathers a lungful of breakfast-scented air and her pretty eyes snap onto mine from across the table, showcasing a glimmer of something. Consideration, perhaps?

"I told you I was falling for you last night, Rossi," I say. "But I lied." With my heart galloping in my chest, I say the words I've said a hundred times before but never actually meant until now. "I love you."

Chapter 37

Rossi

"I'M SORRY, WHAT?" I swear I misheard him.

"I love you," he utters those three little words again, the ones I was certain I hallucinated a second ago. Only this time he says them louder, enunciating each syllable.

But before I have a chance to process it a second time, Lucia grabs a fistful of banana, smears it into a handful of strawberry yogurt, and proceeds to run her goopy fingers through her already-messy bed head hair.

"I need to clean her up." Without missing a beat, I swoop her out of her high chair and carry her to the bathroom. Snapping her out of her bib and onesie, I adjust the water and place her in the tub, gently scrubbing the food from her tiny body and silky onyx hair.

When I was younger, I had an idea of what my dream life would be. Mostly it involved my first love (before I knew he'd grow up to cheat on me when we were barely out of the newlywed stage). But fate had other plans for me

—better plans. I would marry a hundred cheating Bretts if it meant they would all lead me here ... to this sweet, simple life with my beautiful little girl.

For the past nine—almost ten—months, our life has been perfect.

No drama. No complications.

Netflix and baby bottles.

Stuffed elephants and gummy grins.

No broken hearts—only overflowing ones.

The idea of uprooting all of this just to take a chance on a man I barely know makes my stomach tangle into seven hundred sailor's knots, but what if this is nothing more than fate wrecking my plans once again because there's something better in store for us?

There's a chance that maybe this new life could be better than any life I've ever dreamed of.

I rinse the baby shampoo from Lucia's hair, inhaling the sharp, sweet, powdery scent.

Maybe we didn't meet and fall in love and start a family the old-fashioned way, but it doesn't make us any less of a family.

Draining the water, I lift my baby out of the tub and wrap her in a downy soft towel.

"Come on," I say as a tickle of butterflies floods my center. "Let's tell your daddy the good news."

Chapter 38

Fabian

"YOU'RE NOT GOING to believe this," Phoebe says over the phone while Rossi and Lucia are down the hall.

"What?" I clear the table.

"So one of my interns was zooming in on Tatum's ultrasound pic—the one she posted on Insta last week. Don't ask me why, but hear me out. She noticed that the gestational date and the date on the ultrasound didn't match up with the due date Tatum's posted. They were off by a little over three weeks."

Phoebe speaks so fast, I can hardly keep up, but I'm all ears.

"Anyway," she continues, "so my intern plugged the gestational age and date from the ultrasound into this due date calculator online, which also gave an estimated conception date."

"Where are you going with all of this?"

"Fabian, the baby was conceived when you were in Melbourne back in January!"

The plate in my hand crashes into the sink. "Are you sure?"

The last time I slept with Tatum was in December. The Melbourne tournament was the second half of January.

"She's lying about how far along she is so you'll think you're the father," Phoebe says. "God, I *cannot stand* that weasel. You have no idea how much fun we're going to have with this—"

"Is everything okay?" Rossi appears by the fridge, bouncing a freshly bathed Lucia on her hip. "I heard a crash …"

"Phoebe, I'll have to call you back." I end the call and turn toward my girls. "I … I'm pretty sure I'm not the father of Tatum's baby …"

Rossi's expression softens and she fights the twitch of a relieved smile. "Oh my god. Are you sure? Do you know for sure? How do you know?"

"I'm being told she lied about her due date. I was out of the country when she conceived. And before that, we hadn't been intimate in weeks."

Rossi steps toward me, a hand clamped over her beautiful mouth. "This is a good thing, right? You're happy about this?"

"I feel terrible for the kid," I say, "but yeah. This is good news for me, not having to be tied to that psychopath for the next eighteen years."

As the space between us closes, my daughter reaches for me. Scooping her up, I kiss her chubby cheek and inhale her warm, damp, baby-fresh hair.

"That offer," Rossi says. "About moving all of us to California … did you mean that?"

"If it means having my best girls with me year round,

I'll do anything," I say. "I know I'm asking a lot from you, but I know this can work. I've been around the world more times than I can count, Rossi, and I've never met anyone who makes me feel half the things you do."

Despite knowing I could give her the entire world if she asked, the stubborn, independent woman standing before me has no need for me—a fact that only makes her that much hotter in my eyes.

Leaning closer, she presses her body against mine, tipping her chin up and staring so deeply into my eyes I feel it in my fucking soul.

"You're crazy," Rossi says as Lucia grabs a fistful of her hair.

"Crazy for you." I claim her rosy lips before turning my attention to my daughter. "And you, too."

With my entire world in my arms, everything I need—and everything I'll ever need—are finally mine.

Chapter 39

Rossi

"PUT YOUR PHONE DOWN ..." I drag a naked thigh across Fabian's equally naked torso and moan against his bare chest. Ever since I gave him the green light yesterday, he's been making phone calls, sending texts, and coordinating arrangements with various staff out west. "You've been on that thing all day."

"Just trying to make this as easy for you as possible." He places it on the nightstand, rolling back toward me and slipping a hand between my thighs. His finger slides along my seam before plunging inside of me. "I've got an entire team of people whose sole purposes are to make my life easier—no reason why you shouldn't reap the benefits of that."

I'm wet—and deliciously sore—but it still sends a shiver down my back and a buck to my hips. A few more minutes of this, and I should be fully recharged ...

"We haven't even told my sister yet," I remind him as

our lips crash. "Or my parents. It's okay to go slow with this …"

"More than happy to slow down once we get to California." He nibbles my ear.

"Just seems like it's all happening so fast." I trace a finger down his undulating abs. "Question."

"Shoot."

"Am I going to be the only person without an eight-pack in Malibu?" I ask. "Not that it matters. And not that it's a deal breaker. I just want to know what I'm getting into … and are they going to make fun of me if I order ranch dressing? I heard they make fun of Midwesterners who order ranch. Do I need to get highlights? Isn't everyone blonde out there?"

I'm half kidding, but also very much curious.

I've lived in Illinois my entire life—born, raised, educated, and established.

Sliding his fingers from my sex, he rolls me off of him, turns me onto my stomach, and smacks my ass with a playful swat before following up with a nip.

"Promise me something, Rossi," he says. I careen back toward him, studying his face in the dim lamplight of my humble bedroom.

"What?"

"Never change," he says. "Stay exactly the way you are." Tracing his fingertips along my hips until my nerve-ending spark electric, he adds, "This. This woman with the curves and the hard-hitting questions and the wild dark hair. This is the woman I love."

My heart swells, and I swear it grows larger with every beat as I stare into the eyes of a man so crazy about us he's rearranging his entire life to fit us in. From the moment I told him "yes" yesterday, my emotions have teetered between excitement and fear to everything in between.

But a wise, very handsome tennis player once told me, decisions rooted in fear are almost always the wrong ones.

"I love you." A month ago, I never dreamed I'd be saying these words to my daughter's donor—nor did I dream I'd be agreeing to pack up everything I own in the back of my Subaru so I could move out west to be a family with him.

He runs his lips against mine, his fingers lacing through my hair. "I love you, too."

Once again, fate ripped up the plans I had—and offered me something better instead.

Chapter 40

Two Weeks Later ...

Fabian

"OKAY, you should be good to go." Taylor rocks on her Converse-covered heels, hands deep in the back pockets of her cut-off shorts as she plants herself in my kitchen. "The baby-proofer just left, and I cleared out that section of your closet and those drawers in your dresser like you asked. Dinner's being delivered at seven." Her lips press together as she stares at the ceiling. "That should be it."

The driver will be arriving with Rossi and Lucia any minute.

It's been a week since I left them back in Illinois.

A painful, tortuous one-hundred-sixty-eight hours.

I'd have brought them on the first flight back if I could, but Rossi wouldn't have it. She wanted time to get her affairs in order. Break the big news to her family. Meet with a real estate agent. Figure out what to pack, what to store. Not to mention, she still needed to sign the final settlement with the fertility clinic. In my opinion, their screw-up was worth more than the two million they offered, but their legal team was holding firm and pushing back on it would've only eaten into our legal fees.

In the end, we both decided to place that money in an investment account for Lucia, bury the past, and focus on the future.

Besides, I've got more than enough money for the three of us.

"Appreciate it," I say. "You're good to take off for the night."

"Text me if you need anything," her voice trails as she heads for the back door.

"You know I will," I call out.

For a moment, I debate stopping her. Rossi has only met Taylor via FaceTime once and it wouldn't hurt to properly introduce them since Taylor's still here. But I've been working her to the bone the last couple of weeks. She deserves a night off.

So I let her go.

Once Rossi gets settled, the two of them will have ample time to get acquainted.

I stare at the golden bottle of Cristal chilling in a silver-plated bucket of ice and the two pristine flutes Taylor set up on the kitchen island before she left. I hadn't even asked her to do that—she took the initiative herself.

As soon as the dust settles, I'll give her a raise.

It can't be easy working for me, and already she's proving to be worth her weight in gilded tennis trophies.

Heading to the front of my estate, I watch for the driveway gate to swing open and the chauffeur-driven

Escalade to pull up with my precious cargo. I'd planned to meet them there, at the tarmac, but traffic this time of day is notoriously unpredictable, and I wasn't sure when I'd be finished interviewing Coach's replacement.

Turns out, he knew about Tatum's pregnancy—and he was well-aware of the fact that the timeline didn't add up. The two of them had conspired to try to pull one over on me, each with their own agendas. Tatum, of course, was hoping it'd make me "see the light" and reconcile with her. Coach was hoping it'd get me out of Illinois, which he felt was a distraction.

While I owe much of my success to Coach and it pained me to let him go, the betrayal and manipulation was a non-negotiable for me. I've worked too hard, come too far, and respect myself too damn much to tolerate that sort of behavior.

As much as I wanted to confront Tatum, per Phoebe's advice, berating a pregnant woman wouldn't be the wisest move. And I agree. So instead, she issued a public statement from me to the press, denying paternity and providing the proof that it couldn't be me.

Tatum has since deactivated all of her social media accounts.

It's only a matter of time before she springs back—a narcissist can only go so long without the affections of her loyal followers, but she's the least of my concerns.

The driveway gate swings open and my lips spread into the widest grin as I wait for my favorite girls. The Escalade parks by the fountain, and I trot up to the backdoor, which swings open before I have a chance to get it for her. A second later, Rossi is flinging herself into my arms, and I'm swinging her around, like a scene from a damn romance movie.

I've never been this guy—until now.

Once we settle down, I place her feet on the ground and claim her rosy mouth with a slow, soft kiss. The taste of spearmint on her tongue and berry lip balm on her lips sends my heart into overdrive.

"I missed you so damn much." I breathe in her sweet vanilla scent. The way we're acting, you'd think we hadn't seen each other in years. Funny how a single week can feel like an eternity when it's keeping you from the one thing you want more than anything else.

Doesn't help that I'm not accustomed to waiting for things …

"I missed you too," she says. The intensity of her blue irises are magnified in the California late afternoon sun. From the car, Lucia giggles. "I think someone has been missing her daddy …"

Without hesitation, I unbuckle my daughter from her car seat, scooping her into my arms.

"Welcome to your new home, baby girl," I say.

In the coming weeks, we'll work on getting the rest of Rossi's family out here, but for now, it's just the three of us. And between training for my next tournament, I'm planning to devote every waking minute to these two.

The driver unloads the trunk, assembling a line of luggage and baby gear while we head in.

"Oh, guess what?" Rossi slips her arm around my lower back as we walk side-by-side. "You're never going to believe this."

"What?"

"We were leaving today when I saw a Realtor putting a sign in Dan's front yard." She bites her lip. "So I guess he's moving?"

"Actually, I *do* believe that." After the stunt he pulled two weeks ago, I pulled one of my own. Turns out I know someone who knows someone who knows Dan's boss in the accounting division of the large "Fortune 500" corporation where he works.

All it took was a couple of phone calls and the bastard was canned.

"Wonder where he's going to go?" she muses, a hint of sadness in her tone.

But I don't feel bad for him. He got exactly what he deserved.

"As long as he keeps his delusional string-bean ass out of California, I don't care where he goes," I say.

Rossi swats me as we step over the landing and into the foyer of the expansive home that will no longer be quiet and smudge-free from this moment forward—something I'm one-million-percent okay with.

Gasping, she stops, clasping a hand over her chest. "Oh, my god."

"What?"

"This view …" She takes a couple of steps before stopping, transfixed by the rolling ocean view out the two-story window ahead. "How do you live here? How is this real life?"

She chuckles ambling into the next room, her pretty mouth agape.

I'd given her a handful of tours over FaceTime, but apparently I didn't do this place justice.

"Welcome home," I say to my girls.

I think they're going to love it here.

And how could they not?

It's truly paradise on earth; nirvana.

Epilogue

Five Years Later

Rossi

"WHERE WOULD YOU LIKE THIS, MA'AM?" A uniformed mover hoists a small box labeled BARBIES on his shoulder.

"Top of the stairs, second room on the right." I point. "Oh, have you seen my husband? And was he with a miniature version of himself, by chance?"

"Just saw him out back on the court with the little guy," he says before climbing the stairs to deliver the dolls to Lucia's room.

I waddle toward the back sliding door, peering out onto the expansive grassy acre nestled under a shady grove.

For the past several years, we called his Malibu house our home, and we fell asleep every night to the sound of the ocean waves crashing on the shore, but with Lucia and little Frankie getting older and the newest baby Catalano on the way, we wanted more greenspace for them to run around, an extra bedroom, and a second office for me.

We also managed to find a smaller house a few blocks from here in an adjacent neighborhood. Fabian purchased the place as an anniversary present for my parents, who moved out here with us five years ago without giving it a second thought. No convincing necessary. My father's in heaven with this weather, bragging to his friends back home that it's like "being on vacation 24/7." Mom has happily taken over Carina's nanny duties while she gets her first Plant Parenthood location off the ground.

Chuckling, I watch my husband attempt to place a miniature tennis racket into our two-year-old son's chubby fists. He's determined to make him the next Catalano tennis champ, but only time will tell.

Checking my watch, I head to the front of the house to wait for Mom to pull up with Lucia, stopping first to set out an afterschool butterscotch pudding cup for my busy, curious, pig-tailed kindergartener.

In a few short months, we'll be a family of five—something I never dreamed possible.

"Mom! I'm home!" The sound of tiny sneakers tromping through the front door of our new house is music to my ears.

"In the kitchen," I call out.

"I don't know where that is …" she shouts back, sing-songing. Always yelling, this one. Like her father. I'm finding she's got a temper to match, too.

"Follow my voice," I sing-song in response.

A second later, she barrels around the corner, her glittery purple backpack bouncing as the biggest grin takes up half of her face.

"Did you remember to pack my pudding cups?" she asks.

I point to the one sitting on the island. "One step ahead of you, Luc."

Ditching her bag, she sidles up to a bar stool and digs in as movers shuffle in and out of our house with boxes and sofas and questions.

"I can't get over that view," Mom says from the living room as she watches my two favorite fellas play tennis out back. "All those trees. That sparkling pool. All that space."

Sighing, I do a mental run of my to-do list. Fabian's sister-slash-biological-mother is coming to visit next week. They've been attempting to reconnect these last few years, though I think Frankie still has it in her head she's better off leaving him alone. We offered to move her out to California to be closer, but she refused. She doesn't want to "leach" off of Fabian's success—her words.

I'm hopeful that with a little more time, she'll come around.

For now, they're a work in progress.

Baby steps.

It's funny when I think back to the beginning of all of this, when fear and doubt paralyzed my every decision. Because this life? This beautiful, perfect, amazing, dreamy life? Was nothing to be scared of.

Nonna always said everything happens for a reason.

Who'd have ever thought my reason would be Fabian Catalano?

SAMPLE - ENEMY DEAREST

Chapter 1

Sheridan

I sink to the bottom of the glimmering midnight pool, the cashmere-soft water swallowing me whole. With a lungful of sticky night air held tight in my lungs, I wait until my toes scrape the concrete bottom before floating to the surface.

My father always says, *"Nothing good ever happens after midnight."*

But it's 1 AM.

And this is divine.

I brush a ribbon of chlorine-soaked hair from my face, take a deep breath, and close my eyes, letting the full moon paint my body as I float on my back. Muscles liquid. Mind emptied of the day's worries. Naked as the day I was born and as free as a dove.

I could stay here forever—which is ironic because I shouldn't be here in the first place.

Technically, I'm trespassing.

Eyes shut, I inhale the distinct scent of pool water and nearby rose bushes, and try to imagine what it must feel like to be a Monreaux, growing up behind these privileged iron gates, a world away from us ordinary locals.

Not that there's anything wrong with being ordinary.

In fact, I'm quite content being a nobody.

There's more to life than having the world at your fingertips. It's okay to struggle, to want for things. Mama says it builds character; gives us the grit we need to get through the runaway rollercoaster that is life. Or maybe that's what she's had to tell herself all her life to get through the myriad of inflictions God saw fit to gift her—a rare vagus nerve disorder that makes her body overreact to even the mildest stressors, a weak heart that makes everyday tasks feel like scaling Everest, and just this year he thought it'd be fun to throw in a bout with Guillain-Barre syndrome.

And Mama also said no one ever promised life would be fair for everyone. We all have our crosses to carry and comparing them doesn't do us any good. She also said that if all we have is each other, that would be enough. We don't have much in terms of money or possessions or bragging rights, but we have our loyalty and love, and for us, it's all we need to get through this life.

Squinting, I study the blanket of stars above, distracted by Cassiopeia's flickering constellation and the rich section of Milky Way that runs through her—until a light flips on near the back of the Monreaux estate.

A second later, a door slides open with a jarring slick before slamming shut with so much force the sound echoes off the water. My heartbeat ricochets in my chest before whooshing in my ears so loud it drowns out my panicked thoughts.

Righting myself, I swim to the closest ledge, half-obscured by a manmade waterfall trickling over a boulder grotto.

Heavy footsteps pound the pavement, growing louder, closer.

I hold my breath—as if that could possibly make me invisible—and pinch my eyes shut.

"Show yourself," a man's voice booms over the trickling water splashing around me. "I know you're out here."

This morning I ran out for coffee for Mama and overheard someone talking about how the Monreauxs were on their annual trip to St. Thomas this week—which was partly why I saw fit to scale their six-foot fence and dip my toes into these forbidden waters. That and it's been hot as Hades all week, and our air conditioner decided it'd be the perfect time to kick the can.

More footsteps.

I wince.

It has to be a property caretaker. Or maybe a house sitter. People like this don't just leave their massive homes sitting empty while they're snorkeling off some island in the Caribbean. Their staff doesn't take a vacation just because they do. I know that. I guess I figured whoever was here would be fast asleep this time of night …

"You can't hide in there forever," he says with a voice too sharp, too young-sounding to be someone left to tend to a multi-million dollar estate in its owners' absence. He exhales, shoes shuffling closer. "Come on. I don't have time for this. Get your shit and get off my property."

He must've spotted my dress, bra, and panties, resting in a heap on one of the lounge chairs.

I swim out from behind the waterfall, keeping everything below my neck beneath the surface. Scanning the length of the mystery man, I start at his designer sneakers and trail up his ripped jeans before stopping for a brief detour at his broad shoulders, which are hardly contained in his gray t-shirt. Lastly, I arrive at his moonlit glare.

His dark brows angle in as he captures my stare, his expression unreadable. A warm breeze plays with his mussed, sandy blond waves and star-cast shadows frame his chiseled features.

He's beautiful, obscured in moonlight and all.

But his eyes glint, unamused.

And he doesn't smile.

I brace myself for a lecture or a cruel handful of words to be thrown in my direction, but the handsome figure simply takes a swig from the thick beer bottle in his hand, keeping his attention trained on me. My gaze falls to the complicated mess of tattoos covering the exposed skin of his left arm. And when I dare to meet his cold stare, I discover two small barbells piercing his right eyebrow.

This is a man who gives zero fucks.

"I'm sorry." I'm not above apologizing. I'm in the wrong. I shouldn't have come here tonight. Shouldn't have scaled his fence. Shouldn't have stripped out of my clothes and dove into his luxurious swimming pool like I owned the place. "If you'll let me get my things, I'll be out of here in two seconds. You'll never see me again. I promise."

His full mouth arches into a devilish smirk, and his silence sends a shiver down the back of my neck.

I've got less ground to stand on than a mouse who wandered into the den of a ravenous lion.

"You're August, aren't you?" I take a friendlier approach.

There are three Monreaux boys. Soren's the oldest and a bona fide rock God. I'd know his face anywhere thanks to the billboards all over town anytime they tour through

Missouri. Then there's Gannon. I've never seen him, but I know he's quite a bit older than me. August is the baby of the family, though if it's truly him standing before me, there's nothing infant-like about him.

He was only two when his mom died. She was jogging —near our house actually—when she was struck by a car and left to bleed out on the side of the road.

His father tried to blame *my* father for her death.

They have a history …

A dark, rooted, tragic, ugly history that I don't dare discuss around him and Mama unless I want to see his eyes turn cloudy and send Mama off to the bedroom in a fit of tears. A history so shrouded, I don't even know the half of it—I only know that we don't talk about it.

If my parents knew I was here, they'd kill me. Figuratively, of course.

My entire life, it's been made abundantly clear that the Monreaux family is off-limits in every sense of the word. I'm not to go near them, not to breathe their toxic air. Not to so much as even whisper their name under our roof.

Being here, in these waters, on this property, is blasphemous to the Rose family name.

I didn't come here out of spite.

I didn't come to hurt anyone or to prove some kind of point.

But if my parents found out, they'd be devastated.

"I'm the one who should be asking questions, don't you think?" He takes another drink, his gaze all but penetrating my soul.

He isn't wrong.

This isn't the time to be friendly. Last thing I need is August telling his daddy that the Rose girl broke into their back yard and was skinny dipping in their pool. Word would get out. Phone calls would be made. Coronaries would be had. My parents probably wouldn't believe it anyway, but that's not a risk I'm willing to take.

Before I have a chance to utter a single word, August makes his way to a stone-covered cabana and returns with a fluffy white towel. Crouching by the ledge, he hands it to me. It's a simple exchange, yet the uneasy flutters in my chest do double-time when our fingers graze.

"So what name should I give the police when they arrive?" He rises, towering as he peers down. "You look like a … Harper to me. Chloe. No. Addison. Definitely an Addison."

Pretty girl names … or are they basic?

Is he trying to flatter or insult me?

I draw in a hard breath as I climb out of the water and quickly wrap my body in the soft warmth.

He tosses back another mouthful of beer, this one more generous than its predecessor.

"You're not going to give them *any* name." I keep my tone sweet as I tug my sundress off the chair, and then I turn my back to him and pull it over my damp body.

"What makes you so sure of that?" His words are subtly slurred. I imagine this isn't his first beer of the night.

I face him once more, hardening my confidence. "Because if you're who I think you are, you're not twenty-one. You're not going to be calling the cops with liquor on your breath."

His head cocks to one side, as if he's studying me from a new angle. "If I'm who you think I am, then you should know … my family pretty much owns the cops. Sorry, Sugar Tits, but I've got nothing to be scared of in this scenario. You, on the other hand …"

Either he's trying to get a rise out of me or he truly is as big of an asshole as they say …

I may be known to keep sweet, but I'm not going to stand here and let someone objectify me because I made one bad decision.

"Sugar tits? I guess it's true what they say—money can't buy you class."

He laughs, unfazed, as if my insult merely ricocheted off his steely exterior.

"So what *should* I call you then?" His penetrating stare falls to my chest before skimming back to my eyes.

"You're seriously going to turn me in? I didn't steal. I didn't break anything. I didn't hurt anyone. I only went for a swim …"

I fold my arms across my breasts, which I'm quite certain are standing at full attention, and toss him a frown.

"You trespassed on private grounds," he says. "Last I checked, the police don't take kindly to illegal activity in this part of town."

This part of town …

Of course. The southwest quadrant Meredith Hills is the "rich" section of this godforsaken town. Anything south of LeGrand Street and west of Sunderland Avenue is *the* place to reside. It's an interesting layout too—the streets almost designed like spokes in a wheel, all of them poking out from the Monreaux residence, as if it's the capitol complex of this great-and-powerful city.

I roll my eyes. "Spoken like a true Monreaux."

August chuffs. "What's that supposed to mean?"

I lift a shoulder. "You're your father's son. *That's* what that means."

I'm bluffing. I know nothing about his father besides the fact that he's a wealthy, powerful, and resourceful man and people tell stories and give warnings. I don't know what he's truly like behind closed doors—and I never intend to find out.

August takes a step closer, though I attempt to pay him no mind. I also try to ignore the throbbing pulse in my ears and the nausea swelling in my belly. I have no idea what he's capable of, but I'd be wise not to put anything past him.

I gather my bra and panties and stuff them into the pockets of my dress before sliding my feet into my faded flip flops. "Get over yourself. I said I was sorry and now I'm leaving."

Making my way toward the fence line, my steps falter —I'm going to look ridiculous climbing it in nothing but this soggy sundress. But I force the thought from my head, ignoring the weight of his stare on my backside growing heavier with every step.

I don't care what he thinks.

The Monreauxs might own this town, but at the end of the day, August and I are nobody and nothing to each other. We've gone nearly two decades like two passing ships in the night. No reason we can't continue on that way.

"Hey …" he calls after me, his voice cutting through the dark.

I keep going.

"Hey, I'm not done with you." His words are edgier this time, louder.

I pick up my pace, sprinting so fast I hardly feel the ground against my feet.

The fence is just a few meters away, almost in reach when the shattering of glass stops me in my tracks.

I glance over my shoulder as he collapses onto the edge of a pool chair, shards of his beer bottle broken at his feet.

Did he smash it … on purpose?

A hundred Monreaux stories dance through my head all at once, rumors indistinguishable from facts swirling together in a sea of uncertainty. Most of the time people like to exaggerate for the sake of telling an interesting story, but Mama always says every lie is rooted in truth.

All I know is most people say that family is as dangerous as they are powerful, as unpredictable as the stormy sea. Dysfunctional yet loyal to a fault. And thick as thieves. Locals stay away from them for good reason.

I once overheard someone claiming that getting into bed with a Monreaux—figuratively or otherwise—is like playing a game of Russian roulette. Odds are you'll come out of it alive, but you'll never be the same after.

Unfortunately, those odds weren't in my Aunt Cynthia's favor when she dated August's father decades ago. She didn't come out of it alive—which is exactly the reason my parents forbid me from going anywhere near this family.

I steal one last glimpse of the wickedly handsome Monreaux boy, at his broad shoulders and chiseled jaw and messy hair, at the shiny fragments broken glass surrounding him, and I make a running leap for the fence.

Within seconds, I'm dashing home, to the side of town where people keep bars on their windows and police sirens double as bedtime lullabies. Where air conditioners break and water bills sometimes go unpaid. Where no one hires house sitters because vacations are the kind of thing you only do when you win a little bit of cash from a scratch-off card or your tax refund is a little more than you were anticipating that year.

By the time I get to our little gray bungalow on North Fifth Street, the soles of my feet are on fire, and my lungs burn in sympathy. I toss my tattered flip flops in the garbage can by the back door and sneak inside.

My father is working nights, and Mama's asleep in her

room, the TV blaring and ceiling fan whirring. They'll never know about my little escapade tonight, thank goodness.

On my way to my room, I catch my reflection in the mirror in the hall, cringing at my blonde waves that have dried into a frizzy lion's mane of a look. A second later, I peel off the damp dress and toss it on the back of my desk chair.

Tiptoeing to the kitchen, I fill a plastic cup with ice water from the fridge and drink it all in one go. Returning to my ninety-degree room, I crack a window, switch on a box fan, and collapse on my lumpy mattress.

My breath eventually settles despite my adrenaline-soaked blood, and the events of the past hour play in my mind like a surreal fever dream.

Everything happened so fast.

Half asleep and semi delirious, I stare at the stained ceiling above as a loopy grin claims my face. The whole thing is kind of funny. Trespassing and skinny dipping is the last sort of thing anyone would ever think I'm capable of doing, Monreaux estate or otherwise. In fact, I can't think of a single soul who'd believe any of this anyway.

Guess it'll have to be my little secret …

And honestly, I've always wanted to see a Monreaux. Maybe it was all those times my parents whispered about them when they thought I wasn't listening. Or maybe it was the way strangers always looked around the room before they'd start talking about them in public, like they had ears in every corner of this town. They were a mysterious enigma placed on the highest shelf, just out of reach.

At least now I can say that I saw one.

And if I'm lucky, I'll never see him again.

Chapter Two

SAMPLE - ENEMY DEAREST

August

"Way to go, asshole. Better clean this shit up before Dad and Cassandra get back." I'm awoken by a familiar voice in my ear followed with a sharp kick to the shin.

Gannon.

I sit up from the pool lounger chair, lifting a hand to my throbbing temple as my eyes adjust to the searing sun overhead. Instinctively I reach for my phone, only to find it in my brother's possession.

He waves it. "You can have your phone back when you grow the fuck up."

"Fuck you."

"You're pathetic, you know that?"

I smirk. "That's news to me."

"Maybe you should think about actually doing something with your life instead of chugging stolen beers and getting high by the pool."

I don't get high. I can't stand that head-in-the-clouds, floating sensation. It's too *cheery* for me. But he can think what he wants to think. It's all the same.

"And hooking up with a different girl every night. You forgot that part," I add.

"You fucking wish."

If he only knew …

I've gotten more ass this summer than Gannon's had in his entire life. And that's including the college-aged nanny he lost his virginity to at fourteen.

"Dad's going to be home in a few hours," he says. "Pick this shit up. Take a shower. Put on a clean shirt. Wash your damned hair. You look like you have fucking mange."

I've been called a heartless bastard more times than I

can count, but put me next to Gannon and I'm a purring, milk-drunk kitten.

"At least I don't look like a corporate stock photo." I squint up at him, shielding my eyes from the glare of the sun. It's a Sunday afternoon, but he's dressed in designer slacks and an ironed polo with our country club's crest on the pocket. Ever since he graduated first in his class at Vanderbilt, the stick up his ass has grown exponentially. Just for fun, I add, "The discounted kind with dead eyes."

"You want your phone?" He waves it toward me. But before I can reach for it, he chucks it into the pool with a flick of his Rolex-covered wrist.

It lands with a pathetic splash, barely audible over the trickling waterfall feature my father's girlfriend insisted on adding last year.

I don't react.

I don't give him what he wants.

I never do—and I'm pretty sure he hates me for it.

"What do you think Mom would say if she saw us right now?" I ask.

The Mom card has always been Gannon's Achilles' heel. I was two when she died. I have zero recollection of her. But he was older. He still has memories. And he was the biggest fucking Mama's boy—at least that's what Soren tells me. I've seen it in some grainy home videos too. Gannon has always been … *extra*. Our mother had the patience of a saint to put up with his constant neediness. "Bet she'd be real proud, don't you think? Watching us going at it like a couple of prideful jackasses."

Gannon remains impressively stone-faced, though uncharacteristically quiet for a minute.

"If Mom were here, pretty sure she'd be telling you to get your shit together," he finally responds. "But since she's not, someone's got to do it for her."

"You're doing the lord's work." I place my palms in a prayer position. "Saint Gannon."

My brother opens his smart mouth to respond, only to have his thunder stolen by our weekend housekeeper, Clarice. Gazing down, she toddles to the pool with a dust pan and broom in hand.

"Good morning," she says, crouching to sweep up my mess. Her knees crack and she stifles a moan as she bends. She's way too fucking old for this shit, but she's loyal and efficient so my father will keep her on until her dying day.

Once upon a time, she was our full-time grounds manager with a staff of fourteen hand-picked souls, but time caught up with her, as it does, and my father chose to keep her on weekends rather than put her out to pasture.

No one's ever accused Vincent Monreaux of having a soft spot, but he's good to those who are good to him.

Gannon pinches the bridge of his nose, giving me side-eye while Clarice does my dirty work.

I exhale. "Clarice, you don't have to do that. I've got it."

All of this fanfare over one fucking broken beer bottle —and none of this would've happened if it weren't for the naked chick swimming in my pool last night.

At first, I thought I was hallucinating. I'd had a few beers and I was heading back for more when I heard the splash outside. I shoved the living room curtains apart and peered toward the pool, which was pitch dark except for the faint glow of moonlight on the rippling water ... water that should have been still.

And then I saw her. Floating. Peaceful. Oblivious. *Naked*.

Clearly deranged.

Possibly high on drugs for all I knew.

Or dead.

I've never fashioned myself a hero by any stretch of the imagination, but I'd be lying if I said I wasn't preparing myself to fish a lifeless body out of the pool. But by the time I got out there, she was hiding in the grotto—like I wouldn't fucking find her.

Her clothes and sandals lay in a crumpled pile on a chair, and I yelled for her to show herself. When she finally emerged, it took all of two seconds for me to recognize that face.

She was a Rose.

Sheridan Rose, to be exact.

A vile, disgusting ... *beautiful* ... Rose.

I didn't know her, but I knew all about her—and her parents. So I'd kept a poker face and played dumb. I'd seen outdated pictures of her family before, from archived news articles. And I knew she'd dated a guy from my high school a couple years back. In tagged photos on social media, I'd studied her heart-shaped face for more hours than I'd ever admit to anyone ... because she wasn't just gorgeous, she was forbidden—and that made her unlike the rest.

For as long as I can remember, my father has been obsessed with the Roses and avenging the smear campaign they'd launched against him, his reputation, his business, and our family name a lifetime ago.

We'd almost lost *everything* because of them.

Not to mention my mother's death suspiciously occurred a block from their house, and the bastard who struck her and drove off was never found. To make matters worse, not only was my mother's life taken that day, but so was the life of my baby sister. Mom was twenty-two weeks along, carrying the little girl they'd so badly yearned for. A "sweet little angel" to round out our *perfect* family, as my father stated in a camera interview once.

Without warning, nearly everything my father had ever wanted was taken from him.

Forever.

He almost had it all.

To this day, my father is convinced it was one of the Roses. Someone who saw an opportunity and seized it. Someone with good reason to want to inflict the worst kind of pain and loss onto a Monreaux.

Someone like Rich Rose.

Last night, like a true coward and in true Rose fashion, the naked girl ran off before she had a chance to pay her penance. Like she could just wander in here and walk off like nothing happened …

And then she had the audacity to ignore me when I called after her—that's when I smashed the beer bottle.

All I could think about was how the spawn of the family that destroyed mine dared to waltz her perfect peach-shaped ass onto our property like she owned the place.

The fucking *nerve* of that woman.

Clarice sweeps up the last fragment of glass, and Gannon heads into the house without a word—thank God. I wait until they're both out of sight before fishing my dead phone from the deep end with a leaf skimmer, and then I make my way inside to clean up. Not because Gannon told me to, but because I can't stop picturing the Rose girl's ripe tits and pouty mouth and I need to get my head straight with an ice-cold shower.

She was a sitting duck.

I knew *exactly* who she was.

I could have easily made her atone—in more ways than one.

She's lucky I didn't.

And if she's smart, she'll never set foot on these premises again.

Because I can't promise I won't seize the opportunity next time.

Chapter Three

Sheridan

"I can check you out over here, sir." I wave to a bearded customer Sunday afternoon who promptly deposits a pair of Air Pods and a wireless iPhone charger on the counter before all but tossing his credit card at me.

I scan his items, ignoring the weight of his gaze on my chest, choosing to believe he's reading my name tag instead of eyeing my covered cleavage. I've worked at this cell phone store six months now, and no amount of training could have prepared me for the assortment of general public creeps who come in. But I suppose it's to be expected. Par for the course or whatever. Everyone has a cell phone. "Two hundred four dollars and eighty-nine cents is your total today."

He sighs and nods as if the exorbitant price is my fault, and I slide his card through the reader and wait for the beep.

TRANSACTION FAILED.

"I'm so sorry, sir—" I say until he interrupts me.

"—try it again."

I run the card once more.

TRANSACTION FAILED.

"Is there another card you'd like me to try?" I force a friendly smile into my tone. These situations can be embarrassing, though something tells me this man has no pride and gives zero fucks.

Eyes glazing over my chest, he pushes a hard, stale coffee breath from his mouth before fishing a different card from his wallet.

The bells on the front door jangle, and my attention flicks in that direction. A tall figure fills the doorway, backlit by the sun. He takes two steps in, letting the door glide shut, and scans the store space.

Our eyes lock from across the room, and in a fraction of a second, my blood turns to ice water.

"Hello?!" The gruff man in front of me snaps in my face. "You still with me?"

His transaction goes through, and the machine spits out a receipt. I hand him a pen and clear my throat, keeping a close eye on August Monreaux with a lump in my throat.

"Welcome to Priority Cellular, how can I help you today?" My notoriously bubbly co-worker, Adriana, approaches him before I have a chance to warn her off so someone else can deal with him. Though what could I possibly say that hasn't already been conveyed by his ripped jeans, devil-may-care smirk, and the chilled glint in his eye?

Half-distracted, I place the Air Pods and charger in a bag with the man's receipt. He leaves before I can wish him a lovely afternoon.

From my periphery, I experience their exchange with voyeuristic curiosity. Adriana, forever oblivious, leads him to a display case of phones, plucking the most expensive model from its resting place and handing it off for August to inspect.

"I'll take it in black," he says, his voice carrying across the store. They discuss storage for a second before Adriana disappears into the stock room.

Our gazes catch again, and he won't let mine go. I'm

not sure whether or not to care that he saw me naked less than twelve hours ago. I'm sure he's seen a million naked girls before. At some point, they all probably blend together.

I pull myself out of my own head and wave over the next customer in line. "Ma'am, I can help you over here, if you're ready."

Heat creeps up the back of my neck. I don't have to glance over to know he's staring at me with that piercing cold glare.

I ring up a purple car charger for a middle-aged woman in leopard-print Lululemons and a melting Starbucks iced latte in her hand. When we're finished, Adriana makes her way to my register, August in tow.

"Can you start his ticket, Sher? I just have to activate this. I'll be right back." Adriana brushes her hand against his arm. "You're in good hands. I'll just be a sec."

The silence is profound. Awkward. Intense. It's everything heavy, all at once, anchoring me to the floor and shortening my breath.

No one has ever done this to me before …

I scan the empty box of his new phone and straighten my shoulders. "Can I have your number, please? To pull up your account?"

He shifts, jaw set as if he's attempting to stifle what he truly wants to say.

"Okay, I think we're good now." Adriana emerges after an endless moment and hands August his new phone. "Should just take a minute to load."

"Your number?" I ask again, fingers hovering over the keypad with the slightest tremble.

He hasn't taken his attention off of me for one second.

"Your brother is Gannon, right?" Adriana asks after he finally tells me his digits.

August arches a brow. "Maybe."

"He went to school with my cousin. I think they used to hang out back in the day," she says. To some people around here, running around with a Monreaux gives you bragging rights. "They got busted at a party out at the gravel pit off Highway 50."

"That doesn't sound anything like my brother," he says, monotone.

"Well maybe not *now*." Adriana's overfilled lips curl. "But back in the day, I hear he was quite the wild child."

August sniffs, gaze still trained on me. "Depends on your definition of wild."

"What's he up to these days, anyway?" Adriana continues, oblivious to the fact that he isn't interested in shooting the breeze about his older brother. "I see him riding around town in that electric sports car of his. The matte black one with the gunmetal-gray wheels."

I know the one. I've seen it dozens of times. But the windows have always been too dark to see who was seated behind the steering wheel.

Now I know.

"It's a piece of shit," he says, emotionless. "Pretty to look at. Nothing under the hood worth writing home about."

Damn. Bad blood?

I'd always heard Monreaux were thick as thieves, but I'd never considered they'd have an ounce of inner turmoil. Perhaps they're competitive with one another? Most brothers are.

Adriana and I exchange looks, and she gives an awkward chuckle. "Um, okay. So … your total today is thirteen hundred dollars and fifty-two cents."

He slides a black card across the counter, equidistant

between Adriana and me. We both reach at the same time, hands colliding.

"Sorry, go ahead," I say to her. If ever there was a time to pray for a customer rush, it's now. But the store is dead. It's just the three of us now. The assistant manager is hiding in the back somewhere, as per usual.

She swipes the card, tapping her fingers to the beat of the pop song playing from ceiling speakers while we wait. "I heard your brother used to throw the most bomb parties at your house. My cousin has, like, the craziest stories." The register spits out a receipt and Adriana hands him a pen. "I think he said this one time, you brother—"

"—my brother's parties sucked," he says. "All those rumors you've heard, he probably started those himself. No one fucking likes Gannon."

Adriana bites her lip. "Damn. Okay."

"Speaking of parties, I'm having one this weekend. Friday." He signs his receipt, his silvery gaze flicking to mine. "You two should stop by."

My heart slams to my feet.

I'm not sure what his end game is here, but I have no desire to be part of it. Last night was a mistake. The kind of thing you do when you're young and dumb and delirious from a mild case of heat stroke.

My "no thanks" intersects with Adriana's "oh-my-god-yes."

She elbows me.

"I'm sorry," August says, turning to me. "I didn't quite catch that."

"I can't. But thank you," I say.

His head cocks, eyes narrowing into an incredulous squint. "You can't? Or you don't want to?"

"Sher, come on. It'll be fun," Adriana says. "Just tell your parents you're staying at my place."

August studies me.

"Seriously, it's not a big deal. And you don't even have to drink or anything ... I've always wanted to see the Monreaux mansion ... could be pretty epic ..." Adriana continues to try to sell me on something I refuse to buy. If working with her the past six months has taught me anything, it's that she's relentless when it comes to getting what she wants. It's why she's our top salesperson. She could convince the most discerning soul that the sky is glittering olive green, and they wouldn't bat a lash when she's done. "It would be a dream come true for me."

August smirks.

I'm glad he finds this entertaining.

"I will literally die if you don't go, Sher," Adriana continues. Half joking. Half not.

"You don't want that on your conscience, do you ... *Sher*?" August interjects. My name on his tongue is velvet smooth, sending shivers down my arm.

Ripping a piece of paper from a nearby notepad, August scribbles five numbers. "Party starts at nine. Here's the gate code for the night."

"Awesome." Adriana folds the note and places it in her back pocket like it's the most precious thing in the world. "We'll definitely see you then ..."

August gives me a lingering glance before showing himself out, and the moment he's gone, I exhale the longest, hardest breath.

"Okay, what's up with you?" Adriana asks when we're alone. "Why are you acting so weird?"

"I was up late last night." I grab a bottle of Windex and a roll of paper towels and wipe the already flawless display case behind us. "Just ... tired."

"Too tired to realize we just got invited to the freaking Monreaux mansion?" If her brows were any higher they'd be in her hairline. "Do you realize how huge that is? And how epic that night will be? I mean, I've only heard stories, but, like … all-you-can-drink-booze, weed, hot guys, good music, a pool … it's the perfect summer party."

I toss a used paper towel in the trash. "Yeah, but that's not really my thing."

"Which is exactly why you should go."

"Feel free to go without me. Seriously. Go and have a good time. You can tell me all about it at work next weekend."

Lifting a hand to her hip, she exhales. "Okay, fine. I know it's not your scene, but will you at least go for me? This is literally a once-in-a-lifetime invite, and I want to have the time of my life. I want to get stupid wasted. And if I don't know anyone … I need a safety buddy. Or something."

"A safety buddy?" I laugh.

"Someone to make sure no one slips me a roofie or whatever. Just follow me around like a shadow and make sure I don't do anything I'm going to regret the next day."

"No offense, but that sounds like a terrible time to me."

"Okay, then just go with me, and we'll grab a couple drinks, sit by the pool, and stare at all the hot people doing stupid shit." She shrugs like it's no big deal. "Just to be able to say we've been there, even if it's for an hour, would be amazing. It's literally on my bucket list."

"No it's not."

"It is now."

I chuckle, shaking my head and returning the Windex to the cabinet beneath the register. "Can I think about it?"

"No because I know you, and this is your way of buying time and hoping I drop it or forget about it or let it go," she speaks so fast I can hardly keep up. "But that's not going to happen."

"What about your friend ... what's her name? Molly? Can she go with you?"

"Molly's in Indiana this week visiting her grandma or some shit like that. And before you bring up anyone else, Christa's working Friday night, Harper's going to be with her boyfriend like she is every second of every freaking day, and Lydia and I are no longer on speaking terms as of last Thursday. Sorry, chica, but you're my only option."

"Adriana." I tuck my chin. "Please don't put this on me."

She clasps her hands. "I will get on my knees and beg if that's what it takes. I'll take any weekend shift you want. I'll pay you. I will give you my next paycheck in full."

"I don't want your money. And I need my shifts."

"Then what's the issue? Are you worried about what you're going to wear? Just come to my place and we'll get ready together. We can walk there, and I'll have my sister pick us up when she gets off work."

"Your sister who bartends?"

"Yeah."

I lift a brow. "Doesn't she work until three AM?"

"Fine. I'll see if my cousin can come get us. And if she can't, I'll get us an Uber. Is that better? Then we can leave any time you want."

"Adriana ..."

She places her hands on my arms and gives them a gentle squeeze. "Please, Sher. Please. One hour of your life, that's all I ask for. I'll never ask you for anything else so long as I live. Promise."

The front door swings open, bells jingling, and a boisterous family of four barges in, ending our conversation.

"Please?" she mouths to me as she walks toward the customers.

She won't take 'no' for an answer. At the end of the

day, I'm fighting a battle I won't win. As soon as we close up shop today, she'll start blowing up my phone. She's a little bit psychotic at times, but I also kind of love her. In the short time we've worked together, she's become one of my closest friends.

Maybe one hour wouldn't kill me …

Lord knows she'd do anything for me.

I leave for college in six weeks. I've spent the last eighteen years trapped in the rusted cage my parents built for me the second I came into this world. If last night taught me anything, it's that freedom has a strange kick to it. Kind of like stepping into a foreign land for the first time. It's terrifying and exhilarating all at the same time.

My stomach furls at the thought of lying to my parents, but they can't keep me trapped inside their protective bubble forever.

Besides, I'm a responsible adult.

I can handle myself at a party.

Sucking in a long breath, I hold it. And then I let it go before settling on my decision. As soon as Adriana's finished, I'll share the good news … if one can call it that.

It's one hour of one night of my life—what could possibly go wrong?

AVAILABLE NOW!

SAMPLE - ENEMY DEAREST

Also available and FREE in Kindle Unlimited: THE BEST OF WINTER RENSHAW, an 8-book collection!

About the Author

Wall Street Journal and #1 Amazon bestselling author Winter Renshaw is a bona fide daydream believer. She lives somewhere in the middle of the USA and can rarely be seen without her trusty Mead notebook and laptop. When she's not writing, she's living the American Dream with her husband, three kids, the laziest puggle this side of the Mississippi, and a busy pug pup that officially owes her three pairs of shoes, one lamp cord, and an office chair.

Winter also writes psychological suspense under the pseudonym of Minka Kent. Her debut novel, THE MEMORY WATCHER, was optioned by NBC Universal in January 2018 and her book, THE THINNEST AIR, was a #1 Amazon Kindle bestseller and a Washington Post best seller five weeks in a row.

Winter is represented by Jill Marsal of Marsal Lyon Literary Agency.

Join the private mailing list. <- HIGHLY RECOMMENDED!

Follow Winter on Instagram!

Like Winter on Facebook.

Join Winter's Facebook reader group/discussion group/street team, CAMP WINTER.

Made in the USA
Middletown, DE
27 November 2021